ON THE EDGE

ROY DOLINER is a native New Yorker and lives with his wife and two children in Manhattan.

He has written seven successful novels, most of which involve political scandal and skulduggery in high places: *On the Edge* is the most recent.

ROY DOLINER

On the Edge

FONTANA / Collins

First published in Great Britain in 1979 by
William Collins Sons & Co Ltd
First issued in Fontana Books 1980

Made and printed in Great Britain by
William Collins Sons & Co Ltd, Glasgow

TO MY DEAR WIFE

CHAPTER ONE

Reese certainly wasn't small change. Neither was he a shy man nor by any stretch of the imagination a timid one. He was a New York City Police sergeant with three major commendations for bravery, well-connected politically, confident, and savvy. But with all of that he was nervous and unsure of himself around Ash Morgan.

'Ash is what you've always wanted to be,' Reese's wife once said. 'You hero-worship the big faker.'

'He's no faker,' Reese said. 'Just a success. I admire the way he's got on in the world. I enjoy his company, am happy to do him a favour, and expect one day at the right time he'll put in a good word for me.'

The most recent of Reese's favours was a twenty-four-hour tail on a man named Sullivan. Now one of his men had come in with the news that he'd lost Sullivan. It was Reese's unhappy duty to pass the word to Ash.

He first called him at his home on Long Island. It was one o'clock in the morning and he had to wake up Ash's son, who said his father was out of town. Reese apologized and hung up after leaving his name. He next called the central office of New York Telephone, identified himself, and was given the unlisted phone number for the Sutton Place apartment of Ash's girl-friend. Reese had met her only once, at Peter Luger's restaurant in Brooklyn; but with his cop's memory he was able to recall her name: Eleanor Harmon.

It was she who answered the phone. Reese gave her his name and asked to speak to Ash. She hesitated, finally told him to hold, and a few seconds later Ash came on the line.

Reese told Ash that his man had lost Sullivan. 'It was in Radio City Music Hall. The ten o'clock show. He went in during the movie. My guy had him nicely staked out, eating a Mounds bar with his feet up. Then the lights come up for the Rockettes, and Sullivan's blown. Not a trace of him.'

'Sullivan's a magician,' Ash said.

'I've got two men out looking for him now.'

'Call in your men. Put them to bed.'

'They're my best.'

'They won't find him.'

'I could send more men. Put out a net.'

'I don't want that.' Ash's voice rose. 'All of this is to be quiet. You know that. Some snoop gets hold of this, you've done more harm than good.'

Reese said in a low voice, 'What's it about, Ash? Who is this Sullivan bird?' Reese's wife had a homily for every occasion. Curiosity killed the cat was a favourite. 'Give me something to go on, I might quietly turn him up,' he said.

Ash's tone was soothing. 'You've done well to stay with him this long. I appreciate your work.' Reese felt himself being nudged gently out of the picture. He heard Ash say, 'You've done me a favour. One you can be sure I won't forget.'

Ash hung up. The digital clock on the table at Eleanor's side of the bed showed at one-twenty. Seven-twenty in Geneva. There'd be no one in Roper's office, but there was a night number. Ash decided not to call. Records were kept of overseas calls; they left a trail. And as yet there was no emergency. Sullivan had merely slipped his tail, gone underground. He could've managed that at any time. Whatever he planned, he'd have to go underground first. Ash had him followed in order to know when. He'd made an early-warning system. At the moment there was no alarm. It was only condition white, a mysterious blip on the screen. No doubt red would come in due time.

Eleanor's side of the bed was empty. Ash heard the bathroom faucet. One measures love by tolerance of domestic eccentricity; Eleanor brushed her teeth no less than five times a day.

Ash fetched the flat leather address book that he kept in the inside pocket of his jacket, and dialled a New York City number. It rang three times before it was picked up by a woman, her voice sleepy.

Ash said, 'Is the Senator there?'

'Who is this?'

6

'Ash Morgan.'

'He's in Montana,' the woman said. 'Fishing, hunting, playing gin. You know what time it is?'

'Is there a number he can be reached?'

'No.' Ash heard the click of a lighter, an intake of breath as the Senator's wife drew on a cigarette. 'There probably is, but I don't know it.'

'Did Mr Lemoyne go with him?'

'I don't know any Ash Morgan,' she said. 'How'd you get this number?'

'Is Mr Lemoyne in New York?'

'I'm no celebrity service,' she said. 'Not at one-thirty in the morning.'

'I'm sorry,' Ash said. 'If he is in New York, it's important I find him. It concerns the Senator.'

'Mr Lemoyne is in town,' she said. 'I spoke to him earlier. The Senator told him to take me to dinner but the gentleman found a card game.'

Ash apologized again and hung up.

He began quickly to dress. If Lemoyne had found a game, Ash knew where to look for him, knew it would be all night.

Eleanor came out of the bathroom. 'Who is Reese?' she asked.

'You met him once at that steak house in Brooklyn,' Ash said, 'where you said everybody was too fat.'

'Everybody but us,' she said. 'Now I remember Reese. He wore a beautiful silk suit and carried a gun. You said he was a dick.'

'I suspect that may be true.'

She sat on the bed beside Ash, a beautiful woman, strikingly and exotically so. Her mother had been Thai, so that her features had a romantic and mysterious look which was hard to place. Ash had first thought her Polynesian. He'd thought of the women Gauguin had painted. Yet her features were more refined, with less weight and more grace. Her long hair was swept away from the temples and tied in the back in an elaborate knot. The knot was called by a Thai word which he could never remember. Her mouth was wide, the lips full, but clearly defined. She contrived always to smell sweet. There was about her a certain mystery,

7

something cool and remote, a calmness at the centre, as if she had hold of some eternal secret. He'd lived with her two years and was still drawn to that central mystery. He still searched her large deep-black eyes for the answer.

'What does Reese want?' she said.

'Something came up.'

'Something in the middle of the night? Something only Ash Morgan can handle?'

'So it seems.'

'Is it dangerous?'

'Why should you think that?'

'A man who carries a gun calls you in the middle of the night. And then you call about Lemoyne.'

'He doesn't carry a gun.'

'The little swine prefers poison,' she said.

Ash laughed and kissed her lightly. 'Go on back to bed,' he said.

'I've got some work,' she said. 'I'll wait up.'

'It might take a while.'

'So will my work,' she said.

Ash finished dressing, ran an electric razor over his face, and was met at the front door by Eleanor with a cup of coffee.

'You take care of yourself,' she said.

'I notice you're developing a protective attitude towards me.' He watched her closely and said, 'Does it bother you, my being twenty years older than you?'

Her eyes held his. 'It never has,' she said.

'Still, in your line of work you meet a lot of dashing men.'

'None of them can hold a candle to you, old-timer.'

Ash hailed a cab on First Avenue and gave the driver a number on East Eighty-ninth Street, an undistinguished brownstone, one of several which ran from the middle of the block to East End Avenue. It was now past two and few lights showed on the street; heavy drapes were drawn across every window of the brownstone. As he was paying the driver, the door of the house opened, there was a moment of blazing light, and two men stepped out. The door closed quickly behind them. They spoke French, arguing about something, snapping at each other. The older of the two wore his coat draped over his shoulders like a cape. The other flicked a cigarette into the gutter. The door of a Mercedes waiting at the kerb opened and they were driven off. Ash rang the front-door bell, he was aware of being looked over through a peephole, and was finally admitted by a man in evening clothes with a nose flattened in the centre like an English saddle. This was Jimmy Burke, who had fought for the middleweight championship in 1956 and now did what he could. He'd been known for his courage and speed, but was nothing of a puncher, and with his fair Irish skin, had a tendency to bleed around the eyes. He'd always been popular, was now looked after by several wealthy men, and was a particular pet of the Senator's.

'You're looking good,' he said to Ash. 'Maybe a little heavy.'

'Is your family well?' Jimmy's second son was retarded and all his spare time was spent raising money for the boy's school and arranging programmes for the children.

'Thank God.' Jimmy rapped three times on the top of a wooden table. 'The little champ is making wonderful progress.'

They passed into a long rectangular room, the parlour floor of the house. At one end was a small-bar with an elegant buffet attended by a waiter in a red mess jacket. Closer to the door was a roulette wheel with several players, women as well as men, and a houseman in evening clothes. At another table blackjack was being dealt. The players were a woman who'd been the mistress of a President of the United States and a black man who'd won two track and field gold medals in the 1968 Olympics and was now a television network marketing vice-president.

Ash said to Jimmy, 'Is Mr Lemoyne around?'

'The third-floor poker game.'

Jimmy took Ash to a tiny elevator, rang the third-floor button, but held back the door.

'You ought to come in for a workout,' he said. 'The Senator does, every day he's in town.'

'When d'you expect him?'

'I got a call from his office. He'll want a couple of hours in the gym tomorrow afternoon.' He released the iron gate. 'It'd do you a world of good. If you don't have your health, you got nothing. Am I right?'

The third-floor poker game was in a small room in the back of the house. It might once have been a child's bed-room, but the walls were now covered with a russet fabric resembling velvet. A round table covered by green felt stood in the centre of the room under a Tiffany ceiling fixture. The windows were nailed shut, cool air coming through two large vents in the wall just to the right of the ceiling joint. The room was sealed, there wasn't a sound, and the artificially cold air stank of cigar smoke. Five men played, Lemoyne one of them.

All raised their eyes when Ash walked in. He knew Lemoyne and two others, who nodded and went back to their cards, which had been dealt for draw poker.

Ash waited until a hand had been played. He had no interest in cards. Lemoyne won the hand, but before the cards passed to the next dealer, Ash asked to have a word with him.

'I'm on a nice run,' he said. 'Can't it wait?'

'No. It can't.'

Lemoyne was a trim muscular man, who wore tinted aviator glasses and only recently had begun to dye his grey hair. He'd once been indicted for poisoning his wife; but the case never came to trial, the charges were eventually dropped, and the death was officially called a suicide. He served as a conduit for racket people and others with large amounts of illegal cash, and was the executive producer of record of motion pictures, the owner of record of a large block of stock in a professional football team and a Florida race-track and bank. He washed cash and carried promises between his friends and major political figures. The Senator was his dearest friend and chief client.

The third floor was divided into several smaller rooms used for card games and private parties. Ash tried one door after another, finding each locked. Lemoyne trailed after him.

'What're you looking for?'

'A comfortable men's room,' Ash said.

'Now I know what you got me out of the game for,' Lemoyne said.

Ash found the men's room at last; it was painted dark red, a mirrored wall behind the basin lit by a track of high-power bulbs. Bottles of cologne and hair dressing stood on a shelf below a framed reproduction of the Declaration of Independence. Ash locked the door and turned on the water tap; nothing they said could be recorded.

'I tried to reach the Senator,' Ash said, 'but was told he was in Montana shooting moose.'

'Very nearly true,' Lemoyne said. 'His Holiness is in Philadelphia banging Irma Pearson.'

'I think he ought to know that Jack Sullivan shook his tail tonight,' Ash said. 'That means we don't know where he is, or what he's doing.'

'So what? He noticed the tail and shook him.'

Lemoyne stammered when he was nervous and blinked rapidly. He had a habit of stretching his neck as if his collar were choking him; as if he were at last being hanged, Ash thought.

'You can be sure he knew the tail was on him from the first,' Ash said. 'He shook him because now he's up to something, something he plans to do alone.'

'What?'

'I wish I knew.'

Lemoyne hung his jacket on a hook behind the door. He wore a Browning .380 standard automatic pistol in a holster under his armpit. Ash watched him turn back his shirt cuffs and rinse his hands and face in the cold water from the tap.

'The investigation into Astra is going on,' Ash said. 'It's quiet, but it's moving. We can slow it, but we can't turn it off. We have to give them somebody, and that somebody is Sullivan.'

Lemoyne's face was dripping wet and he groped around for a towel with his eyes closed. 'Would you believe, no fucking towels?' Ash handed him a long streamer of toilet paper.

'A thousand-a-year dues and a man dries his face with toilet paper,' Lemoyne said. 'Sullivan is the logical choice. Fraud, perjury, obstruction. He's the link between Roper and the Senator, and through him to the top. We both know just how far that goes and to whom. Sullivan has got to be made to face reality. He has to be reminded of his loyalties. He has to be apprised of reality.'

11

'You think he's going to march quietly to jail?' Ash said. 'He's looking at three to seven. You want him to go in singing "The Star-Spangled Banner"?'

'I want him to recognize reality,' Lemoyne said. 'We'll do what we can, but the fall has to be his. Maybe three to seven doesn't give him an erection, but what choice does he have?'

'He looks to strengthen his hand,' Ash said. 'He first makes himself strong, and then comes back to renegotiate his deal.'

'My client is clean,' Lemoyne said. 'No-way. No-how. There's not a piece of paper anywhere in the world that connects the Senator to your Roper.'

Ash smiled and said, 'You don't have to convince me, Arnold.'

'My client's name appears nowhere. Not in the incorporation papers, not on a share of stock, not a single memo, not a cheque. Everything is through the Royal Bahamas Bank, all dummy-signed.'

Ash patted his shoulder. 'You protected your man,' he said. 'As God is my witness, Arnold, you did a terrific job. The Senator's money went out smelling of herring. When you brought it back a man could take it anywhere with pride.'

'I think I did a good job,' Lemoyne said. 'I made him a rich man. Ash, even you don't know how rich.'

'The man should erect a statue in your honour.'

'Instead he lets his wife abuse me.'

'She's a nervous woman,' Ash said. 'Frustrated, insecure, unhappy . . .'

'I'd like to push her out of a window,' Lemoyne said, adjusting his cuff links.

'The Senator appreciates how you've protected him,' Ash said as he held Lemoyne's jacket. 'Unless they start to dig.'

'Today nobody makes an airtight package,' Lemoyne said. 'Onassis in his lifetime got burned more than once. Even a Lansky is vulnerable.'

'Nobody can point a finger at you.'

'You'll back me up?'

'One hundred per cent.'

'Ash, I got four fish inside,' Lemoyne said. 'Let me make you a present of twenty-five per cent.'

'I'm going home to sleep.'

'Have a bite downstairs,' Lemoyne said. 'They got wonderful roast beef. Fresh-grated horseradish. Please do me the honour of signing my name on the tab.'

'I have to see the Senator.'

'Tomorrow without fail,' Lemoyne said. 'Clear it with him. Then go talk with Sullivan.'

'Sullivan is a dangerous man,' Ash said. 'And he knows where the bodies are buried.'

'A nice way to get himself killed,' Lemoyne said before he turned off the water tap.

CHAPTER TWO

Eleanor was at her drawing board. Ash had let himself in quietly, thinking she might've gone back to sleep after all. But she was bent over the board, totally absorbed in what she was doing and hadn't heard him.

She'd set the drawing board in a corner of their bedroom, where it caught the first morning light. She wore no make-up, merely scrubbed her face and pulled back her gleaming black hair. Her delicate skin had a lemony tint. Bent over the board, intent, it seemed a mask of cool ivory, marked only by faint shadows below her nostrils and wide black crescents made by her lowered eyes.

Ash didn't move, didn't breathe; his earliest desires came together in Eleanor. It seemed a miracle that she waited for him. At such moments he feared losing her. His passion for Eleanor was fired by this uneasy sense that he would one day lose her.

'How long have you been there watching me?' she said.

'Since I was a kid,' he said. 'Since I first went to the movies.'

'How old were you when you first made love?'

'Thirty-eight.'

'I was fifteen,' she said. 'The prettiest little English boy.

I brought *him* flowers.'

'And I've brought you fresh onion rolls.' He held up a brown paper bag.

'He was heir to a baronetcy,' she said. 'And England is without onion rolls.'

'I was looking at you and thinking that I love you,' he said.

'Then why was the look on your face so unhappy?'

'It wasn't unhappy.'

'Not exactly. But not happy either.'

'Does love make you happy?'

'It doesn't make me burst out crying.'

'You boss love around,' he said. 'Push it around, work it over. I think it's a miracle, a million-to-one shot. Blink your eyes and it's gone.'

'Nothing doing, sweetheart.' She held his face between her hands. 'You blink your eyes, close them, I'll still be here.'

He thought to end it there, and asked about her work. That diverted her. She was always eager to talk about her work.

She had been asked to work up a special design for one of Alan Bedford's most important clients, Lady Gayle, one of the richest women in England.

'The stone is superb,' she said, and held it up to the light between her thumb and index finger. 'A faceted ruby. Three carats. Just exquisite.'

'Who does it belong to?'

'The client. It was ours but we sold it to her, and now she's asked Alan to have me create a setting.'

'What makes the stone so good?'

'The colour. It's called pigeon blood.' She turned it against the light. 'See how it flames. There are much bigger ones that aren't worth a quarter of this one. They haven't the depth or fire.'

She set the stone on a square of black cloth, a yellowish-green stone beside it. She called that a peridot, and circled both with tiny diamonds, which she took from a velvet pouch with a tweezer.

'You have a lust for jewellery,' he said.

'It's the Oriental in me, love.' She flipped the pages of

14

her sketch pad until she came to a design she liked, then arranged the stones on the cloth to match it. 'Isn't it beautiful?'

Her dark eyes glittered, filled with the excitement of what she had created, and at the same time she seemed vulnerable and eager for praise. And of course he did praise what she had done, although it seemed to him simple, an arrangement of bright stones. He marvelled at the thrill it gave her, her enthusiasm and passion for her work. He remembered a time he'd felt as deeply about what he did, but it was long ago, and he'd never again feel it. His work had become tawdry. He picked up the pieces for other men, lined his own pockets. He lived well, loved a beautiful girl, and tried to make a life.

'D'you really like it?' she said.

'It's beautiful.'

'Will Alan like it?'

'He'll love it.'

'You barely looked.'

'It's a step up for you,' he said. 'Doing designs like this. And for Lady What's-Her-Name.'

'Lady Gayle.'

'It's good. Damn good. The Queen sees it on Lady Gayle's finger, it puts her nose out of joint.'

'I'll make coffee.'

'What're you sore about?'

'Nothing. Not a damn thing.'

'I admire you. I envy your enthusiasm.'

'And you patronize me. Whenever you talk like one of your pals, it's to put me down. "It puts her nose out of joint." You're in the real world and I'm not. That's it, isn't it? You and your pals. Were there a God in heaven, every last one would be behind bars.'

'Me, too?'

'You, too.'

She brushed past him and went into the kitchen, leaving the stones scattered on the work-table. Forty-five thousand dollars' worth of stones tossed around like popcorn.

He carefully returned them to the little velvet pouch, pulled the string, and carried it into the kitchen.

'You ought to put this away.'

'It was perfectly safe where it was.'

'What's eating you?'

'Where'd you go in the middle of the night?'

'Business. We had a problem.'

'In the middle of the night? Urgent. Ding-a-ling. Get me Iron Ash Morgan, Problem-Solver.'

'It's a long way from being solved.'

'Big secret, is it?'

'What the hell d'you want?'

'Out there where the men are,' she said. 'The reality. Oh, shit in your hat, Ash. I'm sick of all that strong-silent stuff.'

'Is that what I am, strong and silent?'

'And tough.'

'And tired,' he said. 'Worn out.'

'You're tired of your work,' she said. 'You hate working for Roper.'

'It's okay,' Ash said. 'It's a living.'

'Give it up.'

'I'd like a cup of coffee,' Ash said. 'Also I'd like you to boil me up three eggs, break an onion roll into little pieces and soak them in the eggs.'

'The Justice Department has been snooping around, and now the House of Representatives is talking about a Special Committee to investigate your boss,' she said.

'It's just talk,' Ash said. 'It won't come to anything.'

'They want a better look at Roper, the mystery man.'

'My Aunt Doris used day-old bread and called it birdy eggs. God rest her soul. After I eat I'm going to bed,' Ash said.

'You're not like the others,' she said. 'They're greedy, power-hungry, and corrupt. You're not. They do what they do easily. It's natural to them. It takes nothing out of them.'

'I'm no better. You merely think I am because you love me. It's not possible for Eleanor Harmon to love a crumb. Your touching womanly faith in me is at bottom simple egoism.'

'I don't believe it,' she said. 'Roper, the Senator, and that guy that's always with him, the one you went to see . . . What's his name?'

'Lady Gayle.'

'That's very funny.' She couldn't keep from laughing.

16

'Crazy Arnold Lemoyne, the bloody little wife-poisoner. And that cold-blooded bastard, Sullivan. Are you like Sullivan?'

'Perhaps, a bit.'

'You told me the things he did in Vietnam,' she said. 'Or doesn't it count because he did it to Asians?'

'He hates what he did.'

'And you hate what you do,' she said. 'Cleaning up Roper's dirt.'

'I'm paid to clean up Roper's dirt,' he said. 'I'm corrupt because I choose to be. It's a decision. An act without passion or conviction. A reasoned act.'

The eggs were cold from the refrigerator. She set water to boil but first ran hot water over the shells so that they wouldn't crack.

She said, 'Alan has asked me to go to Hong Kong.'

'Alone or with him?'

'Don't tell me you're really jealous?'

'You go away with Alan,' he said, 'I put my head in an oven.'

She put back her head and laughed. He kissed her lightly and stroked her hair, the smell and touch of it never failed to excite him.

'I'd never run out on you,' she said.

'Then marry me.'

'You already have a wife.'

'You know the circumstances,' he said. 'There'd be no problem getting a divorce. None at all.'

'No marriage, Ash. Anything but tying the bloody knot.'

'If we love each other,' he said, 'then wer'e already bound.'

'Which would seem to make marriage superfluous.'

'Not to me,' he said. 'I'm not only old, I'm old-fashioned.'

'I'm not,' she said. 'I love you. I love you even at times like this. I'm happy with you, even at times like this. You're funny, warm-hearted, clever, and a dear swee' piece of ass. But, God bless you, I will not marry you or anyon? else.'

'Not Alan?'

'I've got nothing going with Alan,' she said. 'I just don't like or want marriage. Not now, not ever. Perhaps it's my childhood, perhaps some cockeyed notion of independence and freedom. Don't laugh! I'm my own woman. I've got my work, and we have enough to keep us from growing sick to death of the sight of each other.'

She put her arms around him and held him, but when he kissed her and moved tightly against her, she edged away.

'I do love you,' she said. 'You're no prize, with your crooked friends and your house calls in the middle of the night, and of course you're not about to win a competition for king of the discos.' He watched her lower the warmed eggs into the boiling water. 'But this Hong Kong thing is for real,' she said. 'Alan wants me to stay there, where all our designs are executed. He'd be here, I'd be there. The craftsmen are Chinese. I'd supervise all that. He's actually prepared to offer me a partnership in the business.'

'You mean go there permanently? Let me see if I understand. You're talking about leaving New York and living in Hong Kong?'

'It's a super opportunity,' she said. 'I really want to do it, darling. And I want you to come with me. You've got money buried, you've told me that. Maybe not enough to quit, but there's no reason why you should quit. Not quit working anyway. There's a million and one things you could do. Import-export. And you do have enough money to keep you while you look around.'

'And what if I don't?' he said. 'What if I tell you I won't go?'

'There's no reason why you shouldn't,' she said. 'Your wife is hopeless; the psychiatrists are unanimous about that. David is grown. In another year, he'll be a doctor. You've done a marvellous job with him and with no one to help you.'

'My work is here,' he said.

'You hate your work.'

'Stop telling me what I hate and don't hate. Where in hell do you find the arrogance to tell me what I feel?'

'Are you going to tell me you like cleaning up Roper's dirt? Or is it that you like men like Lemoyne? Or the Senator? Sullivan? He's a killer, isn't he? Are you going to tell me you approve of men like that?'

'I neither approve nor disapprove.'

'Baloney. You approve and disapprove all the time. You're not amoral. You're a moral man, or you were. Bit by bit,

18

you've chipped away at that. You've done it for money. For your family. For doctors' bills for your wife. For tuition for your son.'

'And for good times,' Ash said. 'For posh apartments, for first-class passage to Europe and the Caribbean. For dandy restaurants, for clothes, for cars and paintings and a beautiful mistress.'

'Is that what I am?'

'It's what you insist on being.' Then he smiled, although his heart wasn't in it. 'Come be my beautiful wife instead,' he said.

'Wife,' she said. 'I hate the sound of the bloody word.'

After he'd eaten, Ash undressed and went to bed with *The New York Times,* which was delivered each morning. The investigation of Roper had moved off the front page. He had to look further on, to one of those inner strips taken from a wire service which ran beside a three-quarter-page fashion ad. A special House Committee was proposed to investigate Roper's political influence, his securement without proper bids of defence contracts during the Vietnam war, a federal bank charter in Maryland, easement rights to the Intracoastal Waterway for a land-development project in Florida.

Ash saw it as a fishing expedition. Nothing hard, nothing in black and white. Talk and more talk. The Justice Department was going in with empty hands. In the Senator's phrase: 'They were throwing nowhere near the strike zone.'

Ash read further: Martin Chase was being mentioned as a possible chairman. Chase was an old crony. Ash saw the Senator's long hand, perhaps even that of the Vice-President. The fox was being brought in to count the chickens.

Ash began to relax. It was a comfort to see the wagonmasters close ranks. Eleanor came in dressed for the office, kissed him goodbye as if there'd been no words between them, and drew the bedroom shades. The room was cool, and with the windows locked and the air-conditioner on, there wasn't a sound from the street. It was blissful to burrow deep in bed while others went to work; Ash had come only lately to the softer, self-indulgent pleasures, and prized them all the more for it.

But then he remembered that Sullivan was loose. He'd known all along Sullivan wouldn't play scapegoat. He wasn't a man to take another's fall. There was something stubborn, hard, and retributive in Sullivan, a just man turned around. A bit of a fanatic. Ash had known it and warned the others. But they hadn't listened. Arrogant men, accustomed to having things their own way; Sullivan was one to take his pound of flesh.

Sullivan would be busy now, setting in motion whatever it was he planned. Ash saw him vividly, as if he were moving about the room, and this brought him wide awake. He lay perfectly still and listened, his heart thumping against the mattress. He'd recently had the front door fitted with a Medeco magnetic lock, which Eleanor habitually secured from the outside. A Medeco magnetic was something to give even Sullivan trouble.

But Ash couldn't relax. He lay in bed, weary, his eyes burning with lack of sleep, tense, his ears straining for the sound of a footstep.

It was absurd. Reason told him there was no one in the apartment. But he had to get out of bed and have a look around. He unlocked his desk drawer and took out his Colt .38 Special. He felt a fool with the gun, barefoot and in his pyjamas. But he still checked the door and every window before he put away the gun and returned to bed.

Sullivan had always made him uneasy. He'd never been sure if he liked him, but then Sullivan wasn't a man to like or even dislike. He stood outside of such judgements. One respected him or not, admired his professional competence, one feared him, and tried to make out what made him tick.

What were his private thoughts? Had he a family? Women? What did a man like Sullivan do sexually?

Ash had heard women call him attractive. Others seemed to hate him on sight, perhaps because they feared him, the hard, self-contained look of a man who could take women or leave them.

But Ash had detected something in Sullivan, the more human side of him. Sullivan wasn't a machine, a solitary, one of the freaks. He'd heard of Sullivan with a woman, one of those around Roper. There'd been an affair which had become something else; Sullivan had a soft spot for her. She'd walked out on him in Paris, and Sullivan had gone off his rocker for a time, tore up a few places, put one or two people in the hospital. It had made a situation which cost quite a few thousand dollars to smooth over.

Ash felt better now, thinking of Sullivan. He was calmer, more confident. He was certain that sooner or later he'd be sent to deal with him. He'd have to persuade the Senator and Roper as well that there was reason to fear Sullivan, that he was a dangerous and desperate man, a violent one, and that a better offer must be made.

He knew that he would be sent, and he'd begun to think that he had a handle on Sullivan. And finally Ash drifted off to sleep.

CHAPTER THREE

Sullivan was the first of Roper's people to catch a whiff of the Justice Department's snoops. The same faces kept showing up in different bars, the click of a recording device when he picked up his phone, his mail delivered two days late, which he took to mean it'd been intercepted, read and duplicated; the friendly, jovial fellow in the next seat buying drinks on the Geneva flight. In a New Orleans bar he was picked up by a beautiful girl, but made his excuses and begged off. He was in bed alone three hours later when she knocked on his door, although he'd never mentioned his room number and had given her a false name. In the course of a long and ardent night, she'd asked several leading questions, although he was able to establish that if she was wired, the device could have been planted only in an inlay of one of her back teeth, that being the only possible cavity not thoroughly probed.

Sullivan brought his suspicions to Roper but got nowhere. Roper spoke of a few middle-level Justice gun-slingers out trying to make a reputation; he referred to himself in the third person. He was a top gun. He played in the Super Bowl. When it suited him, Roper liked to prattle on, mimicking the legal-public-relations, media-marketing types around him. Roper was a parodist. He liked his jokes private and was anything but a fool. Still, his cynicism went only as far as to believe that the country was fixed.

Sullivan picked up where he left off: the country was fixed, but the fixers were bunglers. America had begun to look like Uruguay with an army and navy, and Roper was a Boy Scout, a patriot really, his faith vested in the skill of those in power to get away with murder.

That was one side of it, the other was that Roper and the government people had worked things out between them. The press had got wind of one or two things. There had been bungling, dirty money that had been allowed to track up the carpet, and one or two smelly little piles which the press was quick to howl about.

Justice had begun to bear down. The creaking machinery groaned, coughed, and stirred slowly to life. Jack Anderson ferreted out Roper's windfall in Vietnam, *The New York Times* picked it up, and soon a few congressmen on the other side began making hay. *Newsweek* ran a feature about money-laundering in the Bahamas, the Senator's Banking Committee, and tied it all in with paid congressional jaunts to Europe, floozies in London, and grouse shooting on Roper's Scottish moor.

Justice cleared its throat and announced the creation of a grand jury. Indictments were sure to follow. It was getting time to offer up a sacrifice. Sullivan watched shards of evidence and innuendo fall into place. If the enquiry were to be turned off, someone would have to be thrown to the wolves. When the music stopped, Sullivan would find himself standing without a chair. He was to be it.

He began looking around for means to protect himself. His instinct was to find cover, to go underground, establish a second life. He did this while formulating his plan, while still working for Roper. He'd been trained for the clandestine life, for hunting at night, and by now it was his nature. His years with Roper had done nothing to still the instinct.

He sought out a limousine driver, a black named Lew Snead, operating near the Hilton on Sixth Avenue. The Agency had used Snead from time to time, buying identity kits from him. Pocket litter, they called it; still, it was hard to move without it. Sullivan bought two kits from Snead. The first consisted of a California driver's licence, social-security

22

and American Express cards, an assortment of business cards, and a snapshot of a blonde woman and two small children. The licence and cards were in the name of Donald Bowles and the kit cost five hundred dollars. For the second kit he requested only a French driver's licence, and for that, which took the better part of a week, he paid seven hundred and fifty dollars. It was in the name of 'ean-Claude Morvan. Both were undoubtedly traceable, the American Express card was risky for anything beyond identification, but good enough for his immediate purposes. He didn't much care for the woman and children and tore up the photograph.

Using the name Morvan, he rented a small front apartment in a six-storey building on Forty-fourth Street, west of Eighth Avenue.

From Brooks Brothers he bought a three-piece grey suit and two button-down Oxford shirts, two neat striped ties, and a pair of wing-tip shoes. These were for Donald Bowles. Jean-Claude Morvan preferred a beige Yves Saint Laurent suit, two pairs of jeans, lightweight turtleneck sweaters in assorted colours, and the obligatory Gucci slip-ons. He also bought a tube of Estée Lauder Go Bronze, blue-tinted aviator glasses, and a hair blower.

Some time after all of these things were stored in the West Side apartment, he bought a leather pouch, narrow enough to fit in a safe-deposit box; it came with a light combination lock. He carried it one afternoon to the vault of the Marine Midland Bank branch on Park Avenue and asked for the safe-deposit box that he kept in his own name. In a private cubicle, he opened the box; in it was a blank British passport, just as it'd come from Her Majesty's Printing Office. One took a new name and filled it in, changed hair and eye colour by means of dye and coloured contact lenses. One made a new identity, a new being with an untraceable British passport.

Sullivan had bought it years before from a man named Ruddy, a Special Branch officer, whose cover was in the Economic Section of the British Consulate in Saigon. He paid five thousand dollars for it and put it away in his box, treated it as an investment, something put by for a rainy day. The price of an untraceable blank British passport was bound to rise.

Also in the box was a Swiss bankbook with no name, merely an identifying number and signature code, which showed a balance of one hundred and twenty-two thousand Swiss francs; and a chequebook issued by the Nederlandsche Middenstandsbank of Curaçao – there the balance stood at forty-seven thousand five hundred dollars. Another sixty-three hundred dollars was in cash.

He put all this in the narrow leather portfolio, bought a carry-on bag from Crouch & Fitzgerald on Madison Avenue, and went by taxi to the Americana Hotel on Seventh Avenue, where he checked in under the name of Donald Bowles.

The leather portfolio was deposited in a private box in the hotel safe, which, unlike a bank vault, was available to him twenty-four hours a day, seven days a week.

He had completed these preliminary arrangements when the Justice Department called him in for a talk. It was informal at first, rather friendly. The US Attorney was named Neil Soames. He was about thirty-five, bright as a new dime, rapid-fire, quick to impress with his cleverness, hustle, and ambition. His assistant was named Sheffield; Sullivan didn't catch the first name, didn't bother to ask. Sheffield was no more than twenty-five, with a bit of wispy beard and longish straw-coloured hair. Odd for Justice, unless he worked undercover, a narc or one of those detailed to snoop on the radical college crowd.

Also present was a man named Mark Wells. He was a few years older and far smoother. Wells looked as if he played good tennis. He asked no questions, merely listened and took notes on a yellow pad. Sullivan never asked who he was or why he was there.

The meeting meant nothing to Sullivan. He took it to be a signal, a notice served. From now on he was under the gun. But he told them nothing. That was the only line he could take. Justice was fishing; the US Attorney's questions caromed off the wall.

Had he carried cash? Did he know of numbered accounts? Names and dates were thrown at him. Had he acted as a cut-out between Roper and the military?

Sullivan did little more than shake his head; he knew nothing, had seen nothing.

The US Attorney turned to specifics: 'How long have you

beer employed by Roper International?'

'Eight years.'

'During all of that period have you drawn a regular salary?'

'Yes.'

'Last year, how much was that?'

'I filed a federal-tax return for the period.'

'It would be helpful if you volunteered the information.'

'Seventy thousand dollars.'

'Per annum?'

'Yes. Each annum.'

'Were there other benefits?'

'My expenses were paid.'

'How much per year did that come to?'

'I don't have those figures in my head.'

'But they were sizeable?'

'I travelled extensively. It was in the nature of my work.'

'And you did so first-class?'

'Whenever possible.'

'Anything else?'

'There were bonuses.'

'How much were they?'

'About twenty-five thousand dollars.'

'Per year?'

'Per annum,' Sullivan said.

Soames never noticed the rib. 'And what were these bonuses based on?' he said.

'The profits of Roper International.'

'So that your gross income from Roper International was approximately one hundred thousand dollars?'

'And there was a pension plan.' Sullivan permitted himself a thin smile. 'Something every month when I reach sixty-five.'

'Could you tell me what precisely you did for that?' Soames said. 'What your duties were?'

'I was Mr Roper's personal assistant.'

'Why was your employment terminated?'

'A matter of principle.'

'What were your duties?'

Sullivan cleared his throat. 'Roper International is a

conglomerate, three of whose subsidiaries are directly concerned with the design and manufacture of military ordnance and components. First,' and he struck it off on his fingers, 'is the J. L. Hamilton Corporation, which manufactures small arms. J. L. Hamilton was founded by John Laurence Hamilton prior to the War Between the States. It's located in Tennessee, with additional facilities in Texas and Louisiana. Its principal product is the A-57 automatic rifle, which I personally believe to be the finest assault rifle in the world, although of course there are those who would give that honour to the Russian A-26. Second,' and he struck that off on his fingers, 'is Carver Electronics in southern California, a relatively new company which produces components for the Bell Courier, a lightweight helicopter. And third is Pacific Aerodynamics, which works directly with Pratt and Whitney . . .'

'Mr Sullivan' – the US Attorney held up his hand like a traffic policeman – 'my question was what you did – your duties.'

'I thought I was being responsive.'

'Perhaps if you got to the point.'

'I acted as liaison between management of those companies and the military, who were their chief clients.'

'Is it not true that much of this hardware was sold to other countries?'

'And of course I reported on the state of production and relations between management and the military directly to Mr Roper.'

'You have not answered my question.'

'Which question was that?'

'On material sold abroad.'

'We were licensed to sell all over the world.'

'Are you aware that certain of the contracts between the US Government and these Roper subsidiaries were obtained without benefit of competitive bids?'

'No, I was not.'

'And that cost over-runs have been excessive?'

'There have been cost over-runs. I wouldn't characterize them as excessive.'

'How would you characterize them?'

'I wouldn't characterize them at all.'

'Are you still under contract to the CIA?'

'No.'

'Were you at any time during your employment by Roper International?'

'No.'

It was then that Mark Wells broke in to ask his only question: 'During the time you acted as Mr Roper's special assistant, did you have any professional contact with political figures?'

'Mr Roper has many friends in all branches of the government.'

'Do you recall any political figure using influence in obtaining military contracts for any of Mr Roper's subsidiaries?'

Sullivan looked directly at Wells. 'I have no such recollection,' he said.

The meeting ended with a veiled threat. The investigation would continue. Sullivan would be called again, this time to testify under oath.

It was less than a week after this meeting that the direct surveillance began. At first Sullivan thought it was the Justice Department. But then he found his access to Roper cut off. The surveillance came as a relief. He knew how to handle that. He'd been a field agent from the beginning, from the time they'd recruited him.

Since college Sullivan had had only two jobs. The first was with the Agency, the second with Roper. The Agency had recruited him while he was still in college, in his senior year A friend of his father's had called one afternoon, said he was in the neighbourhood and asked if he might drop by. He was a very old friend; Sullivan remembered him as a golfing crony of his father's, and a senior officer at the Department of State, an ambassador to one of the countries in the Middle East. Later, he'd represented the United States at the United Nations. He was a professional, who'd worked under three or four presidents and left the service only when Nixon came in, and went over to the World Bank. He was retired now, and quite an old man – he'd be ten years older than Sullivan's father – and had produced a book about his years in the service. Sullivan had never read it.

Before the man had called, Sullivan had made up his

mind to go on to graduate school; his field was South-East Asia. His father had urged him to go to Columbia, where there were several fine Asian scholars on the faculty, and to learn Vietnamese. He'd grown up in half a dozen countries and had a talent for languages.

That afternoon with his father's friend, Sullivan came slowly to realize that his future had been well thought out by others. He walked with the older man in Riverside Park along the Hudson River. He felt no resentment, no twinge of rebellion. His father was already dead. Over the years Sullivan was to think frequently of that walk with his father's friend along the Hudson River. It was one of those pivotal moments in a young man's life that stay with him always. He remembered feeling grateful, and thinking fondly of this family friend, feeling a certain warmth, as if the spirit of his father were still looking out for him.

He was offered a job as a trainee with the Agency; he accepted at once. Sullivan belonged securely to that class which implemented American policy. Presidents came and went; men like his father and the man walking at his side had continued. They ran things. Sullivan was one of them; he'd been brought up to serve.

While he was a good student, with a gift for mathematics as well as languages, he'd begun to feel restless and in need of direction. To go to work for the Agency seemed natural and right to him.

He was trained in Maryland and in Guatemala. Latin America was warm then, Vietnam still cool, and his Vietnamese was filed away. He never doubted it'd be needed one day, and he kept it up.

He proved to be very good in the field. From the beginning, he'd been wary and secretive, it was his nature. He was a man never without a fall-back position, an escape route. He was good at making new identities for himself. With his languages, he could move in and out of nationalities. He'd stuff a wad of Kleenex in his shoe to change his walk, something between his cheek and gum to alter the shape of his face and speech. He'd comb his hair different ways, wear different clothes, glasses on and off. He had removable caps made for his front teeth. He was an entertaining mimic;

28

there were people in the Agency who swore he could've done it professionally. He knew his way around the clandestine world: where to go for identity papers and passports, and how much they should cost. He'd had access to Agency files and from them learned the names and MO of the better wiremen, shooters, forgers, pick-pockets, and all the speciality trades. There were biochemists on that list, men able to develop a strain of flu virus of sufficient virulence to debilitate a healthy man and kill him of natural causes in two weeks. There were scores of tame doctors to prescribe drugs, and dentists willing and able to install a tiny radio transceiver in a back tooth. It was a very valuable list and as much a part of his capital as an escape route, and he'd written it all down in a black loose-leaf book that he'd stashed in the secure vault of his bank in Basle.

His first assignment had been in Africa, in what was then called the Belgian Congo. He'd worked against Lumumba, but stayed clear of the assassination team which killed Dag Hammarskjöld. As late as 1965 he was operating in South America; in Ecuador, he had his first experience as a prisoner. Each jail has its own unforgettable stink. Of course he was only an amateur smeller of jails, a hobbyist, but a gifted one. There were men in the profession who, like wine-tasters, could sniff a jail and identify the country of origin.

And they stank in America as well. The physical torture was bound to be less than some, the disgrace rather more. In any case, he wasn't going back to jail. On that his mind was made up. He'd been calling Roper to tell him just that. But Roper hadn't returned his calls.

Dying frightened him less than going to jail. He'd intended to tell Roper that as well; it was the jailers he feared and hated, and they were the same everywhere. The jailers and the jailed; he'd seen both sides of that coin and hated both equally. In Ecuador a prisoner had shown him the damp miserable hole in which he was imprisoned and said, '*La miseria*'.

The prisoner was accused of belonging to a terrorist group. Sullivan had interrogated him. He'd been a student but disappeared from the university in Quito and had been captured during a raid on the terrorist base camp in the

Andean foothills. He claimed to know nothing of the ter-rorists, had heard nothing, seen nothing. He wasn't a Marxist. He cared nothing for politics. He'd studied to be a pharmacist. Why had he left his studies, disappearing from the university, from his home? What was he doing wandering armed in the mountains? He'd gone to be alone, to live simply for a time. He needed to be close to God. He was in the throes of a spiritual crisis. He wanted to know if such problems ex-isted in the United States. Was Señor Sullivan familiar with such matters? He was. Sullivan assured the former pharmacy student that he was sympathetic to all manner of spiritual crisis. He offered him a Marlboro cigarette and let him keep the pack.

The prisoner pointed to his stinking black hole of a cell and said again: '*La miseria*'.

He tried to persuade Sullivan that he was a man without politics. Certainly he was no hero, no liberator; that was his claim. To live in such misery, to face death for a political idea was madness. He was an ordinary man, somewhat selfish and at times petty. He was afflicted with spiritual crises. He had a mother in Quito, and a fiancée. He pleaded with Sullivan to be released. He wanted nothing in life but to be allowed to return to his mother, to his fiancée, and the study of pharmacy.

And he knew nothing of the terrorists, not their names, not their whereabouts. Nothing.

Sullivan gave up on him and he was led back to his cell. *La miseria.*

Sullivan heard later that he was tortured and then shot.

It was years before Sullivan thought of him. One word from him and the former pharmacy student would've been freed. But he'd been the jailer, born and bred to fulfil that role. He was therefore able to perform it effortlessly, without guilt or self-doubt.

When the time came for the roles to be reversed and Sullivan was caught and shut up in a damp black hole, he took as naturally to that role. And it never surprised him.

He was interrogated, starved, beaten, and humiliated. Night after night he waited to be shot. But even then, all through those freezing and interminable nights, he never thought of the pharmacy student, who rightfully belonged to the other side, to the jailed. And as long as Sullivan's character remained intact he remained free of any guilt for what he'd done to the pharmacy student and all the others like him. And if a man is without guilt, he has nothing to fear. He leads a charmed life. His destiny is secure. This was taken by his enemies to be courage. But Sullivan wasn't fooled; he knew it was something deeper and more profound, something essential. One might lose courage, gain it back, lose it again. Fear of death is a day-to-day thing. Sullivan survived as a prisoner because in spirit he remained always the jailer, a man serving the right and lawful side. He was never alone in his stinking black hole, never abandoned. He served a mighty nation, a virtuous people. And finally his faith was rewarded, America took care of its own; he was traded for a whole squad of rebels and set free.

The end of it came in Vietnam. There, he saw horrors committed which shook even his faith and made him ashamed of his part in them. He became confused, lost confidence in America and in himself, and for the first time began to brood on the fate of the pharmacy student and others like him he'd seen imprisoned and shot.

His faith in his country was in fact faith in the virtue, wisdom, and goodwill of men older and more powerful than himself. America was governed, despite occasional lapses, by imperfect but decent men, who believed in a Christian God and recognized and submitted to the law and moved slowly but steadily in the direction of what was just and right. Sullivan had grown up during the Cold War, which the Russians had started and perpetuated. They were engaged in a conspiracy, the object of which was to undermine and eventually destroy the Western democracies. They were expansionists; we were not. We were men of goodwill; they were not. They imprisoned and murdered their own people for acts of dissent. They did these things; we did not. And when the execution of the Rosenbergs was mentioned by one or another of the radicals whom Sullivan knew in the late 1950s and early 1960s, or when they invoked the evils of the McCarthy era, Sullivan answered by saying that there was a Communist conspiracy, which was something quite different from dissent. And if the liberals had more clearly recognized and acted on this distinction, and them-

31

selves exposed and repudiated the Communist conspiracy, men like McCarthy, Nixon, Rankin, and all the rest would never have got started.

Sullivan had been taught his faith in school, in the books he read, by his mother and, to a greater extent, by his father, who had graduated from West Point and spent his life in the army. Colonel Sullivan's faith had never wavered. And neither had that of Sullivan's older brother, who had followed their father to the Point: not until one breathless steaming afternoon in a tent in the Mekong.

Sullivan was part of a CIA interrogation team, detached to CIC, with a temporary rank of first lieutenant. His brother Tim was a captain, commanding a company. Sullivan had been eighteen months in Vietnam, a good bit of it in evaluation in Saigon; Tim had had ten months of almost continual combat.

When Sullivan learned that Tim's company was in the area, he'd hunted him down. He hadn't seen Tim in almost two years and was shocked by how he'd changed. He'd always been the bigger and heavier of the two, the other brother who could lift more weight, throw a ball farther, run faster. He genially set records that Sullivan was never able to match. But Sullivan was never jealous of him, never envious. He was his hero, more so than their father, a distant, godly figure. Tim's touchdown against Notre Dame was the high point of Sullivan's youth.

That afternoon in the Mekong he barely recognized him. Tim had lost twenty pounds, his powerful body looked shrunken and exhausted, his face haggard. And his eyes, which had looked out with a bold and confident glint, now were hollow and fearful; he spoke slowly, in a flat, monotonous voice, his eyes avoiding his brother's. He gave the impression of a man who'd been used up. Slowly, he began to describe the horrors he'd seen. He confided his weariness and fear. He opened his heart. And all in the same flat voice. Suddenly his eyes filled with tears. But he never changed expression, never raised his voice or cried out; only his burning eyes expressed what he'd lived through.

As he spoke, different scenes of their childhood flashed through Sullivan's mind: Tim lifting weights in the garage behind a house they'd lived in for a time in Virginia. And the times they had ridden together on a dappled horse their father had bought them. They'd often slept on bunk beds in the same room and for years Sullivan had fallen asleep listening in the dark to the creak of the springs as his brother moved on the bed above him.

He'd learned many lessons from Tim, and that afternoon in the Mekong, he learned another: Tim had seen the wholesale massacre of Vietnamese civilians by Americans. He'd found the corpses of women and children and seen them hastily buried in mass graves. He'd reported what he'd seen to his superiors and been ordered by them to keep it to himself. The crimes of this war were to be kept secret. Officers in the American Army had done what the Nazis had done, and other American officers, classmates of his father at West Point, had covered up the facts. He'd known of enlisted men who'd murdered their officers but weren't charged or brought to trial because if the press got wind of it, word would get back to the people at home.

'What happened to the enlisted men?' Sullivan said. 'To the killers?'

'We shot them,' Tim said, 'and reported them killed in action.'

Sullivan lowered his voice: 'Did you shoot any of them?'

'I'm no better than the rest,' Tim said.

They spent only that one afternoon together. When they parted, embracing awkwardly and with some embarrassment, for neither was a demonstrative man, Sullivan felt that he'd never see his brother again. Tim had to return to his company and had another month before he was rotated. They agreed to meet in Saigon and hitch a ride to Bangkok. Their laughter was strained. Neither believed the meeting would take place.

It suddenly began to rain, fiercely, in solid sheets, and just as suddenly it stopped and the sun came out, hotter than ever. A rotten smell rose from the steaming earth. The brothers promised again to meet in Saigon.

Two weeks later Tim was killed. Sullivan never learned the exact circumstances of his death.

His brother's death changed Sullivan. He continued to carry out orders, as Tim had, and like Tim, he became a killer, reluctantly at first, and then coldly and without conscience. He became as cynical and ruthless as the rest, at first bewildered by what he saw and then brutalized by it. He came upon the dark side of his soul and for a time found evil easier than he'd imagined. Evil was a piece of cake. It certainly cost him less than it had his brother.

He was made a senior agent with the temporary rank of captain and put in charge of a Phoenix interrogation team with headquarters in Saigon, making frequent trips into the battle zones. He had direct contact with both sides and knew what was going on. He gathered the small, ugly facts of the war and made them into a pattern, which he passed on. It was bad news. We were doing everything wrong. It wasn't working. But no one seemed to be listening. He put defeat in one end of the pipeline and saw victory come trumpeting out the other. Each report he wrote was turned upside-down. At the same time he was commended for his work, his performance record was excellent, and there was talk of putting him to work learning one of the Chinese dialects and promoting him to major. Once or twice he thought he might be going crazy, but realized it was the effect of seeing reality turned upside-down. He dreamed frequently of his brother, vivid, haunting dreams, and more than once, at his desk or in the field, he heard his voice, and even saw him. None of this frightened him. He didn't even think it odd. He uncovered a ghostly mystical soul.

The dead pharmacy student came to him in dreams. 'Are you familiar with a spiritual crisis? Do they have such things in the United States?'

And Sullivan asked him, 'Wandering in the mountains, are you closer to God?'

He believed that the spirit of his brother had survived, and that of his father and of his mother as well, although he never saw them. Perhaps the war had worn him down more than he thought. Certainly he'd changed; some mornings he looked in the mirror and didn't recognize the ravaged face staring back at him.

He suffered most from living in a time and place which made an enemy of truth, and from serving a government which had grown to despise it.

He'd never been a reflective man or an introspective one,

but a technician with a gift for languages and analytic reasoning, and was therefore unequipped to deal with this new order which denigrated the values that he had been taught to respect. He became cynical, dissolute, and hard. He drank and brawled and whored. He became stupid. He read nothing and even the superb athlete's body which he'd built, tuning it like the engine of a racing car, even his muscles and wind went to seed.

But the voice of truth and the ideals of discipline and good work were never completely silenced. His conscience woke him in the middle of the night, reproaching him for what he'd become and reminding him of his true nature. At the bottom of the pit, in the worst of times, he never doubted that his nature was to be as his father had raised him and his brother, and that he'd betrayed them both. His character had been violated by terrible events, and had he lived in a better or at least simpler time, he would never have lost track of himself.

Roper picked Sullivan in Vietnam. Several of his companies sold directly to the military, and he first arrived on an inspection tour in the same party as the Secretary of Defence. He was thick with most of the senior officers and several senators and congressmen. Sullivan was assigned to him early in 1966 and served as his guide and interpreter. They got on well. Roper returned to the United States, the war effort was increased, and he grew richer and more powerful, expanding his influence in Washington and with the military. He kept in touch with Sullivan. Returning to Saigon late in 1966 he asked for him.

Roper was an odd-looking duck, a lanky awkward man, with the build of a basketball player, six feet five or six and skinny, with high bony shoulders. But his long, spidery, freckled arms were strong as steel bands: Sullivan had seen him bend a dime between his thumb and first finger. He had great enthusiasm and boundless energy. Sullivan had never known anyone who could get by on so little sleep or put away so much liquor. He also ate prodigiously, but never regular meals: he'd become involved in something and forget to eat, and then gorge himself on two or three steaks and half a dozen eggs. He seemed never to want anything but steak and eggs and huge quantities of milk. His sexual appetite was also prodigious. He consumed women as he did food, forgetting about them for days and then ravishing them in bunches, like grapes.

But of course his overriding concern was money. He believed in its magical properties; money was like the sun, like fresh water or the soil, part of the natural earthly order of things. He liked the crisp feel of cash, and to roll it around in his fingers; it was miraculous, this generative power of money, a source of all things.

His first serious money had been made in 1951, peddling office machines and the first generation of computers. Four years later, using three hundred thousand dollars of borrowed capital – the man who loaned it to him was later killed in a private plane crash and Roper settled with the estate at fifty cents on the dollar – he founded a company called Dallas Data Analysis – DDA – which leased computers on a long-term basis and rented them short term at far higher rates to small businesses. The business grew rapidly, too rapidly, so that it suffered from chronic undercapitalization. There was simply not enough cash in the till to undertake long-term leases in sufficient number to fill the demand of small businesses to sublease the computers. Still, the potential profit was enormous.

And it was then that Roper discovered his greatest talent, and the one gift which would lead him directly to the upper slopes of American finance, where one played among the centimillionaires: Roper could sweet-talk banks. Later he was to use federal charter rights to create his own banks, to lend himself other people's money.

But in the 1950s he was still putting the money that had begun to trickle in from DDA alongside borrowed capital. He opened salesrooms all over the south-west, hired teams of salesmen, and inside of three years was writing leases on forty million dollars a year. The money rolled in. In 1958, in order to have stock to trade with and acquire other companies, he took DDA public, selling one million shares at twelve dollars a share. With a viable stock and a now-firm credit line, he set about acquiring companies; each acquisition increased the earnings of the parent, which raised the price of the stock and made it easier to acquire more companies, continuing the cycle.

He had arrived at that shadowy intersection where big business and government meet. He began to play in the Washington fields. London came into it, Brussels, Bonn, Paris. He bought ranches and Bahamian keys, shot grouse in Scotland with his Washington friends. He had an instinct for big numbers and his companies moved quickly into military hardware. He was in the Congo and North Africa and the Middle East. Payment was made to a holding company formed in Luxemburg. Its directors were remote, untouchable. The goods were shipped under the Bahamian and Liberian flags. Cash and anonymous cashiers' cheques filled numbered accounts. A rush of money flowed back and forth through undetected channels.

But of course the greatest bonanza of all was Vietnam.

Vast amounts of equipment were needed quickly and accounting was loose. Millions of dollars in weapons, trucks, and ammunition were misplaced. There were instances of cargo which was signed for, unloaded, and then stored in places which either couldn't be found or simply didn't exist. Small arms, ammunition, and rations disappeared by the truckload. Nothing could be done without payoffs all along the line. Americans and Vietnamese made illegal fortunes. It was in this atmosphere that Roper flourished. He raked in vast amounts of money. Nobody knew just how much. Perhaps he didn't know himself.

Roper never bragged, rarely talked about himself; Sullivan thought him the only man in America to make two hundred million dollars without boring the pants off the men he drank with.

But Roper did like to talk about the army, the old army; he was with the first American troops to land in North Africa, and two years later he came ashore with the first waves on D-Day. His eyes lit up when he talked about D-Day and the heroism of the men he'd served with, never mentioning his own. Sullivan had to pull Roper's service record to learn he'd been awarded a Silver Star for action on 8 June 1944, and had a cluster added to it in Belgium five months later.

Soon Sullivan became his pal, his buddy, the brother he never had. And perhaps Roper also became something of a brother to Sullivan. By this time Tim and his father were dead. Sullivan needed someone to replace them, a masculine presence, but one without a conscience, one morally unable to judge him.

Roper liked nothing better than to get himself up in fatigues, strap on a side arm, and drive with Sullivan into the combat zones. For men like Sullivan it was a free and foot-loose war. He came and went as he pleased, reported to no one. Because Saigon disgusted him, he lived most of his time in the field. And Roper was happy to be with him, to sit in on fire fights and go out on patrols. Viet Cong interrogations fascinated him. He witnessed the executions, and once or twice pulled the trigger himself. He knew weapons and was good under fire. He was one of those to whom combat was the very best of blood sports. He insisted on living as the grunts did, that was part of the sport, without special food or comfort of any kind. Roper had a strong stomach.

But finally the war wound down and the Americans began to go home. By that time Sullivan was sick of it. He wanted no more of it. Roper immediately offered him a job.

And what would be his duties?

'Pal, aide-de-camp,' Roper said. 'Personal representative, confidant, right hand.'

'In other words, bagman.'

'Something like that,' Roper said, and looked wicked.

He liked and admired Sullivan, but not so much that he wouldn't rather own him. Sullivan was sick of Vietnam, of the Agency. His conscience was dead. He let himself be bought.

CHAPTER FOUR

Ash slept for two hours, but wasn't at all refreshed. His dreams had been vivid and alarming, a swift, disconnected sequence of portraits, of mug shots. A harrowing gallery of criminals and chief inspectors he'd known over the years. One or two dead uncles and, finally, Sullivan.

He lay awake thinking of him. There was reason to fear him, a man with a closed, spare life, one without women, like Ash's nightmares.

He replaced the receiver of the phone, which Eleanor had thought to remove before leaving for her office. Almost at once, it rang.

It was Louise Vernon, Ash's secretary. Normally unflappable, she was now quite excited.

'I'm sorry to bother you at this number,' she said. Louise had been with Ash from his first day with Roper and she was the only person in the organization whom he trusted. There were, in fact, few secrets that he kept from her.

'Geneva's been burning up the overseas wires. The boss himself got on. Something urgent. He wouldn't say what about.'

Ash knew what Roper wanted: Sullivan. He marvelled at how quickly Lemoyne had reached his people and they had run down Roper.

Louise said, 'And Twinkletoes has been calling every ten minutes since nine. Condition red.' Louise handed out nicknames; Twinkletoes was Lemoyne's. 'You're to meet him at the Athletic Club at five. The Senator will be there.'

'Anything else?'

'He asked me to go to Las Vegas with him,' she said. 'I don't believe he poisoned his wife. I think living with Twinkletoes the lady killed herself.'

'I'll be there in half an hour.'

Ash had a brief cold shower, shaved, and dressed in eight minutes, and went by taxi to Park Avenue and Forty-eighth Street. His office, in one of those steel and glass towers, was on the twenty-eighth floor.

Ash had crossed the lobby and was on the escalator leading to the elevators on the mezzanine when someone came up from behind and touched his elbow.

He was young, somewhere between twenty-five and thirty, with long hair and a wispy beard. He wore jeans and scuffed desert boots, but with a tweed jacket and blue work shirt and tie. It was the tie which caught Ash's eye, a pattern made up of tiny yellow golfers on a brown field, an expensive tie made of heavy silk.

'Mr Morgan, I'd like to talk to you a minute about Jack Sullivan. I hear he's talked to the Department of Justice.'

Ash stepped off the escalator and headed directly for the elevator, looking neither to the right nor left, his jaw set, silent, the young man staying at his elbow.

'I'm with Justice, Mr Morgan. I thought we could have a chat informally, off the record. Nothing logged in or out of your office.'

A security guard stood just to the right of an open elevator door. Ash caught his eye, glanced over at the young man, and shook his head. The guard understood; as Ash stepped into the elevator, the guard moved in front of the young man, blocking his way. The young man tried unsuccessfully to go around him. He called out to Ash, but the heavy steel elevator door slid shut and Ash rode alone in the car to the twenty-eighth floor.

Louise met him at his office door with a cup of coffee. She was forty-one years old and unmarried, originally from Iowa, far from beautiful, but always perfectly groomed and stylishly dressed, with a tall, willowy figure and a dry, low-key wit. She was clever, loyal, and efficient, normally in complete control, the one exception being at an office party one Christmas when she'd got smashed and confessed to Ash her fantasies about sleeping with him. He took her home and rather dutifully took her to bed. It turned out to be extraordinary. In public, she was a cool, sage, and self-contained woman, who never flirted or played the coquette; it took time, experience, and sensitivity before a man noticed her sexuality. Ash had been rather slow on the uptake. Taking her to bed turned out to be a revelation. Under a severe Chanel suit, she wore breathtaking underwear. She was bawdy and experimental, a two-dollar pistol as the old saying went. She described herself as suffering from a courtesan complex, and would stop at nothing to please and titillate Ash. They slept together on the average of once a week after that, usually when working late, and more often than not on the shaggy carpet covering his office floor. It became a cherished spot of theirs, the floor of his office, although late on the memorable night during which Ash successfully arranged the transfer of one and a half million in cash from Toronto to a small boat off Montauk Point, he was inspired to turn her around and bend her face-down over his Louis XIV desk. She was later to demand more of the same, the only demand she ever made, and seemed to want no more from him than he did from her, never permitting their hectic sexual bouts to intrude on daily office routine.

She remained a brilliant secretary and an independent woman with a life of her own. For nineteen years she'd been having an affair with a man known to Ash only as 'My Little Jewish Gentleman'.

One night on the office floor, she told Ash the story.

My Little Jewish Gentleman turned out to be immensely rich, a self-made man with a widowed mother, a German refugee who'd sacrificed everything for her only son. 'She scrubbed floors,' Louise said, 'she waited on tables, she sewed and worked as a maid. Not one day did he appear in law school without a clean shirt.'

By the time he and Louise met, the mother was dying of cancer. Terminal, the doctors agreed, a matter of months, perhaps weeks. The mother begged the son not to marry the Shiksa while she lived. Dead and gone, he could do as he wished. My Little Jewish Gentleman of course agreed to wait.

Once extracting this solemn promise, the mother staged a remission, which, Louise said, 'brought the AMA to its feet, cheering'.

While Ash sipped his coffee in her office, through which one passed in order to get to his, she handed him a wad of pink telephone-message slips.

'Most of them are nothing. I either handled them for you or told them you were out of town. Reese called twice.'

'What would I do if I lost you, Louise?'

'You give that a little serious thought,' she said, 'and see if you come up with a bright answer.'

'What did Reese say?'

'He had nothing. He was still plugging. He'll be in touch.'

'Anything else?'

'Houston called about the deep-pressure drilling bits for Teheran. Should we use our own carrier or Pan Am?'

'Do we have one of our own routed?'

'Not until Tuesday.'

'Tell them to go with Pan Am. But call Hendricks and tell him to keep an eye on them.'

'That's it then.'

'I need ten minutes alone,' Ash said. 'Hold my calls. Nothing. I've got one or two things to think over.'

'There's somebody waiting to see you. He's in your office.'

'I don't want to see anybody.'

'You'll see this fellow.'

It was Dave, Ash's son. He was a half a head taller than Ash, large-boned but skinny, near-sighted, and had a mop of curly black hair, big ears, and a charming and ingenuous smile.

Dave was sprawled on the couch reading the *Times*, a duffel bag and a tennis racquet on the floor beside him, but scrambled to his feet when he saw his father. They put their arms around each other and Ash kissed him; he'd always kissed his son, as his father had kissed him.

'Great surprise,' Ash said. 'But you should've told me you were coming.'

'I called all over town but I couldn't get hold of you.' Dave's smile was crafty; there had been one or two competitive and abrasive years between them, but now he often seemed amused by his father. He loved and respected him, but there was in his attitude a hint of condescension. This was a recent development, one which Ash took easily in his stride, and seemed almost to encourage. Dave's boyish awe of his father had gone on rather long, and there were times, in early adolescence, when he seemed afraid of him. Ash did too many things too well, his forcefulness and competence, the violence in the foreground of his life and 'he trembling respect which Dave often saw in the attitude of other men before his father, could easily have intimidated him. Ash was sensitive to that. He'd seen too many ruined sons of powerful men. So he encouraged his independence and, at times, an easy banter which approached impertinence.

But at the same time he'd been forced to serve as both father and mother, so that he reached out too eagerly to help and protect him. There was certainly a tender, maternal side to Ash's love. He often felt bewildered by the young man standing before him. It seemed a miracle that he was grown up and virtually independent. The achievements and happiness of his son weighed heavily in the judgement Ash made upon his own life.

But this was the kind of thing Ash kept to himself. It was

42

some comfort to imagine that in his own middle years, a father himself, Dave might come belatedly to understand him.

But for the present he suffered these small hints of condescension. Dave was clever and, with this carefully nurtured confidence, had become a brilliant student. He was a son certain he'd gone beyond his father. The men he admired most were doctors, scholars, and scientists, men far removed from his father's experience. He sometimes praised his father's 'native intelligence', a left-handed compliment which took for granted Ash's limitations.

'I stayed at the house last night,' he said. 'There was a call for you about one o'clock. It sounded urgent. I tried to reach you, but I haven't the number of your various hide-outs.'

'I stayed in town at the Athletic Club,' Ash said.

'I spoke to Ben Wade, though,' Dave said. 'My old roommate. He's got classes until three, and then we're going to play a couple of sets. How about you taking on the loser?'

'You think the old man can't whip you?'

'I make you even money for the first set. How about it?'

Ash shook his head. 'There's no way I can get out of here today.' Ash noted that David's disappointment was hollow. For some time he'd gone easy with his father on the tennis court. Their games were close, while both knew he could demolish his father any time he chose to. Ash had come late to tennis, while David had been given lessons and sent to tennis camp as a boy.

Ash was relieved when Louise Vernon buzzed him on the inter-office phone. 'There's a Telex coming through from Geneva.'

'Hold it for me,' Ash said.

'And there's a guy in tennis shoes here. Been hanging around trying to see you for days.'

'Young, with a beard?'

'Name of Sheffield.'

'Give him to public relations.'

'He's persistent. He wants you.'

'I haven't time for an interview,' Ash said. David's eyes were on him and Ash found himself showing off. 'And they're desert boots, not tennis shoes.'

'May I be permitted a personal observation, Mr Morgan?' Louise said into the phone.

Ash glanced at Dave to be certain he couldn't hear. 'You certainly may,' he said.

'You look rather weary this morning,' she said softly into the mouthpiece. 'Neglected and unloved.'

'In that case we may have to work late tonight,' Ash said.

'By the oddest coincidence, it's pinochle night for My Little Jewish Gentleman,' she said. 'And the Good Soldier Reese called again. I put him off.' There was a moment and then Louise said, 'What do I do if Mr Sullivan calls?'

'He won't call,' Ash said.

'We might contact him,' she said. 'Shall I try?'

Ash again glanced over at David; the boy was watching his father with a tolerant, rather supercilious smile; at that moment Ash didn't much care for his son.

'Let's wait on that,' he said and hung up.

'What's going on?' David said. 'I get the feeling I've stumbled into World War Three.'

'I sometimes have the same feeling.' Ash smiled, his voice conciliatory, although David's had been smart-alecky. When the boy was younger, Ash's anger sometimes swept over him without warning, taking him by surprise. The boy would stand helplessly before him, his eyes wide and frightened, fighting back the tears.

'I hear the roof is about to fall in on your boss,' David said.

'I hadn't heard that.'

'There's talk of indicting him, isn't there?'

Ash's smile had faded, but the last thing he wanted this morning was an argument with David. 'He's a controversial man,' he said.

'That was very suave,' David said. 'You really have learned how to skilfully evade a direct question.'

'I know of no indictment of Mr Roper,' Ash said. 'I know of none impending or even contemplated.'

'Well, he should be indicted. He should be punished.'

'For what?'

'For stock fraud. Income-tax evasion. Bribery of public officials.'

'You know for a fact he's guilty of all that?'

'And a great deal more,' David said. 'Don't you?'

'I'm not a lawyer and you're not a theologian. Neither are you much of a moral philosopher. If Roper is guilty of anything, it's of making a lot of money.'

'From the Vietnam war.'

'Which is a moral issue, not a legal one. I suggest you try to keep the two separate.'

'And I suggest you stop defending cut-throats like Roper, and the crooks in Washington who are paid to protect him. Roper's a thief. They ought to drag him back from Geneva, or wherever he's holed up, and put him in the dock. And when they find him guilty they ought to throw him in jail.'

Ash allowed David's outburst to pass. His first anger had faded and finally he said coolly, 'If I thought Walt Roper was a crook, I wouldn't work for him. I'd quit today.'

David met his father's gaze; there was a time he believed everything his father said, but both realized that time had passed. Ash wondered to which of them the loss was greater.

'Look, son,' Ash said, 'the Justice Department has been investigating Walt Roper on and off for years, and they've come up empty. Nothing concrete, nothing which would be grounds for an indictment.'

'Roper owns the Justice Department,' David said. 'That's why they've never come up with anything against him.'

'You studied logic,' Ash said. 'I didn't, but I do recognize a circular argument. The investigations of Roper have provided no hard evidence against him; therefore the investigations are dishonest. There's an alternative possibility, which is that no hard evidence has been uncovered because none exists. But that would mean Roper is innocent.'

But David wasn't listening. 'Roper hasn't been caught because he's rich. If you're rich enough you buy the lawyers, and they thread their way through the law, they stand the law on its head, and if that doesn't work, they buy the men who make the laws.'

'Ah, so that's how it works,' Ash spoke lightly, with a self-conscious raising of his eyes, determined to keep it gay.

'It's all money,' David said. 'America has come to the point where that's all there is. My psych. professor says that's all they dream about. I know it's all they talk about. It's even all they fight about. Last summer when I was in Emergency at Bellevue, every fracas we got was over money. Women, men, kids – all shooting and cutting each other over money. Knife wounds, garrottings, scaldings, acid burns, ice picks, guns, razors – all about money. Where have the crimes of passion gone? Where is jealousy? Envy yes, jealousy no! Give me lust, oh Lord! Give me sexual passion!'

'At these moments you remind me of my Uncle Ralph,' Ash said, 'your grandfather's youngest brother. He was also given to social commentary, indignation, and oratory. A trained optometrist, he settled in Los Angeles, married a Chinese woman, and did very well.'

'Greed is not a joking matter,' David said.

'Neither is it altogether a serious one,' Ash said.

Now David sighed and sat beside his father on the couch opposite his desk, without self-consciousness taking hold of his hand.

'I didn't know your Uncle Ralph married a Chinese woman,' David said.

'Lovely little woman,' Ash said. 'Set a beautiful table and had the smallest feet you ever saw.'

But David didn't find that funny. 'You never will fight with me, will you?' he said. 'And you never really let me get sore at you. Or stay sore anyway.'

'If that's a criticism,' Ash said, 'it's an odd one for a son to make.'

'What're you afraid of?' David said. 'That if we ever start fighting we'll never stop? For years now I've watched you avoid the basic issues.'

'Probably because I don't know what in hell they are – the basic issues.'

'I'm talking about the natural conflict between a father and son.'

'I never felt any conflict. I have always loved you.'

'And condescended to me. Even now you treat me like a kid, one you can't argue with on equal terms.'

Ash said, 'Are you telling me that now that you're a man I should stop treating you as a son? Fat chance, Davey.'

'No. No more than I can stop treating you as a father. But you must remember that you're not the only person who

46

knows what the world is like really. The real world. I'm to be a doctor. Protected. The most secure of all professions. In the meantime you're out in the real world slaying the dragons.'

Ash said slowly, 'I've been told that before. Just this morning, in fact.'

'How is Eleanor?' David said.

Ash managed a smile and said, 'You ought to think about psychiatry.'

'Or palmistry.'

'Eleanor is fine,' Ash said.

'Wonderful girl. You ought to marry her.'

'Thanks for the advice.'

'It's on the house,' David said. 'By the way, have I told you I'll be interning in Houston?'

'No.'

'I was accepted there a couple of weeks ago, I thought I mentioned it. It's the spot I wanted. Houston is tops for cardiovascular. I'll intern there, residency if I'm good enough.'

'We have offices there,' Ash said.

'I don't need anything.'

'In case you do.'

'I won't.'

'But we will keep in touch?' Ash said.

'Of course we will.'

'I'll call you next week.'

'I've got to get going or I'll miss the tennis.'

'Goodbye, Davey.'

After David had left, Louise came in with a Telex message from Geneva.

Ash read it at a glance:

IMPERATIVE LOST ARTICLE BE FOUND.
YOU ARE TO ASSUME PERSONAL CHARGE.
REPEAT PERSONAL. ASCERTAIN CONDITIONS
FOR RETURN. ACKNOWLEDGE. ROPER

Ash spread the Telex on his desk. The ball had been handed to him and he didn't like it. He was not an officer of the Astra Corporation, he owned no stock, had profited by none of its transactions. No deposit slips were in his name, no cheques. Nothing existed to tie him to it. He was merely the guardian of a file locked away in his safe. He could walk away. If the investigation heated up, he might be singed a bit, but nothing serious, nothing he couldn't finesse.

Eleanor seemed to be serious about Hong Kong. David was grown, determined to be on his own, his wife beyond reach. There was nothing here to keep him. He went as far as to calculate how much cash he had, the assets he could quickly liquidate. What brought him up short was the image of tagging along after Eleanor, an older man without a job, living frugally on cautiously invested capital, scrambling to make an extra dollar or two, faintly ridiculous.

Ash struck a match and lit a corner of the Telex. He stood outside of himself, a witness to one of those rare moments of clear moral choice. A question of character. He could lash himself to Roper, cover for him, obstruct justice, bribe and threaten; or he could get out. He could resign. He could say no.

But even now, as he watched himself at a moral crossroads, he knew that his fate was already sealed, his mind made up. There was no real choice. He supported certain vanities and respect of certain men, and was secure where he was. He was pleasures, he'd built his life around the comradeship and not indignant; those ancient fires had gone out. Not a feather of bitter smoke against Roper's blue sky. He doubted that all his early idealism had ever done a lick of unmitigated good.

But if he didn't say no to Roper, neither did he say yes. He simply acted. He called Louise into his office and told her to call the number of an answering service located in a small office in the Empire State Building. He instructed her to leave a message for Mr Weston. He was to call her. She was to tell him his suit was ready for a fitting. Would it be convenient for Mr Weston to come in today? He was to give her a time.

Louise understood. She made a shorthand note of the message without asking Ash what it was about.

Ash went out for a walk and spent an hour in Central Park. He wondered only if Mr Weston was still calling in to the answering service for his messages, and if he would return

Ash's call. And if they met, what Ash would say to him.

Tactics occupied Ash's mind. The moral issues slipped quietly away. While he had said neither yes or no his actions bound him closer to Roper.

It was nearly two when he returned to his office. Mr Weston had returned his call.

'Not personally,' Louise said. 'Not Our Mr Weston.' She knew who Weston was, made sure Ash knew she knew. *Our* Mr Weston. An unmarried woman of forty-one, she fed on these pale unspoken confidences.

Ash saw her apartment, one neat, maidenly room with a fold-up bed and a dining alcove. She had served him dinner in that tiny alcove, an elaborate candlelight affair, the chicken chasseur catered, but served on her very own Minton, the wine in Baccarat crystal. He had been touched by the gravity with which she treated their little dinner.

'An operator at the answering service called for him,' Louise said. 'He'll be in for his fitting at four. He said he knew the address.'

'Four it is,' Ash said.

'The gun is in your safe,' she said. 'You'd better take that.'

That hadn't occurred to him. The idea was absurd, but he chose to humour her. 'You think Our Mr Weston is dangerous?'

'Like a rattler,' she said.

Ash worked at routine matters for another hour. Mr Weston had his suits fitted at the Port Authority Bus Terminal on the West Side. Ash arrived there at 3.55.

Weston was a cover name for Sullivan. Some months before, when both realized the possibility that Sullivan might eventually have to go underground, Ash had suggested an emergency means of making contact. Sullivan had gone along. He'd chosen the name Weston and picked the answering service, paying a year in advance by means of a postal money order. They'd agreed in advance to meet at Teepee Town in the bus terminal.

Both men were professionals with a high degree of mutual respect and some trust. While he fidgeted in the terminal waiting for Sullivan, Ash wondered how much of that trust remained. Sullivan was outside now, utterly on his own, and

Ash knew how rapidly a man on the outside came to distrust everyone.

At four o'clock, the terminal was already busy. There were a dozen ways in and out, a perfect place to lose surveillance. Sullivan would have every chance to see that Ash had come alone.

But Sullivan never appeared. Ash waited an hour and went away wondering what Sullivan was up to, and how he'd go about making contact with him now. He rejected the notion of calling the answering service again.

Ash hadn't eaten since early breakfast with Eleanor and was ravenous. He left the terminal by way of Ninth Avenue and walked past all the food shops until he came to Manganaro's. Between the lunch hour and dinner, the self-service restaurant was nearly empty. Ash had the counterman build a splendid hero sandwich, bought a bottle of beer to drink with it, and only when he turned away from the counter did he see Sullivan. He was alone at a small table in the rear, his back to the wall, facing the door.

'Are you going to eat all of that, Ash?' he said.

'Half is for you.'

'Are there anchovies on it?' Sullivan said.

'D'you like anchovies?'

'Can't stand them.'

'There are no anchovies,' Ash said.

Sullivan wasn't a large man, but he was strongly built, as if he'd worked with weights or been a boxer. His nose had once been badly broken and then reset. He looked as though he'd once played violent sports; after he went to work for Roper he let himself go, drinking too much and putting on fat. Now he looked hard and in condition.

He dressed with some care, leather jackets and turtleneck sweaters. He never wore shoes with laces, always Italian slip-ons; he wore blue-tinted aviator glasses. There was a good deal of actor in him, and he liked to deceive people, to appear different from the man he was. He liked disguises.

His eyes were grey and his hair straight, dark, and neatly parted, and he had the kind of dense bluish beard that needed shaving twice a day, the look of a man built to last, one able to handle things, to endure, who had made up his mind and was ready to play his hand to the end.

'You look well,' Ash said. 'Have you gone into training? You look different.'

'You look the same, Ash.'

'Radio City was a neat piece of work,' Ash said.

'Reese put his hounds on me,' Sullivan said. 'He wouldn't have done that if you hadn't told him to.'

'You've made Roper and the others nervous,' Ash said.

'And the hounds made me nervous.'

'I told Reese to call them off. I told him you could shake them whenever you wanted. But he's stubborn. He's still got them out on the street.'

'Reese is honest. He gives a day's work for a day's pay.'

The notion amused Sullivan, who showed his teeth when he smiled; they were large and white, one of those in the front chipped. There was a story about being kicked by a horse as a kid. He'd told Ash the story in a bar waiting out a storm in the Caracas airport. Both were drunk, and Ash remembered that Sullivan had translated for two whores at the bar. Soon the whores were drunk as well, the storm lashing the panoramic windows of the bar, and Ash thinking about Sullivan's brother, who was buried in Arlington National Cemetery.

'You've got to understand, it's not all in my hands,' Ash said. 'Not any more, Jack. Probably it never was.'

Sullivan ignored that. He seemed not even to have heard. Ash saw that he was abstracted, deep in his own thoughts, his own plans. Sullivan had cut himself free. He'd always made Ash uneasy, but never as much as now.

'Of course Reese is an honest man,' Sullivan said. 'I'm an honest man. So are you. The Senator, Roper, our other friends in Washington. All honest. General Motors makes an honest car.' He smiled again, his eyes flat, showing his chipped front tooth. 'I'm not going to jail,' he said. 'You carry the word to Roper. Tell him that.'

'You're going to have to deal, compromise.'

'Not with a jail term.'

'They can soften it,' Ash said. 'But you have to plead guilty and take the fall. That you have to do for the newspapers, the public, for the voters. You understand. Every day in the week somebody does what you did, but you were nailed. They have to bottle up the investigation. What they can arrange is an early parole. Quietly, when it all settles down. A year, maybe two, two and a half. And all your time done in minimum security. That they can arrange. Don't forget it's federal, which is on your side. Danbury or one like it.'

'Danbury is terrific,' Sullivan said. 'One meets lawyers and accountants, politicians and gentlemen stock swindlers. Thieves of one's own class. But I don't want it. Tell Roper and the Senator, too. Tell them Danbury won't do.'

Ash pushed away his half-eaten sandwich and tore the cellophane from a cigar. He lit it carefully, turning the end over the flame, his second cigar of the day. Ash kept track; since breakfast he'd smoked two cigars, eaten eleven hundred calories, give or take. When the bank opened tomorrow morning he could empty his box of thirty-eight thousand dollars in cash.

'Tell me what you want,' Ash said. 'Lay it out for me and I promise you I'll bring it to them.'

'No jail. No pleading.'

'You want it quashed?' Ash took the cigar from his mouth. 'The Department of Justice? You've got to be kidding.'

'And I want two hundred and fifty thousand in cash,' Sullivan said.

'And then what?'

'Then I disappear.'

'They won't do it,' Ash said. 'They can't. Even the people we're talking about can't do that.'

Sullivan fixed his grey eyes on Ash. 'The Justice Department has been after me to open up. Tell my story. I could do that. Tell them, Ash. I could bring the house down.'

'And do what for yourself?' Ash looked into those unyielding eyes. 'You're not a solitary. Never one of those, not you. You going to spend your life underground? You going to live alone in hotel rooms, a gun under your pillow? You're no freak. You can't take a new name, fill a bag with money and vanish.'

'You've never been in jail,' Sullivan said. 'You don't know what it's like.'

'This is different,' Ash said. 'It's America. There are limits on what they can do.'

'And they'd look after me,' Sullivan said. 'They'd send me the latest books. They'd see I ate steak, a girl when I needed one, maybe a first-run movie.'

'The alternative to jail is that you go underground. And you go alone. A freak. It's not your life. Think about it.'

'I don't think about things any more,' Sullivan said. 'I don't reflect. It's worthless, so I don't bother.' He pushed back his chair and stood up, the grey eyes sweeping the restaurant. 'Tell them what I want,' Sullivan said. 'Deliver the message.'

Before Sullivan could leave, Ash took hold of his arm. Sullivan didn't like that. The arm was thick and hard as steel. Ash relaxed his grip, and asked Sullivan to sit.

'It's pride with you,' he said. 'Pride and revenge. You hate them and you want to hurt them. God's vengeful angel. But it's you who'll be hurt, you who'll be killed.'

'They won't find killing me a rocking chair.'

'Take the fall, Jack. For God's sake, bend a little. Play the game. For once in your life do it the easy way. Two years, three at the most, and you come out smelling like a rose. They can put you in Allenwood, a country club, for Christ sake. Afterwards, there'll be a place for you. I promise you that.'

'And if I don't?'

'They'll send someone after you. Someone like you to find you.'

Sullivan smiled; his grey eyes unnaturally bright. He liked the idea. It was a sport. Ash saw it clearly: Sullivan needed to live on the edge.

Ash's meeting with the Senator was at the Towne Athletic Club, a whitestone Italian Renaissance mansion on Sixty-third Street, just off Madison Avenue. Ash had just given his name to the hallman when Lemoyne stepped out of a small bar and led him inside the lobby.

'The Senator is in the locker room suiting up,' he said. 'I had to give him a bit of a backgrounder on Sullivan. The Senator had no real conception of just how much Sullivan knew, how close to things he was. The Senator liked him, still does. But of course I made him cognizant of the danger, I've made it crystal clear to him.'

The lobby was small, polished wood and brass, a cosy,

discreet place and, at five o'clock, nearly empty. A solitary elderly gentleman sat at a small table drinking a Campari and soda and reading *Foreign Affairs.*

'The Senator knew Sullivan's father,' Lemoyne said. 'They used to shoot ducks together when the Senator represented General Dynamics.'

'In Philadelphia with Irma Pearson?'

'I don't think that's funny,' Lemoyne said. 'It's not what I'd call an appropriate remark. Also a remark like that could get us both compromised.'

Ash said, 'Have you ever been to Hong Kong?'

'What for?' Lemoyne said.

'I could use a little steam,' Ash said. 'Maybe a massage.'

'Somebody is going to have to go and talk to Sullivan,' Lemoyne said.

'Are you getting edgy?'

'If you know something, I think you ought to tell me,' Lemoyne said. 'The thing that must be avoided in situations like this is for the principals to stop trusting each other and exchanging information. Nothing exacerbates a bad situation like everybody looking to protect his own ass.'

Ash said, 'I just saw Sullivan.'

'He came to you?'

Ash paused and then said, coolly, 'He called me at the office.'

'And you met him?'

'I just left him.'

'Is he going to be reasonable?' Without waiting for an answer, Lemoyne said, 'This is a very serious matter. There's something in the wind. I don't think even you know the extent of this.' He gripped Ash's arm. 'We're on the verge of something very big. But all that's going to have to come from the Senator, or maybe from Roper.'

They left the bar and squeezed into a tiny elevator. 'I'm not worried,' Lemoyne said. 'I think Sullivan can be fingered. It's a number. It's got to be a number. And a number we can always handle.'

'And if it's not a number?'

The elevator creaked, the gears turned and it began slowly to rise. Lemoyne ignored that and said, 'I don't want you to be offended, but that shirt you're wearing was in style five,

54

maybe ten years ago.'

'How can you be sure?'

'I'm a fashion plate.'

'Are you happy with my shoes?'

'No fair-minded person would say a thing against them,' Lemoyne said.

Ash found the Senator in front of his locker, lowering his pants. He shook Ash's hand and called for the attendant, who provided Ash with a bathrobe, slippers, and an empty locker. Once the attendant had gone, Ash began to describe his meeting with Jack Sullivan.

The Senator listened without saying a word. He was thought of by his colleagues as a patient man and a good listener and heard Ash out seated in front of his locker in his underwear, absent-mindedly fiddling with the medallion he wore on a gold chain around his neck: one side was a star of David, the other a Saint Christopher's medal, a gift from his closest friend and golfing partner, the Vice-President of the United States.

When Ash had finished, the Senator reflected a moment or two and then said, 'Let me see if I can lay it out clearly: Sullivan was trusted by Roper and is therefore aware of certain confidential matters transacted over the past few years.'

'Since nineteen sixty-eight,' Ash said.

Lemoyne said, 'Everything since sixty-eight?'

'Again, to be clear,' the Senator said, 'are we to include Roper's confidential arrangements with members of the legislative and executive branch?'

'That's my understanding,' Ash said.

'How d'you know that?' Lemoyne said. 'Did Roper tell you?'

'Not in so many words,' Ash said, 'but they were close. Roper confided in him. I know that.'

'And now he intends to double-cross him,' Lemoyne said.

'Sullivan sees it differently,' Ash said. 'He thinks he's the one who's been double-crossed.'

'How d'you see it?' Lemoyne said.

'I'm no umpire,' Ash said. 'My job is to put a lid on it.'

'We all trusted Jack Sullivan,' the Senator said. 'There's an element of risk in all these matters. The rewards are great and the risks commensurate with them. If a man is caught with his hand in the till, it's understood he's supposed to take his medicine and keep his mouth shut. Those are the rules. Sullivan knew that.'

Lemoyne said, 'Does he have anything on paper?'

'He didn't say.'

'Has he indicated to you a readiness to go public with what he knows?' the Senator said.

'Yes, unless the indictment against him is quashed. And in addition he is to receive two hundred and fifty thousand dollars in cash,' Ash said.

'We can do that,' Lemoyne said. 'Yes, that can be done.'

'I wonder if it's been made clear to Sullivan just who the people are he'd be destroying,' the Senator said.

'I think it's safe to assume he knows that, Senator.'

'Perhaps if we appealed to his patriotism,' the Senator said. Ash and Lemoyne exchanged a glance. The Senator never noticed, he was looking off into space, slowly shaking his head. 'Doesn't he realize the irreparable harm he can do this country? If the truth should come out, what happens to public trust? We're a democratic society, and in order to function the people must have faith in their leaders.'

'The stick in the eye is quashing the indictment,' Lemoyne said. 'Offer him a year of bad time and two seventy-five in cash. Take it off one end, put it on the other.'

'I think you ought to go back and talk to him again,' the Senator said. 'Talk to him in terms of his obligation to his country.'

'I don't know if that'll do any good,' Ash said. 'The last few years have made him very cynical.'

'It's the affliction of our times.'

For the first time the Senator looked squarely at Ash; he was quite a handsome man, with a deep sun tan and a mane of white hair. His blue eyes had a cold, uncanny steadiness. Ash could not hold that stare long. Busying himself with a shoelace, he heard the Senator's words: 'Has it become naïve to talk about love of country? Am I old-fashioned? Out-of-date? Are the notions of self-sacrifice and dedication superannuated? Sometimes I get the feeling that nobody believes in anything but making money and sexual exhibitionism. Materialism and hedonism. Jack Sullivan was a

56

dedicated and patriotic boy. He had certain values. I knew his father. I just can't believe he's become as cynical as you seem to think.'

'We're going to have to face certain unpleasant facts,' Ash said.

The Senator slowly shook his handsome head. 'It's a terrible and rather depressing state of affairs.'

'He ought to be shot,' Lemoyne said. 'The man is nothing more than a traitor.'

The Senator stepped out of his shorts and pulled his undershirt over his head. His head and trunk were large for his legs, which were short but thickly muscled. A mat of curly white hair covered his broad chest. Sixty-one years old, he bore with pride the physique of his father, who'd started life hauling sides of beef in an Omaha slaughterhouse.

'I was very fond of Jack Sullivan,' he said. 'I always wanted a son like that. God rest her soul, Phyllis was never able to conceive. She was what, twenty-nine, thirty when she had the hysterectomy.'

'Nineteen fifty-six,' Lemoyne said. 'The year the other side beat hell out of us.'

'We talked a lot about adopting one,' the Senator said. 'Phyllis was for it, but I couldn't see it. It's tough enough pulling them through when they're your own flesh and blood.' The Senator pulled on his supporter, made a cup of his hand and laid himself gently to rest in the elastic sling; he dressed in a blue warm-up suit with the club logo over his breast. 'I certainly admire the job you've done with your son,' he said to Ash. 'He's a doctor, isn't he?'

'He's in his final year.'

'We're going to need a decision about Sullivan,' Lemoyne said. 'For all we know, he could be talking his head off to the US Attorney.'

'We've got some good friends there,' the Senator said. 'I'm sure they'd let us know if he were opening up.'

A black porter sauntered by carrying a suit in a dry cleaner's plastic bag, the fingers of his free hand deep in a pair of newly polished shoes. Ash and Lemoyne followed the Senator up a flight of stairs to the gym, where Jimmy Burke waited for him. Together they went through a series of light calisthenics. Once he was loose, Jimmy helped the Senator into a leather headguard and tied the laces of the big sixteen-ounce gloves. Jimmy was devoted to the Senator, who helped him whenever he could, and had even appeared at a benefit Jimmy had organized at his son's school for handicapped children.

They sparred three two-minute rounds, with four minutes of rest between each. Neither struck the other above the shoulders, and Jimmy tapped the Senator only on the arms, occasionally cuffing him on the leather headguard with an open glove if the Senator made the mistake of dropping his left.

The Senator had been captain of his college boxing team and it was still his favourite form of exercise, but only with Jimmy Burke, who knew just how hard to work him, and whom he trusted never to lose his head or hit him a solid punch. The Senator loved all sports, and could be seen at the big football games, the World Series, basketball, and ringside at the big fights. On his office wall were many photographs, most of them politicians and heads of state, but some were of famous sporting figures.

After the boxing, the Senator swam twelve laps of the thirty-metre pool before stretching out on the top bench of the sauna. He was of course recognized by other members, but after a brief greeting wasn't disturbed; when he'd sweated enough, Jimmy put him under the shower, dried him down, and dusted him with Johnson's Baby Powder. Ash had had a massage and joined him smelling of rubbing alcohol; he carried the *New York Post* and wore rubber clogs and a terrycloth robe.

Jimmy put the Senator on the scale. 'One sixty-five on the nose,' he said.

'I was afraid I'd picked up a couple,' the Senator said. 'I felt a little bloated.'

'Did you move your bowels?' Jimmy said.

'This morning.'

Ash said, 'There's tomorrow's headline.'

It was a second or two before the Senator remembered he was a man able to take ribbing from old friends.

'The Senator don't weigh five pounds more than he did as a middleweight in school,' Jimmy said.

'Let's have you weigh in,' the Senator said to Ash.

58

'Mr Morgan don't take care of himself like he should,' Jimmy said.

Jimmy brought two pewter mugs in which were mixed equal parts of freshly squeezed orange juice and Fresca, and left the men alone. Lemoyne was locked up with the club podiatrist.

'You're going to have to go back and talk to Sullivan again,' the Senator said. 'Tell him we're going to do all we can for him and to keep his mouth shut. Not a word. Nothing. He knows nothing. Roper paid the money to him and only to him and it went no higher.'

'It's not credible, Senator.'

'Nevertheless, that's his story.'

'How high does this go?' Ash said. 'Sullivan said he could bring the house down.'

'He threatened that?'

'I wouldn't say it was a threat.'

'What would you say it was?'

'A statement of fact.'

The Senator rattled the ice in his mug. 'There's nothing like regular exercise,' he said. 'Boxing is marvellous. Swim, a little steam. That and you watch your diet and no smoking.'

'He's a tough kid, Senator,' Ash said. 'And I get the feeling he doesn't give a damn. He's desperate.'

'Then what's your advice?'

'Give him what he wants.'

'I don't think we can,' the Senator said. 'I'm going to have to take this higher. There's a shindig at the Waldorf tonight. There'll be two tickets at the desk in your name. You know the Vice-President, don't you?' Ash nodded and the Senator said, 'I've got to fly to Washington, but you go by and say hello. I'll have spoken to him.'

CHAPTER FIVE

After he left the Senator, Ash went directly to the Sutton Place apartment to change to dinner clothes and to ask Eleanor to join him for dinner at the Waldorf with the Vice-President.

But she wasn't alone. Ash was surprised to find himself in the middle of a small but lively party. These were friends of Eleanor's, people with whom she worked, and while he'd met all of them at one time or another, he felt awkward with them, and they with him, so that conversation was meagre and bland, as if forced through a sieve.

All her friends were a generation younger than Ash; most of the women were younger than Eleanor, who reigned as queen of the hive. The men and women were a lean, chic, handsome, clever bunch, confident and friendly. They practised good manners and good taste. They were nearly as careful about what they said as what they ate; Ash was treated with kid gloves; the women feared Eleanor and didn't flirt with him. The men knew he'd once been a captain of police, but weren't quite sure what he did at the moment. They could see it was lucrative, and they imagined it was shady. He was thought to move in that clandestine world, which most Americans know exists, but few actually see. It deals with politics, big business, and crime; it is international, large amounts of cash are involved. Swiss banks come into it. The commodities range from Turkish dope and Belgian rifles to American jet aircraft. People are shot to death in Paris, Amsterdam, or New York. Once in a great while someone goes to prison.

Eleanor's friends believed her middle-aged lover belonged to that world.

And Ash looked back at them with envy, at their care-free sexual lives, the tennis and ski weekends, the hand-tooled boots and faded jeans worn on Air France First-Class to Paris. They made him feel old; worse, he felt stiff and foolish – square – in his neat dark suit.

He'd been raised to wear a necktie, and to make something of himself. Each of them was something to begin with. They earned money so easily it seemed nothing at all of which to be proud. Pride in his own success was made to seem vulgar.

He was born in a puritanical time, when sex was still a ceremony, an event, either a sacred act of love or a triumphant one of seduction. He went back to the time when the sight of a naked woman was heady stuff.

He accepted a drink, in his own apartment, and loosened his tie. The truth was he liked Eleanor's friends, and wasn't in the slightest disapproving. He simply envied them, regretted his years and rigidities, a burly middle-aged man trying his best to be friendly to the beautiful young without kissing their asses.

The conversation was about a new Italian movie. He'd seen it and thought it a fake. Everyone else seemed to have liked it. The critics had raved. Ash kept still. The conversation turned to restaurants, the prices of things; he was aware of being handled deferentially, as if he were someone's father from out of town.

He soon began to grow restless, and then unhappy. He was in danger of becoming surly. But Eleanor was a clever girl; she saw all of it, and rushed to protect both her friends and him. She refilled his glass and led him away to the kitchen.

'I tried reaching you all afternoon,' she said. 'I wanted you to know they were coming by. Louise didn't know where to find you. Please don't be angry.'

'Louise knew how to get hold of me.'

'She wouldn't tell me.'

'There's been a lot going on.'

She touched his cheek with her fingertips. 'You look done in.'

'There's a dinner at the Waldorf tonight,' he said. 'I've got to go and I'd like you to come with me.'

'They're all here,' she said. 'I can't walk out. Alan is in the bedroom hanging wallpaper, and then he's going to make his lasagna.'

'Tell them something came up,' he said. 'You forgot a prior engagement. Tell them to stay and eat Alan's lasagna.'

'I can't do that,' she said. 'You should've given me more notice.'

'I didn't know until an hour ago,' Ash said. 'We'll be with the Vice-President.'

'Which Vice-President?'

'Of the United States.'

'I just wish you'd have told me earlier,' she said. 'I know, I know. It just came up. You didn't know yourself until an hour ago. The Vice-President. But look at it this way, love, I just can't walk out on my friends.'

'Not on Alan's lasagna.'

'Please don't take that attitude.'

'What attitude is that?'

'That I put my friends and work above you. That I divide my life between my career and you. And that you get the short end of the stick.'

'If a woman puts her damn work first,' he said, 'it's she who gives herself the short end.'

'And what about a man? Is it okay for him to put his work first?'

'It's not fair, is it?'

'No, it's not.'

'But it is true,' he said.

'In a pig's ear it is.'

'A man would've said, "In a pig's ass".'

'You're a wise guy,' she said. 'A fucking wise guy. How's that for man-talk?'

A fashion model stepped into the kitchen, looking for more ice. She glanced from Ash to Eleanor, excused herself, and quickly ducked out.

'I'm sorry,' Eleanor said. 'I really don't want to fight. I'll try to understand and you try to understand. Politics, the Vice-President. It's not my kind of thing anyway. And let's face it, showing up with the yellow peril on your arm isn't about to do you a whole lot of good.'

'For a smart girl,' he said, 'you do talk a lot of crap.'

'Well, to tell you the truth, I wouldn't exactly bring my autograph book to meet your Vice-President.'

'What if I told you Nureyev was going to be there?'

'Is he?'

'And Richard Burton and Jackie O.'

62

'Wheeeee.'

'And Solzhenitsyn and Mel Brooks.'

'You're funny, Ash. By jingo, the world's funniest ex-flatfoot.'

'Now I've got to get dressed.'

She followed him into the bedroom, pulling on his sleeve. The room was a mess, the bed and bureau heaped in the centre of the floor, lamps, books, chairs, and small tables piled on the bed. And above it all, halfway up a ladder and bare to the waist, was Alan Bedford, hanging wallpaper.

He leaned down to shake Ash's hand, first wiping his own clean on the seat of his jeans. He was about forty, but looked ten years younger, a taut muscular man who worked daily with weights and travelled with a folding incline-board to do sit-ups; he played tennis and did karate. He flew his own plane, had earned a graduate degree in oceanography and produced a movie about sharks, which had been shown at the Museum of Modern Art. He was a self-made millionaire who collected early American art and furniture, owned the finest wine cellar in New York, and Alfred Dunhill held for him in their humidor a thousand pre-Castro Montecristo cigars. His teeth were perfect, his hair naturally blond and, although the most gentle and polite of men, he could probably break Ash's neck with a single karate blow.

Now he'd formed a company to manufacture wallpaper of his own design. 'Alan has it blocked by hand,' Eleanor said. 'And then rolled on an original Dubellant press. Bloomingdale's has ordered it, and Sloane's and Neiman-Marcus.'

'Neiman-Marcus isn't set,' Alan said. 'I'm going to have to fly out next week and try to nail them down.'

'How can they refuse?' Eleanor said.

'Easy,' Alan said. 'The buyer doesn't have to like it.'

'But it's beautiful.' Eleanor waved her hand at the wall Alan had been working on. 'Isn't it lovely, Ash?'

It was textured pale-yellow paper with small highlights of darker yellow woven into the silky fabric. It was beautiful and Ash said so.

'It's a gift from Alan to us,' Eleanor said, her eyes shining. The wallpaper delighted her; she clutched Ash's arm, anxious that he say the right thing, that he do nothing to offend Alan. And she was also concerned that Ash not be jealous. It seemed to Ash that she'd never looked more beautiful, and certainly he'd never valued or loved her more.

'I'll take a break in about an hour and do the lasagna,' Alan said. 'I remember how crazy you were about it last time, Ash.'

Eleanor said, 'Can you stay, darling?'

'I wish I could,' Ash said. 'Alan is the best Italian cook I know.'

'You thank my mother, Mrs Bedini,' Alan said.

'Ash is having dinner with the Vice-President of the United States,' Eleanor said, and put her arm around Ash's waist.

Ash left the apartment in an unhappy frame of mind. He was in evening clothes but decided to walk. He couldn't shake the mood, and at first neither could he understand what had caused it. And suddenly it came to him that he was losing Eleanor. She had shielded him with Alan. The remark about his going off to meet the Vice-President was a kindness, an attempt to bolster an ego which she believed sagged in the presence of Alan Bedford. She was a clever, kind woman. But Ash had lived with her long enough to understand her. She had begun to feel sorry for him. Beside Alan Bedford, he must seem old and rather grey.

Ash arrived early at the Waldorf, picked up his two tickets to the dinner, and went to the Bull and Bear Room for a drink. Then he telephoned Louise Vernon.

He told her where he was and asked if she wanted to dress and meet him.

'Ordinarily, I'd say no,' she said. 'My Little Jewish Gentleman is with his mother in a Chinese restaurant, so I've got the night off to wash my hair.'

'I thought he was playing pinochle.'

'And I thought we were working late.'

'Please meet me,' Ash said.

'You sound rotten,' Louise said. 'Why is it I only get to pick up the pieces?'

'Does your friend Millie Parker still go around with the Vice-President?'

'You didn't answer my question,' Louise said.

'I'll answer all your questions,' Ash said. 'First come down and pick up all this old man's pieces.'

'You'd better give me an hour,' Louise said.

At the bar, Ash ordered a second drink, sitting so that he faced the entrance. Four other single men were at the bar, two with afternoon papers and one smoking a pipe. The fourth combined pretzel sticks and peanuts to make a design on the surface of the bar. Ash was caught between reels, squirming in his seat waiting for the movie to pick up where it had left off. The pretzels and peanuts on the bar turned out to be a replica of the American flag. Its creator was a stout, florid gentleman, drinking a Martini.

When he smiled, Ash said, 'It's very nice.'

'I'm a descendant of Betsy Ross,' the stout gentleman said.

'There's every reason to believe she'd be proud of you,' Ash said.

'On my father's side,' he said. 'My name is Calhoun.'

Ash told him his name and the conversation would certainly have gone further, but Ash caught sight of a familiar face pass in the lobby. He excused himself to Calhoun and dashed out to retrieve Sid Green and fetch him in for a drink.

Ash and Sid had grown up in the same neighbourhood and had been at the Police Academy, same year, although Sid was six years older. Sid had done his twenty years and then angled an appointment as a marshal in the US Attorney's office.

'Are you here for the Vice-President's speech?' Ash said.

'They've got to fill up the hall,' Sid said. 'So they press-gang the federal offices.'

Sid had been a good amateur boxer and captain of the NYU wrestling team, a big powerful man, who'd once been surprised by two hold-up men in a Brooklyn supermarket and shot both to death. He still carried a fragment of .38 slug just under his left lung.

Ash said, 'Is your boss around? The Honourable Neil R. Soames. I've got one or two matters to discuss with him.'

'Out of town,' Sid said.

'I've got to talk to him.'

'The US Attorney is a very busy man,' Sid said. 'Perhaps one of his assistants.'

'Where is he?'

'Beats me.'

'In Geneva?'

'What's in Geneva?'

'Walt Roper.'

'Now why should the US Attorney be talking to Walt Roper?'

Ash held Sid Green's eyes. 'Lay it on the line with me,' he said. 'I need your help.'

Sid slowly shook his head. 'Ash . . .' He laid his heavy hands on Ash's shoulders and brought his face close to Ash's. For a moment Ash thought he was going to kiss him. 'My dear friend,' Sid Green said. 'Thirty years we know each other. Kids together. Remember we used to go to the fights Friday nights. And before that in the five-buck seats at the second Louis-Schmeling. What was the name of that squarehead played centre for Boys' High?'

'I always called him Kraut,' Ash said.

'He bet ten bucks on Schmeling and when Louis wiped him out, he broke down and cried like a baby. He was a German patriot.'

'It was the ten bucks,' Ash said.

'True, he was tight with a dollar,' Sid Green said. 'He didn't care much for Jews, but otherwise he wasn't bad to be around.'

'He's dead,' Ash said.

'Him, too?' Sid Green looked gloomily into his glass. Ash pressed a cigar on him. Sid Green put the cigar away in his pocket. A dollar cigar, he'd smoke it after Sunday dinner, give himself a treat. Ash made a mental note to send him a box. Calhoun had broken up the American flag and now used the peanuts and pretzel sticks to fashion a warship.

'Ash, you made the right move,' Sid Green said. 'When you first left the Department and went over to Roper I thought you were making a big mistake. You were an idealist, never on the take. An honest man, but no fool. I remember how you used to take your annual leave and go South with Martin Luther King, and getting the hell beat out of you. You weren't one to take the narrow bread-and-butter view of life. And then out of the blue there you are in bed with Walt Roper.'

'You want another drink?'

Sid Green shook his head. 'The truth is I'm working,' he

said. 'The Secret Service is short and they got us spread out all over the place.'

'You still got your place up at Candlewood Lake?' Ash said.

'You don't want to talk about basic things.' Sid Green had never been stupid. 'I'm saying you were right. There's not a dime's worth of difference between Roper and my people. Except I get eighteen thousand a year to look after my mutt and you get fifty to look after yours. Maybe I will have that other drink.'

After it was served, Sid said, 'I left the Department because I couldn't take it out in the street any more. In the hospital after I got shot, I promised my wife I'd finish my twenty and get out. But it wasn't just for her. It's murder out there. I know how you felt about the Negro people, but even you've got to admit they've got way out of hand. Not that the whites are any bargain. Today even decent people steal all they can. Look at the White House. Look at Congress. You really want a laugh, look at the City of New York. The only thing is what do we do, Ash? Where do we go?'

'You got your place in Candlewood Lake.'

'How'd you stand it?' Sid Green said. 'Look at our country. I mean, doesn't it break your heart?'

'Only when I talk to an old-timer like you,' Ash said.

Sid Green sipped his drink; he'd never been much of a drinker, but in 1946, the week they'd both been discharged from the army, they'd run into each other at Fort Dix, and went out together and got drunk in a bar in New Jersey.

'What is it you want to learn from Soames?' he said.

'If he's talked to Jack Sullivan.'

'I hear they met,' Sid Green said. 'Once I know of, maybe twice. I don't know what was said. But it wasn't official, I know that much. There was no stenographer, nobody was sworn, none of that.'

'What was said?'

'I told you I don't know.'

'C'mon, Sid.'

'You're fast using up your credit with me, Ash.' Then in a gentler tone: 'I'm not close to Soames. He's a smart kid, ambitious. Arrogant. He knows everything, you know nothing.

A Harvard Law prick. Not that he doesn't know how to conduct an investigation. That is, if he wants to.'

'What is that supposed to mean?'

'You take it any way you want.'

'Let's see if we can talk straight for a second, Sid. Are you saying Soames isn't conducting a proper investigation?'

'Don't talk like a child,' Sid said.

'Is he or isn't he?'

'I would've thought you'd know if he weren't,' Sid said. 'If there were pressure on him, it'd be coming from your people. Or is it that they don't tell you everything?'

'There's nobody who knows everything except Roper,' Ash said. 'But nobody gets to talk to him any more. Tell you the truth, I'm fed up with the intrigue.'

'The kind of money you're pulling down, I wouldn't kick,' Sid said.

Louise Vernon came into the bar, looking her best. There was a pause in the conversation, a moment of respectful silence as all eyes were raised in the direction of this elegant and self-possessed woman in beige silk. Calhoun halted work on his warship.

More than anything Ash felt comradeship, pride in the way she'd turned herself from a plain woman into an attractive one, and great relief that she'd come. He was more comfortable with her than with Eleanor, surer of himself, and more at ease. If he lived with her, they'd eat out every night. She had no friends. With Eleanor he'd gone beyond himself. It was a mismatch. And in a moment of memorable clarity he saw that if he were to be happy, he must not be governed by dreams or search out views of Paradise.

Louise made her way around the horseshoe bar. Ash rose and kissed her lightly. He introduced her to Sid Green, whose eyes sparkled as they shook hands. She declined a drink. From the next stool, Calhoun smiled and pushed his glasses along his nose. Louise, who always handled herself well in bars, complimented him on his work with the peanuts and pretzel sticks.

'It's the *Graf Spee*,' Calhoun said modestly.

The dinner for the Vice-President was to be held on the Starlight Roof, the largest of the Waldorf's ballrooms, reached by elevators guarded by the Secret Service. In the lobby, guests in evening clothes showed their invitations to polite young men, each with a transmitting button plugged into one ear. One knew they were armed and noted how watchful they were, a clean-shaven brotherhood of ministers' sons, Special Forces cadre, courteous, and hard as nails.

Under Secret Service's scrutiny the guests were subdued and went under escort meekly to the elevators, and from them to a large square room, brilliantly lit and brightened further by elaborate arrangements of early fall flowers. Photographers mingled with the guests, their electronic flashguns blinking. Waiters brought around trays of assorted drinks and others followed with canapés.

But the mood of the guests remained subdued; there was a good deal of uneasy chatter and whispered jokes, for they were uncertain whether or not they were there to enjoy themselves.

A receiving line was set up, and within a few minutes the Vice-President strode in, escorted by four agents, like a fighter entering the ring among his handlers. There was a splutter of applause, which flickered briefly and then died out. The Secret Service went among the guests with name tags and numbered slips of paper, assigning the order in which they were to present themselves in the receiving line.

'Like the numbers they hand out in a bakery,' Louise Vernon said.

The Vice-President was a tall, burly man, his bulk minimized by a flawlessly cut dinner jacket. He was deeply tanned, his hair styled and cunningly dyed, so that folded silver wings swept the tops of his pink ears. His collar fitted perfectly. His teeth flashed brilliantly; he was unblemished, polished, and gleamed like a prize apple. Ash saw something fascinating and gruesome. Certainly the impression was of an intense theatrical presence, a face recognized at once. But recognized by way of newspaper photographs and television. In the flesh, he seemed less real. Ash couldn't shake the odd feeling that he belonged in that other dimension, a face flickering on a screen, and not a man out walking around in the world.

And that feeling persisted, even as Ash passed through the

receiving line and pressed the large, warm, soft hand, and came under the rays of that incandescent smile. But the Vice-President knew Ash, remembered his name, and why he had come.

'I talked to the Senator just a few minutes ago.' He spoke softly, without moving his eyes or extinguishing that smile. But he held fast to Ash, his small hard eyes glittered under the strobe lights. 'And from what he said, you and I are going to have to sit down and have a nice little heart-to-heart.'

The Vice-President nodded his head, the expression in his eyes now one of calculation, the intense light bouncing from his moist forehead. Then he flexed his jaws, flashed his splendid teeth at the lens of a camera, and released Ash's hand.

He dallied some seconds with Louise while Ash went off and had himself a stiff drink.

Some time later the doors to the dining-room were opened and the call came to be seated for dinner. Ash found Louise and they squeezed in, searching among the tables for their names.

'We're invited to a private party,' Louise said. 'My old room-mate Millie Parker and the Vice-President. His suite in the Towers, right after the speech.'

'I've always liked Millie,' Ash said. 'The best-looking Rockette ever to come down the pike.'

'She's had a distinguished career of public service,' Louise said. 'Eighteen tops when she ran off with that ball-player, then the Governor, and after that comes Al Larson.'

'Even Roper's learned a trick or two from Al Larson.'

'And the navy flier, the one Nixon made White House doorman.'

'And now the Vice-President,' Ash said. 'Did she invite you?'

'He did,' Louise said. 'He said he wanted a word in private with you. He said it was confidential, you know. national security, and then he pinched my ass.'

They shared a table with a banker from New Jersey and his party. They had just returned from Iran and had nothing but praise for the industry and energy of the people and the far-sighted wisdom of the Shah. The Vice-President entered the dining-room followed by the National Party Chairman and the same Secret Service agents. Everyone stood and applauded and a pianist played 'God Bless America'. The Vice-President smiled broadly and clasped his hands over his head.

Dinner consisted of shrimp cocktail, filet mignon, over-cooked vegetables, pineapple upside-down cake, and coffee. Two Californian wines were served. The food tasted much like that served aboard aeroplanes and the wines were sugary and unpleasant. Ash noticed that the Vice-President didn't pretend to eat or drink any of it.

After coffee, the party chairman introduced the Vice-President, who spoke twelve minutes, making some pretty good jokes before issuing a plea for party unity and the need to reduce government interference with business.

He finished to applause that was now sustained and enthusiastic, shook hands with everyone he passed on his way out and left the room by way of a door to one side of the dais encircled by the ubiquitous Secret Service. At the back of the room, Millie Parker stood up and slipped quickly out a side door.

A private elevator led to the Towers. Ash and Louise were met by yet another Secret Service agent and escorted to the Vice-President's suite. He was already there, his jacket and shoes off, a drink in his hand. Millie sat with her feet tucked under her, on a couch covered in yellow silk. She had exquisite ivory skin, although her hair was jet-black and her eyes a deep-violet blue. No man could look into those eyes and not wonder how it would be to take Millie Parker to bed. This was in part due to her teasing manner, for she made sport of men and of herself as well; she was a girl who loved a good joke, a girl of evident good nature, gifted with a laugh which could be sly. intimate, and deadly when breathed into the ear, or just as easily ring out like a bell celebrating good times in a public place.

'Tell me the truth,' she said to Ash. 'D'you remember me?'

'Only as well as I do the first time I checked into the Carlton Hotel.'

She liked that, although the Vice-President looked bewildered. She took his hand and pulled him down beside

71

her on the couch. Away from the spotlight, the Vice-President was an awkward man; although he'd lived for years in the best hotels, and with the rich as a pampered house-guest, he'd been wandering around aimlessly with a drink in his hand, not quite knowing where to sit until she showed him. He was quite happy beside her and put his feet up on a low table for Ash to admire his silk socks.

'I didn't know Ash when we roomed together,' Louise said to Millie.

'And I'm talking way back before that.'

'I'm not sure I want to hear this,' the Vice-President said.

'Ernest is very jealous.' She squeezed his hand. 'Darling, what would you do if you found out I was running around on you?'

'I'd have you killed.' The Vice-President put back his head and laughed with his mouth wide open. 'I'd have them bury your body in the foundation under that new federal office building we're putting up in Houston.'

'One thing, Ernest.' Millie bit the Vice-President's ear-lobe. 'Promise you'd never have me put in a garbage compactor.'

'That's for the gentleman I catch you with,' the Vice-President said.

Louise said, 'Where was it you met Ash?'

'Well, Ash and I go back to when he was a cop,' Millie said. 'And I'm going to tell you something, I had one flaming crush on this fellow. You never knew that, did you, Ash?'

'I knew I didn't like this guy,' the Vice-President said.

'I was a kid, Ernest,' she said. 'A pisher.'

'Pisher,' the Vice-President said. 'One who wets one's pants.'

'You see why I love him,' Millie said. 'A Vice-President of the United States, and he's not too big to know what a pisher is.'

'Your mother was Fay Parker,' Ash said. 'First manicurist at the Dawn Patrol barber shop.'

'A legend on Broadway,' Millie said. 'And a great manicurist.'

'I certainly hope the years have been kind to her,' Ash said.

'With her life savings she opened a magnificent place in Palm Springs,' Millie said.

'I've always admired a well-run barber shop,' the Vice-President said.

'It folded,' Millie said. 'All the old-timers are dead or home shaving themselves.'

The Vice-President had another scotch, the girls drank vodka, and Ash toyed with a glass of white wine. Millie began to reminisce about the great men whose hands her mother had tended and the shows she herself had danced in; the Vice-President admitted a life-long weakness for show business and told a story about being taken as a boy to shake the hand of Louis B. Mayer.

Then he took Ash aside and said he wanted a word. He led him through a door of polished brass and oak into a small study with an antique desk and two phones, one a white console and the other a single black instrument without a dial.

'The black one goes straight to the Boss,' the Vice-President said.

'Is he going to run again?'

'He'll announce in a month or two.'

'I've heard talk he's not well.'

'I don't know where those rumours got started,' the Vice-President said. 'I've seen the medical reports and I've played golf with him. Hell, he's sixty-two years old, with the toughest job in the world, but the man's strong as a bull.'

'You told me you talked to the Senator,' Ash said.

'He said you had reservations about laying it on the line with Roper's man. What's his name?'

'Jack Sullivan.'

'I saw Roper last week,' the Vice-President said. 'Had to sneak down to some little sandpit. But we caught some wahoo and had a good talk.'

'I thought Roper was in Geneva,' Ash said.

The Vice-President gave Ash a sharp look. 'He's got his jet and the big boat. He moves around.' He freshened his drink from a decanter on a side table. 'The Senator told me you were inside, Ash, and that you could be talked to. Here it is – we're trying to straighten things out for Roper. Bury this and that. Piss on the fire, if you know what I mean.'

'I guess Walt Roper can hurt a lot of people,' Ash said.

For a moment he feared he'd gone too far; a reckless mood had overtaken him. But the Vice-President smiled and nodded thoughtfully. 'Yes, I believe he can,' he said.

'I think we ought to sit still and let it blow over,' Ash said.

'We don't want to.'

'And Sullivan doesn't want to go to jail.'

'Nobody wants to go to jail,' the Vice-President said. 'It's just that Sullivan has no choice.'

'Yes he does.'

'You mean talk?' The Vice-President laughed as he had earlier, when talking of burying Millie under a federal building in Houston.

'Make himself a deal with the US Attorney? No, I don't see Jack Sullivan shooting his mouth off,' he said. 'I don't see him taking what he knows public. I see that as bluff. Bluff, pure and simple.'

'I don't think he's bluffing,' Ash said.

'You mean he's ready to take on all of us?' the Vice-President said. 'You must think he's crazy!'

'Probably a little crazy,' Ash said, 'but more than anything else he just hates us.'

'He's one of us,' the Vice-President said. 'He must hate himself as well.'

'There's no doubt of that,' Ash said.

The Vice-President said, 'I like to take a more practical point of view. Not talking, he makes friends. Loyal friends.' The Vice-President's small hard eyes flicked up and down Ash's face. 'Money. He's got to have money. When he comes out of prison, he's got to live. He's been with Roper quite a while; how much you figure he socked away?'

'I don't know.'

'You worked with him. You were his friend. How much have you got?' the Vice-President said. 'Let's use that as a yardstick.'

'We were in different areas,' Ash said. 'He did his work and I did mine. I put him next to the Senator, but that was it. We were friends. I liked him. I still do.'

74

The Vice-President was smiling, but his eyes were steady. 'Are you a rich man? How much have you got, Ash?'

'And you, Ernest?' Ash said. 'How about you? You take yours out first. We'll play show me.'

'The Senator said you were a scrapper.'

'Don't ask me to go to Jack Sullivan and tell him to roll over and lay still for five years.'

'It won't be five years.'

'How many?'

'Two. Two is tops.'

'You personally guarantee it?'

'Better than that.' The Vice-President tapped the black phone.

'You're right about one thing,' Ash said. 'Whether or not he goes to jail he'll need money. A new life. Far away and brand-new.'

'You want to run with him, Ash?' The Vice-President sipped his drink; over the rim of the glass his eyes never left Ash's face. 'Are you tired?'

'No.'

'How old are you, Ash?'

'Fifty-two.'

'I got three years on you,' the Vice-President said. 'I have the people I deal with researched, and you've done a lot to be proud of. Civil rights work, anti-corruption. You were never an ordinary cop, Ash. Never a hard-nose. A firm believer in self-improvement, the work ethic. You worked yourself up, and you can take pride in that. Am I any different? Is the Boss? Self-made. But men like us have a problem in middle age. We tend to ask ourselves, "What's it all about? What's it all for?" Ambition. We work our butts off and never learn how to enjoy it. Sit back, Ash. Enjoy the rewards of all that sacrifice, all that hard work.'

'I told you I'm satisfied,' Ash said.

'Maybe there are ethical questions,' the Vice-President said. 'You were an honest cop. Idealistic. Martin Luther King's pal. He was a great man, Ash. King, Jackie Robinson. Trail blazers. This administration wants to do what's right, Ash. And you're part of it. I respect you. The Senator, even the Boss, everybody respects and appreciates the work you've done.'

Ash glanced at the black phone without a dial. There wasn't a sound in the room, silence carefully maintained, hushed and sacred. The Secret Service guarded the door. Herbert Hoover had lived in the Waldorf Towers and so had Douglas MacArthur. As a young cop, Ash had once been posted at the Fiftieth Street entrance. He'd seen MacArthur, a sour old man wearing a black homburg.

'Or is it personal problems?' the Vice-President said. 'Is that what's bothering you, your wife's health?'

Ash looked up; his eyes held the Vice-President's.

'Maybe something more personal,' the Vice-President said. 'Your young lady. She has some very strange friends.'

Ash said, 'Are you having me looked over?'

'You mean surveillance? That sort of thing? Certainly not.'

'You think I may be in this with Sullivan? That between us we cooked up a way to milk you?'

The Vice-President slowly shook his head.

Ash said, 'You mean the thought never crossed your mind?'

'Oh, it crossed my mind.'

'I don't like being manoeuvred out front on this thing,' Ash said. 'I'm Security Chief. I'm not a negotiator. And if it comes down to it, I'm no tough guy. I wasn't in Astra from the beginning, and I don't like finding myself out front on it now.'

'But that's where we need you,' the Vice-President said. 'Speaking of your young lady . . . she's not an American citizen, is she?'

Ash said, 'You're coming at me in the wrong way.'

'What way is that?'

'Putting your weight on me.'

'Oh, no. Ash . . .' The Vice-President spread his hands, as if to show they were empty. 'If I gave you that impression, I'm truly sorry. We need you. Your loyalty.'

'Then tell me what you want, Mr Vice-President,' Ash said. 'But without the bullshit.'

'Go back to Sullivan,' the Vice-President said. 'Tell him we'll go to two hundred and seventy-five thousand. And tell him he'll do no more than two years. Tell him that's a promise.'

In the living-room, Millie Parker played the piano and sang old songs. Louise sang along in her thin, reedy but sweet voice. She looked grave when she sang, like a child in church, and Ash was moved by that, and by her voice. She stood beside the piano, one arm resting gracefully on it, and Ash thought she'd never looked prettier. But then the Vice-President joined in the singing, and soon his bass voice drowned out the others. After a few minutes Ash said good night.

Louise offered to go with him, but she was obviously having a good time and he urged her to stay. At the door, she took him aside.

'Let me go with you,' she said again.

He shook his head. From the far end of the room, the Vice-President sang 'Some Enchanted Evening'.

Louise said, 'What is it they want you to do?'

Ash smiled and kissed her lightly on the lips; a gesture to turn her aside. She understood it, and a pained expression crossed her face.

'The stakes have got very high, haven't they?' she said.

'You stay clear of it.'

'You, too.'

'Too late for that,' he said.

'Come home with me,' she said.

He thought of the dinner she'd served him, the good china and silver laid in the tiny dining alcove. Her nervousness, the trouble she'd taken. A single woman trying to make a life. She'd wrung Ash's heart.

He said, 'David is spending the night at the Long Island house. I thought I'd drive out.'

When Ash had gone, Louise joined Millie and the Vice-President at the piano. They were singing something from *Annie Get Your Gun*, the first Broadway show she'd ever seen. Ethel Merman had sung in it with Ray Middleton. A room-service waiter wheeled in a cart with late supper. The Vice-President was jolly and sang at the top of his voice. He put his arm around Louise, and she also began to sing. She smiled over at Millie and winked.

Millie was a lucky girl; the Vice-President was a wonderful guy. Maybe a bit of a schmuck, but when all was said and done, a wonderful guy. Generous.

CHAPTER SIX

Sullivan had left Ash convinced that his conditions would not be met. They would probably agree to pass money to him under the table, bargaining a bit on the amount. But if backed to the wall, they could come up with nearly any number. There would be promises of clemency or an early parole, a soft berth later on. They had long memories; loyalty was always rewarded. *We take care of our own.* In Vietnam, they flew the dying out in helicopters, and were there with hot food for the human wrecks who staggered in and out of the Delta after Tet. He'd known a lieutenant whose career had been made because he'd kept still about a superior who passed the wrong co-ordinates to the air force and called down a napalm strike on his own men. Eleven of them were burned to a crisp, but the lieutenant was persuaded to omit the error from his report and finished his tour a captain with a letter of commendation in his service folder.

Sullivan knew that all he had to do was to keep his mouth shut, plead guilty, and go to jail. He must go remorsefully, a penitent, begging forgiveness. He was a sacrifice; the people would have his warm heart.

But Sullivan was not yet ready for that. It wasn't that he much honoured freedom, or even life, his or anyone else's; like others who'd cheated death, he had about him a resigned fatalism, of living on by way of a miracle, in a state of grace. It was as if he'd already died and was now on stolen time. He both cherished life and held it cheaply. It was an old paradox, but hardly uncommon. One saw it in soldiers too long under fire, in those who'd survived death camps, in holy men.

Sullivan's moment of death had come, passed like a cold wind, and he'd gone on living. He'd bowed his head, clenched his teeth, and closed his eyes, thought of odd things, and waited for the blow which would separate him from life. But he hadn't expected it to end there. He never expected silence. In death the air was sure to be light. He expected to float eternally. He expected to rise and soar away.

But the blow never came. Sullivan opened his eyes. He first saw the paddy mud and the deep scars made in it by truck tyres. The stink of burning plastic, metal, and flesh. The sweat ran into his eyes and blinded him.

He lived on. He grew together. He even came again to love a woman.

And after he left Ash, he thought of Lorraine. Roper had brought them together, knew they'd hit it off. He was something of a matchmaker, as he had become an enthusiastic collector of wines. Both were entertainments. But in choosing Lorraine, he was right.

With her Sullivan came slowly to life. He had her and lost her. He wanted another chance with her. But that was a secret, an ache buried deep in his heart.

Lorraine had promised to come back. He'd waited for her on the terrace of La Colisée in Paris. She'd not come then, but one day she would.

Lorraine was his first reason for not letting them put him in jail.

The second came from his hatred of men like the Senator and the Vice-President. He wouldn't go contritely to jail while they stalked the land trumpeting about how well the system worked.

He expected them to tell him that it wasn't in their power to keep him out of jail. He wouldn't buy that. It was in their power, but it would cost them in reputation and career. Money was easy, as were promises of a job later on. All easy. But he must find a way to make them pay the higher price.

And so he decided to go ahead with a plan he'd worked out six or seven months earlier, when he first realized he was to be sacrificed: he would break into Ash's office, force open his locked file cabinet, and take the Astra documents.

He knew exactly what was in them.

In order to do that he'd first need a better look at the security file in Ash's office. He'd seen and recognized it, taken note that it was a standard Government Security Agency file and guaranteed against surreptitious entry. It was made of half-inch-thick steel, a formidable piece of equipment, and if he was going to get inside, he'd need some additional information.

While still working for Roper, he stayed late several nights

79

in order to make friends with the cleaning woman, a Ukrainian with whom he was able to speak Russian. He soon had her charmed and, one night after waiting until she'd finished with both his and Ash's office and had settled down for a sandwich and a cup of tea in a small room just off the secretarial pool, told her he'd forgotten his key and locked himself out of his office. He assured her there was no need for her to interrupt her meal. If she would let him have her ring with all the office keys, he'd return it in just a few minutes. The conversation was conducted in Russian, she teasing him all the while about his Saint Petersburg accent. As for the keys – she handed them over without a word and went back to blowing on her tea.

Sullivan needed only a few minutes' access to Ash's open file, which Louise Vernon maintained in her office. The security file was a recent model, purchased by Ash within the last eighteen months. He wanted a look at the invoice, which took four minutes to find. Louise Vernon had filed it under the manufacturer's name. Sullivan quickly copied the serial number of the security file, replaced the invoice, closed the open file, locked the office door, and had the keys in the hands of the Ukrainian woman before she'd finished her sandwich.

These files were made by the Hercules Safe Company under US Government specifications, and were designed to be used only by government agencies for the storage of classified material, or by companies engaged in government work.

All the Agency's closed files were of the same design, most of the same model, and Sullivan knew enough about the equipment to be sure he couldn't open it without help. He kept the serial number and date of construction of the file in Ash's office and, after his meeting with Ash at Manganaro's, he went looking for a man named George Knapp.

George had worked for Hercules, Diebold, Mosler, even Chubb & Sons in England. For a time the Agency used him whenever they wanted something particularly difficult opened. But George Knapp was hard to handle. He drank and he beat up women. He was a mild, scholarly, soft-spoken little man, who in his time had assaulted some formidable women. George Knapp liked his women large, and he liked them fat and pink, and then he liked to beat hell out of them.

George Knapp had a dark side. He went off for days at a time, drunk and yearning for a fat pink woman, and when he found her there was sure to be a brawl; he'd be arrested and bring in the Agency, which was embarrassing. George Knapp was a genius, there was no doubt of it, but the dark side got in his way, and eventually the Agency had no choice but to let him go. Hercules, Diebold, and Mosler had come to the same conclusion, and with all the lovely fat pink women in Britain, he must have driven them crazy at Chubb & Sons.

The last address Sullivan had for George was on West End Avenue near Seventy-seventh Street. George had moved, leaving a forwarding address with the superintendent. It turned out to be only a few blocks away, a converted brownstone on Seventy-fourth Street, just off Riverside Drive.

Two names were on the bell: George's and someone named N. Svare, who answered Sullivan's ring, and turned out to be the largest and by all odds the most formidable of George's fat pink women. N. Svare was a bit taller than Sullivan and fifty pounds heavier. She was blonde and apple-cheeked, fresh off the bus from Minnesota, and gave every indication that with her George Knapp had at last met his match.

'George is in bed at the moment.' She dimpled when she smiled. 'He's recuperating from having fallen down a flight of stairs.'

Sullivan found George propped up in bed with his stamp collection – philately was another of his obsessions – his left leg in a cast and one eye swollen shut.

There was a minute or two of polite chatter while Nadine Svare fussed with George and offered to brew tea. But both men declined and George said, 'Nadine, Mr Sullivan is a very old friend and business associate, I'm sure he's come to discuss one or two matters of a confidential sort.'

It was Sunday morning, time for Nadine to go off to church. She promised to return in time to prepare George's lunch and invited Sullivan to stay.

'You've got to try my Swedish pancakes,' she said.

'The batter is beaten for twenty minutes by hand.'

'Like one or two other things around here,' Nadine said.

After she'd gone, George turned back the covers and opened the buttons of his pyjamas; he was bound in elastic bandage from his armpits to just above the waist.

'She cracked three of my ribs,' George said. 'I think this time I'm really in love.'

George buttoned his pyjamas and painfully drew himself up to a sitting position. The time had come to get down to business, and Sullivan described the security file and his need to open it.

'Will this be a surreptitious entry?' George said.

'It will.'

'And you're no longer with the Agency?'

'This has nothing to do with the Agency.'

'Oh, my.' George sighed and reached under the covers to scratch himself. 'You wouldn't have a cigarette, would you? Nadine doesn't let me have any.' Sullivan gave him instead one of the small Dutch cigars that he smoked. 'How much time will you have?' George said.

'Ten minutes. No more than that.'

'What light would you have?'

'Portable high-intensity.'

'This is a class-five cabinet,' George said. 'The top of the line, Irish. Hercules is the best. I worked nine years for them. They've got a guarantee written out on a prissy little plaque bolted to the inside of the top drawer of every cabinet they make. I can give it to you word for word.'

George Knapp closed his eyes and began to recite in a faint Irish brogue, and with the Hercules guarantee set to metre, as if it were a poem.

'This is a US Government Security Container class-five cabinet, which under the tests defined in interim Federal Specifications A-A F-three-five-eight-C affords protection for:
Thirty man-minutes against surreptitious entry.
Ten man-minutes against forced entry.
Twenty man-hours against manipulation of the lock.
Twenty man-hours against radiological attack.'

Sullivan offered him a second cigar and said, 'That was beautiful, George.'

'Cheeky, those Hercules chaps.'

'Your years at Chubb & Sons were well spent.'

'Happy, happy years,' George Knapp said. 'Among great, pillowy women with flawless complexions.'

'Tell me about the safe, George.'

'A piece of cake, Irish. And a pleasure to give their come-uppance to the arrogant swine at Hercules. You're going to have to manipulate the lock, feel the numbers in your finger-tips. You know some of it, I'll teach you the rest.'

'Can it be done in ten minutes?'

'If you have the serial number of the particular cabinet, and the date of construction as well.'

'I have both.'

'Then you can do it in under ten minutes,' he said. 'The tumblers are set in sequence. Three numbers. Hercules changes the sequence every couple of months. But if we've got the serial number and the date, we can begin to zero in. Shorten the odds and the time it takes to hit the number. You remember the Mosler seven hundred I did for you in Bang-kok? Same principle.'

'You'll need access to the Hercules files.'

'Or a cabinet manufactured between the same time brackets where we know the combination. But you leave that to me. I know a fellow keeps good records.'

'And a cabinet for me to practise on.'

'A good used one will cost you about five hundred bucks,' George said. 'Another thousand for my troubles.'

Sullivan took two single hundred-dollar bills from the in-side pocket of his jacket and handed them folded to George Knapp. He put the money away without glancing at it. Money had never meant much to George Knapp.

'You come by Tuesday night,' he said. 'I'll have the cabinet, and I promise you'll be opening it in less time than it takes Nadine to boil an egg.'

George Knapp was as good as his word. Tuesday morning he called with word that the goods had been delivered, and that Nadine would be out that night between six and ten. She'd be at her macramé class at the YWCA.

Jack arrived to find George up and hobbling about with the aid of a crutch. He'd shaved and dressed; George was a dapper man with a weakness for silk scarves knotted loosely around the throat. The front of his trousers was pleated and his fly, Sullivan observed, fastened by means of buttons. The years with Chubb & Sons had made an Anglophile of George Knapp.

He sparkled with confidence and good spirits, the notion of embarrassing the Hercules Safe Company having restored the colour to his cheeks; he led Sullivan directly into the bedroom, where the file stood, a great steel column looming over George and Nadine's bed. It had four drawers and was made of steel half an inch thick, a duplicate of the one in Ash's office.

'This model was first manufactured in nineteen sixty-five,' George said. 'And they haven't changed a thing since. Quite pleased with themselves at Hercules. We get to opening this brute in under ten minutes, you'll do as well with the one you're after.'

Sullivan came prepared with a stethoscope, which he'd bought earlier in a medical-supply shop near Bellevue Hospital, a small pair of pliers, and a pencil flashlight. The stethoscope was wrapped tightly around the pliers and made a neat package, fitting in the inside pocket of his jacket. The pencil flashlight was clipped to the seam of the pocket.

George approved of these items. They were all Sullivan would need.

The cabinet lock was a three-number tumbler system; in this case, right, left, right, as were all those manufactured under the serial number of the one in Ash's office. The number sequence was, however, different; it was manufactured during another time bracket.

To test his skill, Sullivan was told only that the first digit was between three and seven, the second between twelve and sixteen, and the last either twenty-seven, twenty-nine, or thirty-one. The last digit had to be odd and it had to be one of those three numbers. Hercules had cut corners a bit with the tooling for its microlathe, and by that bit of penny-pinching set a series limit on the system. It was a serious flaw.

But Sullivan's first time dropping the tumblers with the stethoscope was a disappointment. He missed the first two digits and twice had to circle back. George held a stopwatch on him: twenty-one minutes, eighteen seconds.

But George remained confident. 'Not bad time at all. How long since you last manipulated a safe?'

'Ten years.'

'Well, there's your answer. You've good hands, Irish. I swear you have, or I wouldn't waste my time.'

'You want to beat Hercules, don't you?'

'Boastful, that guarantee of theirs,' George said.

'Twenty-one minutes and we haven't touched the second lock.'

'That's nothing at all,' George said. 'A simple spring affair set to snap when the tumblers are set. It's only to slow down your Mr Sticky Fingers in case some fool hasn't spun the dial.'

They worked together for several hours for the next two nights. George kept the bedroom curtains drawn, the lights out. After the first few hours, Sullivan had no need of the pencil flashlight. George trained him to work with a blindfold. He came to know the mechanism intimately, each threaded calibration of the dial, the play in the wheel. He learned to anticipate each tumbler's fall, and to hold his breath until it fell with a decisive dead thud. Blindfolded, listening through the stethoscope, each tumbler sounded big as a boulder.

As George had promised, the second lock offered no problem; Sullivan used the pliers to hold back the spring, and George made him a present of a number-three stainless-steel pick to work the lock.

Midnight of the fourth day, after eleven hours of practice, George again held a stopwatch to him: he had the Hercules open in nine minutes flat.

The rest of Sullivan's time was spent planning how to enter the building surreptitiously and make his way to Ash's office. His preference was to go in late in the working day, just before five o'clock, lie low for an hour or two behind the door of a fire exit or the crawlway of an elevator shaft, and be in Ash's office and out again before the cleaning women. But he was too well known to get into the office by one of the usual ruses – posing as a messenger, or to fake an appointment and masquerade as a client with business. He'd have to go in at night, when the security was toughest. This in mind, he reconnoitred the building; it was served by three elevator banks, eighteen cars in all. But between six at night and eight-thirty the next morning only one car operated in each bank. The control panel and monitoring console for all the elevators was built into a large communications terminal at the south end of the lobby, thirty-eight feet from the revolving door opening on to Park Avenue. A second lobby entrance, this a series of two doors, one push and the other pull, led to Forty-eighth Street. This was locked at six in the evening, and monitored by a large mirror set high on the wall above the central communications terminal.

The terminal was manned all night by a single security guard. At his disposal were radio-telephone hook-ups with building guards at the underground garage and garbage collection exits, security staff's locker room, and off-duty shack in the first basement. In the same way he was in contact with all of the private security personnel, those hired by several of the corporate tenants in the building.

Ash had hired security from Burns International, two men on alternating shifts stationed at a desk just outside the door of the main office on the twenty-eighth floor. After six o'clock, the door of the night elevator opened eleven feet from that desk.

Sullivan had a careful look inside the night elevator. Besides the telephone link to the central console in the lobby, there was an electronic control board; like most modern elevators it was operated by means of a thermal touch system, the body heat of one's finger triggering an electric impulse on the floor selector.

He found he was able to free the panel on the roof of the elevator car and scramble through the opening on to a beam, which led to a steel ladder rigged the height of the building inside the elevator shaft. Clearance between the ladder and the wall of the elevator car was three and a half feet.

To continue his surveillance of the Park Avenue building, he checked into the Waldorf Astoria, again using the identity of Donald Bowles, requesting a room with a view of Park Avenue.

From Willoughby Peerless he bought a pair of seven-by-fifty wide-angle Nikon glasses, designed for night vision, and spent two nights at the window of his room, familiarizing himself with the security procedure. He clocked the courier, whom he knew met the eight o'clock Swissair flight with the confidential pouch from Roper's Geneva office. The courier was in and out of the building in less than ten minutes. Sullivan confirmed that the pouch was given by the courier to the Burns guard stationed outside the office door on the twenty-eighth floor, and that the guard left his post to carry the pouch to the mail room and lock it away. That would take three or four minutes, ample time for Sullivan to enter with his key and make his way to Ash's office.

Only two offices in the building operated with a night staff. One was the central records repository of Bankers Trust Company on the mezzanine, reached by escalator from the street floor. The second was on the sixth floor, where the daily stock transactions of the country's largest brokerage house were processed by an elaborate system of computers.

Security in both offices was tight. All personnel were obliged to show identifying badges when entering and leaving. But the employees of Bankers Trust were fewer and more familiar to the guards. There was more of a turnover at the securities-processing office. People would appear at odd hours, identify themselves, and be admitted to the building. In some cases they stayed only an hour or two. The bond transactions were more numerous and complicated, and the computers needed were consequently more sophisticated. Sullivan knew something of how these things worked; the irregulars were computer-maintenance people sent by the company which leased the computers.

There were only two computer-leasing companies in New York big enough to handle equipment that costly and complicated. From the library of Standard & Poor's, Sullivan drew the annual report of both companies. Each listed its major clients. The company he wanted was Computer Data Leasing, its executive offices in the World Trade Centre.

He checked out of the Waldorf, paying for his room with cash, retrieved his possessions from the Americana's safe, and took a cab to La Guardia Airport.

In a pay toilet in the airport washroom he transferred Donald Bowles's driver's licence, social-security and American Express cards to a compartment in his suitcase before removing his Brooks Brothers suit, button-down shirt, and striped tie; from his suitcase he took a brown turtleneck sweater and an Yves Saint Laurent suit, which he'd bought in Paris. He quickly slipped on the French clothes, exchanged his English wing-tip shoes for Gucci slip-ons, and folded away the Brooks Brothers suit, shirt, and tie. He brushed his black hair forward on to his forehead and used some of the Estée Lauder Go Bronze to darken his skin. A pair of blue-tinted aviator glasses completed the transformation.

When he left the washroom, it was as Jean-Claude Morvan, the name which appeared on the second identity kit bought from Lew Snead. It was as Morvan that he registered later that afternoon at the New York Hilton on Sixth Avenue.

He rented space in the Hilton safe and deposited the locked leather pouch. From a pay phone on Sixth Avenue he called Computer Data Leasing and, using a French accent, represented himself as an importer of European dental supplies and equipment in need of computer services to control his inventory. He was connected to the office of a man named Shank. He spoke first to Shank's secretary and was told the gentleman was out of the office at the moment.

'Can I be of help?'

She had a pleasing, rather husky voice with the trace of a Southern accent.

'I'm sorry. I didn't quite get your name.'

'Blackmur. Janice Blackmur.'

'Is it *Miss* Blackmur?'

'It sure is.'

'Perhaps you could be of some help,' Sullivan said. 'I'm not at all familiar with New York. And of course it's somewhat overpowering.'

'I know just what you mean.'

'You're not from here?'

'Oh, no. I guess you don't know American accents well. Virginia, originally. But I've been here in Fun City three years.'

'I take it it's not all been fun.'

'You learn to take the good with the bad.'

'What I was going to ask was rather personal. And of course we've never even seen each other. No, it's really too much.'

'That's a devastating French accent you're tossing around, mister.'

'I apologize. It's remarkable you can understand me at all, Miss Blackmur.'

'Janice.'

'My name is Jean-Claude.'

'Oh, my heavens.' She took a deep breath and said, 'What is it you wanted me to do?'

'My ex-wife has remarried. An American fellow, living in Los Angeles. I want to send a little gift. Something silver or crystal. Something not for her alone, not wishing to intrude myself. You understand. Something for the marriage.'

'That's very nice, Jean-Claude.'

'I wish her every happiness.'

'I think the place to go is Cartier. Maybe Tiffany.'

'On Fifth Avenue?'

'Tiffany's on Fifty-seventh, and Cartier is a couple of blocks south. That's downtown.'

'You've been very helpful. I would like to thank you personally.'

'Mr Shank is free tomorrow at ten-thirty,' she said. 'Could you come in then?'

He spent the night as a Jean-Claude Morvan, choosing the Café des Artistes for dinner, where his French was quite good enough to fool the native staff. He was in his room at the Hilton by ten o'clock, requested a showing of *Last Tango in Paris* on pay television, but was able to watch only fifteen minutes of it before drifting off to sleep.

Sullivan was awake at six-thirty the next morning. He showered and dressed quickly; it was a brilliant fall morning and he decided to walk from midtown to the World Trade Centre at the southern end of Manhattan, pausing for a breakfast of freshly baked Italian bread, cheese, and two cups of capuccino on Grand Street. He gave up his Dutch cigars and bought a pack of Gauloises from a cigar store on the Bowery south of Canal Street.

Promptly at ten, he presented himself to the receptionist of Computer Data Leasing, and asked to see Mr Shank. Janice Blackmur came out to show him in. She was a tall, handsome, confident girl, who looked as if she played good tennis and skied. She had splendid white teeth and a forthright handshake. Sullivan sensed a happy childhood with a prosperous and adoring father, one of a large and boisterous family in which she was the only girl.

They chatted briefly just outside Shank's office. He told her he'd taken her advice and bought his ex-wife's wedding present at Cartier. An antique crystal decanter. He made a small joke about new husbands in old bottles, and then stood back to see if she understood what he was talking about. She did. She was clever. Her face at first glance had seemed open and frank – wholesome was the word which came to mind, but now he saw her clear blue eyes go quickly over each of his features, the way he moved and the clothes he wore; she knew how to take an inventory and draw conclusions. And she liked what she saw. But then Sullivan was used to that; he had learned to accept casually the attentions of a wide variety of women. He handled his attractiveness easily, and put it to good use, like a man who'd grown up with a large trust fund.

'How long will you be in New York?' she said.

'I'm opening a branch here,' he said. 'To get it running well should take a year, perhaps longer.'

She'd taken pains that morning with her make-up and the green Anne Klein smock was the best thing she could wear to the office without attracting attention.

Shank turned out to be older than Sullivan had imagined.

Computer people tended to be young, bright, and cocksure; the Agency and Roper both relied heavily on these young men with graduate degrees in the measurement sciences, bland, tidy, and infallible. Shank turned out to be something else altogether, a man on the downgrade; he looked as if he drank, he was a fat, grey-faced and unhealthy man, lighting one Salem cigarette after another.

From Sullivan's point of view the meeting went well. Shank was either persuaded or too uneasy to question the representation Sullivan made of himself. He handed over a variety of specifications on the entire computer line. He spelled it all out for Sullivan, gathered his hand in a flabby wet handshake, and turned him loose.

Janice Blackmur was at her desk just outside. She seemed to have little to do, a clever girl in a dull and undemanding job. She was certainly bored and could do with a little adventure.

Sullivan said, 'Do you know of a good French restaurant

in the neighbourhood?'

'Must it be French?'

'It would help if it were.'

'Help whom?'

'Help me to show you a good time.'

They wound up eating fresh oysters and drinking white wine at Sweets near the Fulton Fish Market. That night he gave her a marvellous dinner at Chez Pascal and afterwards took her to a club where they danced, listened to music, and he got her to talk about herself. He was a good listener, it was part of his training, and of course the less he talked the less chance there was for a slip in his cover.

He was right about her coming from a large family, and her father had been prosperous. But her mother had developed cancer and the prolonged treatment had taken nearly all of his money.

'He was okay as long as he had to take care of her,' she said. 'As long as he had to cope. But after she died, he just fell apart. He started to drink and neglect his law practice. One of my brothers went into the navy, and the other is a lawyer married to a little Queen of the Cotillion in Richmond. They have a little girl and she's expecting, so they're naturally hoping for a little boy. And of course my brother is doing very well, thank you. Thirty years old and he's already got himself his first Cadillac.'

'You make it sound' – he groped for the word in English – 'futile.'

'I'm unfair,' she said. 'It's not futile. It need not be. My brother and his wife are decent people, living the best life they know how.'

'But that's not enough for you?'

'No. Work, family, money. No, that's not enough for me.'

'But what else is there?' he said.

'Oh, I think you know,' she said. 'I think this is some kind of test you're giving me. What else is there? There's excitement, risk, and danger. Danger is best. Then at least you know you're alive.'

'You found me out,' he said. 'I was testing to see if you were at bottom as conventional as the rest of your family. The way you described your father's inability to comprehend tragedy. That's a conventional man, a mediocre one. And that's not you.'

He saw the suspicion come into her eyes. She had sensed that he was angling, that he wanted something. She was indeed a clever girl. He was glad of that.

'I don't know what kind of life is right for me.' She pretended to a fluent gaiety. 'I tried Washington for a while. San Francisco, now New York. Certain things are out. I won't work in any of the hospitality professions, or live in Los Angeles, Miami, or any place in the State of Texas. The Southern Rim.' She pretended to shudder. 'Nixon territory. I was one of those kids in the New Hampshire snow for Eugene McCarthy.'

'Eight years ago,' he said. 'You don't look old enough.'

'I'm twenty-nine.'

'Have you ever been married?'

'Don't believe in it.'

'What would you do if you fell in love with a man?'

'That's easy,' she said. 'I'd fuck him until his ears fell off.'

Sullivan's laugh was sincere. He'd begun to enjoy his work.

'Did I shock you?'

'Not nearly as much as you hoped to.'

'But your ex-wife would never have said that.'

'Certainly not. She's a conventional woman, obviously with no sense of tragedy, since she divorced me.'

'And clearly she believes in marriage. Marriage and again marriage.'

'We forgive her that,' he said.

'This radical guy once told me that putting down marriage was really Marxism, step one. Marriage is possessions. Houses, furniture, cars, people. You think that sounds simplistic?'

She was playing at being serious, at using certain words like a child dining out and ordering her own dinner. But suddenly she laughed, and deliberately tossed her hair, a stagey gesture, but effective; she was an attractive girl with one eye slightly off-centre and a fondness for breezy self-scrutiny.

'I'm just lazy, self-indulgent, and restless,' she said. 'The longest I ever lived with one guy was three weeks. Weekends, one-night stands. Oh, the usual thing. The politics of commitment, vegetarianism. Now I ski. I work only to put enough bread together to go somewhere and ski.'

'You sound bored.'

'And if I am?'

'Then I must find some way to entertain you.'

But it was she who undertook to entertain him. She belonged to a private club in a renovated hotel on the Upper West Side. It was an all-night party with food, drinks, unisex fashion shows, singers, comics. Drinks and organic food were served around a large baroque swimming pool. The swimming was nude. There were saunas and squash courts. Men and women used the same showers and locker room. There were homosexuals, but not enough to write the bylaws. The mood was cool, androgynous; many of the men were bodybuilders and there were quite a few extraordinary women, but one was expected to do nothing before this naked beauty but admire it. One dared not be heated or graceless. The word was soft, soft-pedal, soft-spoken. Glasses tinkled around the pool, polite laughter. Sullivan did his best; between Janice's legs there flashed a patch of warm russet hair, gorgeous as autumn leaves.

She drank her second cognac, dipped her fingers in the glass and wet the tip of his penis. 'A penny for your thoughts,' she said.

'I was wondering how you came to be a member of this club?'

'This man I used to ball bought me a lifetime pass for Christmas.'

They swam and showered together and went twice to the sauna. It was nearly two when they left. He took her to his hotel room, where they made love several times during the night and slept until mid-afternoon.

It was Saturday and they walked across town to Maxwell's Plum for an early dinner, and then went to a movie. They ate ice-cream cones from Baskin-Robbins and to avoid the trip to her apartment in Greenwich Village for a change of clothes, he bought her some things in Ted Lapidus and from the boutiques along Third Avenue in the Sixties and the side streets between Third and Second avenues.

He noticed that she accepted gifts easily, that it flushed and excited her, that it was a passion with her, and the finer and more expensive the gifts, the better. She was greedy; he was certain she'd make a good thief.

On Sunday, they rented bicycles and rode through Central Park. Lunch was on the terrace outside the cafeteria across from the sea lions' pool.

She said, 'Could you make love to me now?'

'On the terrace? In Central Park?'

'Is there a time you don't want to make love?'

'Not to you. Not so far.'

'But the time will come?'

'If we stay together long enough.'

She was looking into a brilliant early-afternoon sun. He noticed her skin, which was lightly tanned, flawless. The touch of it lingered on his fingertips. The pupils of her eyes were contracted, the iris an intense blue.

'And will we stay together?' she said.

'What's on your mind?' Then he laughed and said, 'A penny for *your* thoughts.'

He watched her dip her fingertips in a glass of water and then flick the drops at him.

'You know what I've noticed about you?' she said. 'You do it all my way. Yet I don't think you're that kind of man. And sexually you've been so marvellously obedient.'

'I like to please.'

'I don't think so,' she said.

'Are you interested in hearing what I've noticed about you?' he said.

'Only if they're good things.'

'Wonderful things,' he said. 'First, you're really a very good cocksucker.'

'And second?'

'Give me enough time,' he said, 'and I'm sure I'll think of something.'

'I want to make love,' she said, 'but not at your brassy hotel. I'd like a nice, raunchy fleabag. Some place really crummy. Can it be done?'

Her eyes never left his face; she was serious. One met an ordinary American girl and quickly uncovered such odd things.

He took her to a transient hotel near Gramercy Park, a favourite of streetwalkers who prowled lower Park Avenue after dark. The desk clerk was about twenty-five with a great black beard, wearing a khaki field jacket with a 102nd Airborne patch. He was reading a paperback edition of *The Gulag Archipelago*. Sullivan paid ten dollars and was given a key.

The room had a weary, faded look, the bed and single chair were relics of the early 1930s and falling to pieces. Ancient plaster moulding framed the arch above a double window on which the name Roxy had been written in the dust.

It was just the place she wanted and quickly tore off the pretty clothes he'd bought her at Ted Lapidus the day before. He was still fully dressed, examining the bed for bugs. Because he was slow to begin, she became impatient. She'd come to play the whore. He didn't like that, didn't want it. He wasn't at his best, but went at her mechanically, his thoughts elsewhere, a man rolling behind a wooden stick.

Afterwards, he made her smooth her new clothes, and dress, and he took her as far away and as quickly as he could: he chose the Palm Court at the Plaza for tea.

As he'd noted before, she was clever: 'Who are you really?' she said. 'Jean-Claude. Is that your real name?'

'Yes.'

'You're not a Frenchman. The accent is terrific. The clothes were bought in Paris. I checked the labels once, while you were asleep. But you're no Frenchman. I don't know what you are, but you're not French.'

He beckoned a waiter and asked for more lemon and some hot water. His tea was cold.

'Tell me why you think that,' he said.

'When I mentioned Gene McCarthy in New Hampshire, you knew just what I meant. The nineteen sixty-eight primary.'

'I'm political. I read the Paris *Herald Tribune* to practise my English.'

'And you watch everything you say. You weigh every word. Your eyes. You are in fact one calculating bastard.'

'I do have one or two things to hide. And it's true I've not just come from Paris.'

'And you're not in the dental-supply business. Not you. Where does your money come from?'

'I'm a thief.'

'Now we're getting somewhere,' she said. 'Are you working on something at the moment? Is that why you came to Shank? The dental supply is all cock and bull, isn't it?'

'Yes.'

'And the crystal decanter and the ex-wife in Los Angeles. More cock and bull?'

'I've never been married.'

'And you and me are just a put-on?' There wasn't a hint of tears. Her face was white with anger. She was a hard one. He liked her for it, it made things easier.

She said, 'What I mean, Jean-Claude, is that you've been fucking me under false pretences.'

'Not at all. I've put my plan off because I don't want you involved. The risk is very slight, but I decided to protect you even from that.'

'I don't want to be protected,' she said. 'I've outgrown it.'

'And I've outgrown using people I care for.'

'And you care for me?'

'I'm a professional thief,' he said. 'And I've put away a very good scam for you.'

She hesitated, then asked softly, 'And you and me? Was it all fake?'

'Only at the very beginning. I was going to use your boss, and to get near him through you. But then we started up and I changed my mind.'

She nodded and laid her hand on his. 'You needn't look so miserable. I believe you. Last night I woke up and saw that you were awake, staring at the ceiling. You didn't know I was watching you and wondering what you were thinking. That's when you changed your mind about using me. I can see that now.'

'I should've told you from the beginning.' His deep, luminous eyes held hers. 'I've ruined things for us.'

She looked away, then smiled and said, 'I think I knew all along. Now I feel something I didn't before. You're a dangerous man. But I'm not afraid. Not in the least.'

'I wouldn't blame you if you got up and walked out now,' he said.

'Would you let me?'

'No. I'm faking again.'

'Tell me what you had planned. What were you going to steal? Is there much risk?'

'Not much as these things go. There's always some danger.'

'Would it be violent?'

'No. No guns, nothing like that. A small, neat swindle. And the victim is a bank, a balance sheet. The numbers are moved from one column to another, nothing more personal than that.'

'I never have liked banks,' she said.

The waiter brought a pot of hot water and a saucer with half-moons of sliced lemon. She freshened his tea.

'It's a simple swindle, but a nice one,' he said. 'I use a different name to open a minimum-balance chequeing account, make a deposit and ask for an extra supply of deposit slips. The ones with my alias won't be delivered for two or three weeks. I tell them I'm in the mail-order business and expect a lot of small cheques which need to be deposited. They'll give me a packet of one hundred slips. The thing to remember is all of these will have my account number magnetized so that the computer will be able to read it.'

She was leaning forward, her elbow on the table, her chin cupped in the palm of her hand, listening intently to every word.

'It's a large bank,' he said. 'There are twenty-nine branches in Manhattan alone. I go around to each of them and put a couple of the deposit slips with my number in with the regular stack.'

'And people who've forgotten their deposit slips come in and use them, thinking they're blank. But in fact the money they deposit goes into your account.'

'I had planned to do it on the fifteenth of the month. Pay day. The tellers are busy and the cheques tend to be larger. Then wait three days, time for all but the out-of-town cheques to clear, ask for a statement of my account. Draw cheques to cash in that amount, and be gone.'

She thought a moment and then said, 'If I use one of those blank slips to make a deposit, I write my own account number on it.'

'With a ball-point pen,' he said. 'The computer is unable to read the numbers. It's coded only to separate those with handwritten numbers from the pre-printed, magnetized ones. Later on, the written ones are collected and credited manually. The computer is your company's Six-twenty. Easy enough to recode so that the handwritten slips pass with the magnetized ones.'

'But you'd have to get into the bank data-processing centre.'

'That's right.'

'And that's where I come in?'

'I'd drop about one hundred slips. Average it out at three, four hundred dollars each. Six months' first-class in the Alps. After that Greece, North Africa. It'd do for a year.'

'And when that's gone you do it again?'

'If not this, something else. Opportunities turn up, one thinks of things.'

'And what part do I play?'

'Three or four sheets of stationery with the letterhead of your company.'

'Just that? Blank sheets? Nothing more?' She was disappointed. 'I've got stacks in my desk drawer. Envelopes, airmail, regular bond. Take your pick.'

'Regular bond will be fine. Perhaps an envelope or two.'

'Whose signature goes on the letter you're going to write?'

'Shank's.'

'I can get you that. At least a copy. I'll trace it off one of his regular letters.'

'I don't need it.'

'The specs. of our Six-twenty. I can get you that.'

'I know how it works,' he said. 'But I do wish there was something more I could ask you to steal.'

'Do you think I'll make a good thief?'

'I'm certain of it.'

'Will we travel on our own names?'

'Why not? No one will be looking for us.'

'Could we get different papers if we had to? If the cops or somebody came looking for us. Could we change our names? Become somebody else?'

'It can be done.'

'Have you ever lived that way, with a fake name and passport and all the rest?' She was excited and eager to begin. 'Tomorrow is Monday. You'd better not come by the office

98

again. Meet me in Battery Park at twelve-thirty. I'll have the stationery then.'

'You're not bored any more, are you?' he said.

'I'm going to like being a thief,' she said. 'I'm going to like it even more than I do skiing.'

CHAPTER SEVEN

The Vice-President had laid it out clearly; Ash was to contact Sullivan and tell him his demands had been rejected. They would pay, the money deposited anywhere in the world, in any hard currency, but that was as far as they would go. They would do nothing to quash the indictment. Sullivan would have to plead guilty. He would keep his mouth shut and go quietly to jail. For that he would be paid two hundred and seventy-five thousand dollars.

The Vice-President had made the decision. Perhaps the President was involved, certainly the Senator and Roper. Each for his own reasons had an interest in burying the Astra file. Roper, the Senator, the Vice-President, the President himself, there was no telling where one ended and the other began.

Ash hated them, but he worked for them, all of them. Roper paid his salary, but who paid Roper? Whom did Roper pay? It went round in a circle, Ash in the centre.

He was one of them. He'd joined with his eyes open. Ash was a new cop, who had learned Spanish and earned a degree in sociology at night. He had nerve enough, but was never brutal. He neither hated nor feared. He believed in the goodness of man and the perfectibility of his institutions. It was a million years ago.

On the streets he saw terrible things, violent, cruel, corrupt. But he hadn't yet begun to question the notion that evil was a social problem, curable by better and more humane government.

He spent his vacations working for Martin Luther King, in the vanguard of that honourable revolution, and served during the violence in Mississippi and Alabama; he'd been bloodied in it, dragged from a car and beaten senseless on a country road outside of Oxford. The men who beat him carried shotguns and pistols and he never understood why they hadn't shot him. He carried no gun, nothing to protect himself with, although he did fight back, landing only one punch before being overwhelmed. At least he had the satisfaction of feeling one bastard's nose squash under his fist. But that only infuriated them, and all the while they were beating him, and the beating went on and on, it seemed for hours, he believed they were going to kill him. He never lost consciousness, he saw the face of his son, of his wife, and father, he was certain he was going to die on that desolate country road, and through it all he repeated to himself that he was right to have come to Mississippi, and given the chance and knowing that he would die, he would do it all again.

He was in a hospital for nearly two months, and when he returned to New York, it was as one of the few white policemen trusted by the black community. When the riots of the 1960s started, he was in the centre of things, and was rapidly promoted. He was honest and smart. The time was right. There was even talk of his going into politics.

It was just about then he began to lose heart. It began around the time Martin Luther King was shot. He first heard about it over the radio of a police launch on the East River, supervising the search for the body of a man who'd doused himself with gasoline, set himself on fire, and leaped from the Williamsburg Bridge.

The commissioner summoned him to a meeting with the mayor and all of the top city brass. The talk was of civil war in Harlem and Bedford-Stuyvesant. A plan existed to bring in the State National Guard, and the mayor put in a call to Washington in the event federal troops were needed. The mood was one of panic.

Ash was on the streets of Harlem seventy-two hours without a break, napping for fifteen or twenty minutes at a time in the back of patrol cars. He argued and pleaded and screamed until he was hoarse. He flattered and threatened. He bargained and made promises, and it worked. There were no major riots, no looting, the lid had been kept on, and the city came through it rather well. More than any other man, he was responsible.

The following year he was promoted to captain. But by that time the passionate belief in his work had disappeared. It was a gradual, subtle process, this erosion of faith. There was nothing dramatic about it. No electrifying truth was revealed to him. The murder of Dr King seemed only to speed up a process already well under way. He could remember no one event which caused him to lose faith. Not the Kennedy murders, not that of King, not the war in Vietnam, but at the same time each of these played a part. Each chipped away a precious bit of his faith.

One day he saw the corpse of a three-year-old boy whose mother had sewed up his rectum before beating him to death. Now the woman who did that was a monster. She was evil, and the evil was in her soul, in each cell of her body. He could find no way to hold time and place responsible for such evil. It wasn't a social problem. It wasn't because she had been raised in slums or deprived of education or even because she had been herself mistreated as a child. It was because she was evil.

But Ash was a fair and thoughtful man with a long memory. In his years as a cop he'd seen other terrible things, which his faith had survived. No, it wasn't a single dramatic event. One day he simply believed that all evil was born in man, part of him, always and for all time, more in some men than in others, and there was damn little to be done about it. And after that Ash's faith simply shrank, broke into pieces, and slipped away. One day it was gone.

Now his choices were narrowed. It was really quite simple: either you have faith in something, a vision; or you put on your pants and make as much money as you can as quickly as you can.

Ash and the Senator had been friends for years. Ash had put him alongside the black movers and shakers in Brooklyn and Harlem, where the Senator was known as a liberal. The Senator was grateful. He introduced him to Roper. And of course Roper had a nose for idealists when the milk had gone sour. He scooped up Ash, as he had Sullivan. Ash became head of Roper's security, his salary twice that of a police captain. There were bonuses, and creamy little pearls of stock-market wisdom, insider's information it was called. Strictly speaking, it was illegal, but Ash was taught how to profit without ownership of record. One bought through friends and foreign banks, an investment trust incorporated in Panama. And there were other friends in Washington to feed a tame SEC.

Roper flattered Ash until he was one of them, until his monthly nut couldn't be supported elsewhere, until he had grown used to the luscious life and was dependent on Roper.

Now the price to get out was too high. Could he trail Eleanor to Hong Kong, a middle-aged man on an allowance, a has-been, waiting at home with a drink, wondering in whose bed she'd spent the lunch hour? Quit Roper, say no to the Vice-President of the United States, and he'd be unemployable. They'd hound him, cut him down, perhaps kill him. He thought of David, an intern in Houston. The young speak easily of hard moral decisions.

Ash first tried to contact Sullivan in the usual way. He called the answering service in the Empire State Building with a message for Mr Weston. Twenty-four hours passed without Mr Weston returning the call. Ash tried the answering service again, this time speaking to the supervisor. Mr Weston had cancelled his service. A postcard had been received that morning.

Sullivan had gone underground. Ash reasoned that wherever Sullivan was he'd need a name, an identity, a driver's licence, and all the bogus pocket litter that went with it.

Sullivan would be fussy, a careful shopper, he'd insist on a cold identity, paper without a traceable history. He had money and he was certain to have kept up his connections. Sullivan would buy the best: there weren't that many sellers at that level. Ash knew them all.

Reese's surveillance report was helpful. On the first day he was followed, probably before he'd spotted the tail, Sullivan had spent an hour and a half – between three and four-thirty – over a drink in the bar in the lobby of the New York Hilton. At four-fifteen he used a pay phone to make a local call. He was on the phone less than a minute and then ordered a second drink, but left it unfinished. A man – black, five feet ten, slender build, about thirty-five, in chauffeur's livery – came into the bar for him and they left together. The investigator followed them outside where they entered the driver's car and sat together talking for about ten minutes. The investigator didn't know the driver's name, but the car was a 1976 Cadillac Fleetwood limousine, New York licence number EQZ-103.

Ash called Reese and asked him to run the number through the Motor Vehicle computer.

'That's a limo number,' Reese said. 'The hack bureau would have it and they're faster these days.'

Twenty minutes later he called Ash back. 'It's registered to a Lewis Walker Snead. Mr Snead is black, thirty-eight years old, five foot ten inches tall, and lives at Two hundred and six, West One hundred and Sixty-eighth Street.'

Reese paused, Ash plainly heard the creak made by the unoiled steel spring of Reese's swivel chair.

'You just leaned back and put your feet up on your desk,' Ash said. 'That means you're deciding whether to ask me what I want with Lewis Walker Snead.'

'And also if I should stick in my big schnozzola,' Reese said.

'I got the licence number off the surveillance report,' Ash said.

'I already know that.'

'D'you also know what Mr Snead has on his sheet?'

'Three arrests, two selling of stolen property, one possession of firearms. All dismissed. LOE. He's a ragpicker. Buys and sells soft goods mostly. Now and then iron, but the speciality is high-quality paper.' Reese's desk chair squeaked again. 'How else can I be of help?'

'Call Snead. Tell him to expect a call from me. I'm going to want the answers to certain questions. You tell him.'

'I can do better for you,' Reese said. 'Snead works for a Cuban named Benny Alvar. Benny is a prodigy. Good connections in Central America and the Caribbean. Coke traffic and weapons, with documents as a sideline. That's where Snead came in. Benny is a major figure, Ash, but after your time.'

103

'I know the name,' Ash said.

'His father was President of the Cuban Senate in Batista's time.'

'That'd be Máximo Alvar,' Ash said. 'You tell Benny, Ash Morgan would like to talk to him.'

Early the next morning, shortly after he arrived at his office, Ash received a phone call from a man who didn't identify himself, but spoke as if he'd learned Spanish before he'd learned English. Could Mr Morgan be ready in half an hour? A car would be waiting in front of his building.

Ash was prompt, but the car was already at the kerb, a dark-grey Mercedes with diplomatic plates. One man was at the wheel and a second leaned against the rear door, his arms folded across his chest. He recognized Ash and opened the door for him; the driver started the car, went down Park Avenue, and turned east on Forty-sixth Street.

The man beside Ash was about sixty, carefully dressed in a lightweight dark suit. He was short and broad and his skin had a dark-coppery tint with the wrinkled, weather-worn look of an Indian elder. His hair was slick and unnaturally black. He said nothing, but Ash supposed he was the one who'd telephoned. He had an odd way of sitting with his arms folded across his chest, his hands tucked out of sight under his armpits.

The Mercedes continued east to First Avenue, and then north, past United Nations Plaza, and into the garage built under the Secretariat Building. They slowed for the security guard, who nodded to the driver and passed them in. The driver parked near an elevator and turned off the ignition. The man next to Ash motioned for him to follow; as they climbed out of the car, Ash noticed that he was missing the thumbs of both hands.

Benny Alvar was at a table in the third-floor executive lounge. He was younger than Ash had expected, certainly no more than thirty, a handsome man, one would have called him beautiful, with the pampered good looks of a Latin singing star. He looked nothing like his father, but then Ash remembered that one of old Máximo's early wives had been a Mexican actress.

'My father asks to be remembered to you,' Benny Alvar said.

'Is he well?'

'He had a small medical problem, an enlargement of the prostate, which required surgery.' Benny Alvar rapped the wooden table-top with his knuckles. 'He came through it very well.'

'Your father is a very strong man.'

'He's been warned against salt, shellfish, and sorrow,' he said. 'But the hardest problem for such an active man is retirement. Inactivity. At first he felt bored and useless. And the loss of the prostate gland only made matters worse.'

'I'd heard he bought a ranch in Florida.'

'The ranch changed everything,' Benny Alvar said. 'It's there he became interested again in his pineapples.' He brought out two cigars, the largest size made, Churchills, nearly black and full strength. He gave one to Ash and lit the other himself, biting it with his fine white teeth; as an afterthought, he passed a third cigar to the henchman without thumbs, who sat behind him, his arms folded across his chest.

'Agriculture has always been a hobby of my father's,' Benny Alvar said. 'In Cuba, we owned some of the best land.' He spread his arms to indicate the extent of the family estates. 'Mangoes, citrus fruits, sugar cane, of course. And now, in Florida, he hopes to develop a new strain of pineapple, one as economical as the Puerto Rican and at the same time as delectable as those from Hawaii.'

'I'm sure he'll be successful,' Ash said. 'And please tell him that I think of him often, always with affection and respect.'

Benny Alvar nodded and released the immense cigar briefly from between his teeth.

'My father has asked that I oblige you in any way that I can,' he said. 'I asked Reese and he told me what you wanted to know. Snead sold Sullivan two sets of papers. One was American, nothing out of the ordinary. Snead put the kit together himself from fresh blanks and names out of the phone book. Now he claims he can't remember the name he picked.'

The man without the thumbs nodded and spoke for the first time. 'It's true he doesn't remember,' he said. 'I vouch for that.'

'But the other set of papers had a foreign driver's licence,' Alvar said. 'That he does remember. The name was Morvan, and the licence was French.'

'He thinks your man has a place on the West Side,' the man without the thumbs said. 'In the Forties, near Ninth Avenue. Snead saw him there one morning, shopping in a grocery store. He thinks Sullivan was using the French papers.'

'What made Snead think that?'

'He was wearing European clothes.'

'When was this?'

'Two days ago,' Benny Alvar said. 'Sullivan had combed his hair differently.'

The man with no thumbs said, 'Also sunglasses, and he'd darkened his skin somehow.'

Benny Alvar said, 'If you like, we can find Sullivan for you.'

'No, I'll do it myself.'

'Anything else we can do?'

'You've already been very helpful.'

Benny Alvar pushed back his chair, and Ash rose with him. He was shorter than Ash had thought.

The man with no thumbs said, 'I mentioned the name Sullivan to an old comrade. He'd heard of him. He said he was dangerous.'

'I suppose he is.'

'That's your affair,' the man with no thumbs said. One of his front teeth was fitted with a gold cap.

Ash declined a lift to his office. He needed to walk, to be alone to think things through. He had the uneasy sense that events had taken hold of him, and that he'd been too easily manoeuvred to the end of the limb. Benny Alvar had been a fraction too co-operative, Reese too quick to step aside. Reese was an ambitious man, ready to go around him when the time was right. How many years had he been on the force? Eighteen? Nineteen? He'd be thinking of moving into something soft that paid well. He wondered if Reese had spoken to Lemoyne. If Benny Alvar had. They were a devious, murderous bunch, a nest of spiders.

And Sullivan *was* a dangerous man. And somehow Ash

elt he'd been set up with him, one-to-one. How neat if he and Sullivan could be made to cut each other down and let he game go on.

He walked for some time, and finally, just after twelve-hirty, found himself in front of Eleanor's office building. He needed to talk, and while he believed she normally ate cotage cheese and yoghurt at her desk, he thought he could persuade her to have lunch with him.

The other offices were empty. The receptionist wasn't at ner desk, and only one jeweller was at his bench, gnawing a chicken leg while listening to *Rigoletto* on a cassette recorder.

The door to Eleanor's office was open, but she was nowhere to be seen. Ash went in and was immediately aware of the faint scent left by her cologne. He stood quite still for several seconds, thinking how quickly the time had gone, the three years since they'd met. He couldn't quite remember how he'd been before. Then he began to browse slowly in her room, picking at the few books, one a French-English dictionary, another on gems. He studied the photographs of models wearing jewellery she'd designed, and advertisements for her things cut from *The New York Times* and *The New Yorker*. She'd framed a photograph of Lady Gayle, curtsying for the Queen of England, wearing an Alan Bedford necklace. He saw a strip from 'Peanuts', which had one of the characters choosing a diamond ring, trying to etch a Coke bottle with it, and then bringing it back for a refund. He read it over twice; an inside joke, not at all funny to him. He looked through a sheaf of designs on her work-table, a vat of jeweller's glue, a Swiss Army knife, sharpened pencils, tweezers, scissors, a bowl of tacks. One perfect yellow rose stood in a narrow crystal vase.

He sat heavily on the high, hard stool behind her work-table. It was an uncomfortable seat and he wondered how she was able to sit on it. He wondered where she was and with whom.

'Mr Morgan.' The receptionist stood in the door of the office. 'I must've been away from my desk when you came in.'

She held a china mug, the wet cardboard tab at the end of a tea bag string drooping over the side. A pretty black girl, for a moment Ash couldn't remember her name. Abbie. That was it. Abbie Frazier, the same as the heavyweight fighter.

'Twelve-thirty, I put on my Telo-mate, and get my lunch,' she said. She was very pretty, and cleverly dressed, sexy, fresh as paint. Alan Bedford's receptionist was cute and black, just as his car was a Bentley with right-hand drive.

'Eleanor has gone out to lunch with Mr Bedford,' she said. 'Any message?'

'Only that I was in the neighbourhood.'

'They're just around the corner, at the St Regis.' Her pink tongue flicked like a serpent. 'The King Cole Bar, that's their favourite place.'

Ash set about to find Sullivan alone. He asked Personnel for a photograph and had an artist who did work for the company re-do Sullivan's hair with an airbrush. He had copies printed with dark glasses on and off. Then he began the laborious legwork, tramping the West Forties between Eighth and Tenth avenues, showing the picture to mailmen and the janitors of every brownstone, tenement, and rooming house. He checked with all the small shopkeepers, but got nowhere. Once or twice he thought he saw a glimmer of recognition, but could get no one to talk. It was a tough neighbourhood, with a sprinkling of fugitives and illegal aliens, and people learned early to mind their own business.

By five o'clock of the second day, he'd worked his way as far south as Forty-second Street. He was weary, hot, and thirsty, and stopped for a Coke in a bodega on Eighth Avenue.

There were a few other customers, men as well as women, all of them black or Hispanic, and Ash at once felt their enmity; he was an outsider, a white American, and he smelled to them of cop.

But he sensed something more in the woman who ran the place. Her glance had a teasing, sexual glint. She was a handsome woman with a broad, open face and prominent cheekbones. Ash thought she must be Spanish or Spanish-American. But she was tall and her eyes were light brown with flecks of gold in the iris. There was a child, a little girl in a playpen behind the counter, picking nuts from a paper cup and delicately putting them one at a time in her mouth. And near her was a large mongrel dog, dozing in the sun, its muzzle on its paws.

Ash waited until he and the woman were alone before showing her Sullivan's photograph.

She glanced from it to Ash's face; again he noticed the specks of yellow in her eyes. He was certain she'd recognized the photograph.

But she shrugged and handed it back. 'Who are you?' she said. 'Are you a police?'

She spoke English slowly, with difficulty. Ash tried his rusty Spanish. 'I'm a friend,' he said. 'I want only to talk to him.'

'If you're a friend, you ought to know where he lives.'

'But you do know him?'

She hesitated; she neither trusted the police nor lied easily. A peanut caught in the child's throat and she began to cough. The woman scooped her up and began gently patting her back.

When the coughing stopped, Ash repeated the question. 'You have seen him?'

'Maybe. Once or twice, but not for a while.'

'How long since you've seen him?'

'A week. Maybe more.'

'Where does he live?'

She glanced east, across Eighth Avenue, in the direction of Forty-fourth Street. But then she shrugged again, the baby squirming in her powerful arms.

'I don't know where he lives.' The baby's tiny hand began to explore its mother's face, first the nose, then the mouth. She let her baby do as it pleased. Soon it began to laugh and tugged its mother's hair. 'A man buys a loaf of bread, am I to ask him where he lives?' the woman said. 'You bought a Coca-Cola, Señor. Where do you live?'

The woman in the bodega had given Ash a bit more than she knew. He thought it more than likely that Sullivan, perhaps using the name Morvan, had rented an apartment somewhere on Forty-fourth Street. He went up and down the block checking mailboxes and talking to every janitor, but got nowhere. He'd already checked the phone book and all the new listings without turning up a Morvan in the neighbourhood. Now that he had something more to go on, he called an old friend in the phone company and had him search all the unlisted numbers: there was none under the name of Morvan.

'Is there a way of checking the unlisted numbers by street? Or any recently installed unlisted number on West Forty-fourth Street.'

'There's no breakdown by street. The reverse directory has numbers by address, but only those which are listed. I'd have to look through every unlisted number in Manhattan and pull any I found on Forty-fourth Street.'

'Not only Forty-fourth,' Ash said, 'but Forty-fifth and Forty-third. But to make it easier, just check the exchanges that service the area. There couldn't be more than three or four.'

'There are six.'

'I wouldn't ask you if it wasn't important,' Ash said. He was told it would take an hour or two.

Ash returned to his office, where Louise Vernon was clearing her desk, about to call it a day.

'You look all in,' she said. 'And in need of a drink.'

'Any calls?'

'Only urgent ones,' she said. 'Matters of life and death, of world-wide implication. Nothing that can't wait.'

She made two stiff Jack Daniels and water, joined him in his office, and when the drinks were half gone, she said, 'Would you like to hear my troubles?'

'Only if it's something I can fix.'

'Oh, you can fix it,' she said. 'It has to do with my alleged personal life. I kissed off My Little Jewish Gentleman.'

For several seconds their eyes held and neither spoke. Ash began slowly to smile, saluted her with his glass, but before either could speak or move the phone rang.

'He took it very well,' Louise said.

'What did he say?'

The phone rang again. 'That he was taking his mother for a week to Palm Beach.'

She picked up the receiver. 'No, Mr Lemoyne. I haven't had a chance to deliver your messages.'

She glanced at Ash, who slowly shook his head. 'He's not

110

here. No, I don't know where he is. I'll give him your message as soon as I speak to him.'

She hung up. 'He's called three times. Also the Vice-President's counsel, Mark Wells. He wants you to call him in Washington. And Geneva called. The Imperial Wizard wants to know what you're doing about Sullivan. They want you to work with Lemoyne, and you're to put Wells in the picture.'

'Is it final,' he said, 'you and the Little Jewish Gentleman?'

'Yes.'

'Why now? Why after all these years?'

'I don't want to be with him. I can't go to bed with him any more.' She took a deep swallow of her drink, tilting the glass until the ice clattered against her teeth. 'Because I'm in love with you,' she said.

'Eleanor is moving to Hong Kong,' he said.

'Permanently?'

'She's been offered a big new job. She wants me to follow along.'

'I don't think that's your kind of play.'

'It's not.'

'One thing about My Little Jewish Gentleman,' she said, 'you'll never move him out of Central Park South.'

Ash finished his drink. 'I've got some calls to make. Go home and take one of your mineral baths. Turn on the whirl-pool. Get dressed up. Nine o'clock I'll meet you at the Pen and Pencil for a steak.'

After she'd gone, Ash called his friend at the phone company who'd turned up some useful information.

'I tapped the computer for unlisted numbers installed during the past twelve months. There were two hundred and eleven in the six exchanges that touch your area. One hundred and sixty-three are still in service. Are you with me, Ash?'

'I'm listening.'

'D'you appreciate all I'm doing for you?'

'I'm going to take good care of you,' Ash said. 'Particularly after you tell me how many are on the streets I'm interested in.'

'Eleven. But I think I can narrow it down a little bit. I pulled the payment records of those eleven. But don't ask for long-distance records: disclosure without a court order is a violation of federal law. What I'm doing for you now is bad enough. The point is that a couple of these unlisted numbers sound like dead drops. That's when the party has a phone installed only to receive calls, not to make them. The bill never exceeds the minimum, so it's the same every month. I got two numbers like that.'

'Is one on Forty-fourth Street?'

'Between Eighth and Ninth Avenue. One black instrument, no extension. It was installed eleven months ago. The bills are sent to a box in the Empire State Building.'

Mr Weston had used an answering service in the Empire State Building. Ash knew he'd found Sullivan.

The contact said, 'I don't want to ask questions that are none of my business. Kidding aside, I'm glad to be able to do you a good turn.' He inhaled, as if lighting a cigarette. 'There's a cute little twist to this. This is a tricky guy,' he said. 'And it looks like he's daring you to come and get him.'

'What're you talking about?'

'The name on the phone,' he said. 'It's yours. The listing is A. Morgan.'

CHAPTER EIGHT

Sullivan arrived at Battery Park fifteen minutes early and spent the time checking to see if the area had been staked out. It was clear.

He saw Janice arrive, alone and on time, carrying a nine-by-twelve manila envelope. She waited for him at the old ferry slip, looking out at the narrow channel to Staten Island. He stayed back, studying her face; it was an old habit of his to wonder at the pauses in people's lives, those brief intermissions spent dreaming in the mountains or before bodies of water. But she was a puzzle, rootless and detached, clever, strange and cool, a person from a generation once removed from his, and her reveries were a mystery to him.

She smiled when she saw him and handed over the envelope;

the stationery was in it.

'You can have this back,' he said. 'You can change your mind.'

Near them two small blond boys in blazer jackets, each with the same school crest, were playing with a penknife, throwing it blade-first into the soft earth at the base of a tree. They'd traced squares in the earth and each aimed to divide the other's square. Jack remembered the game; it was called Territory.

'I want to do this,' she said. 'Truth is it sounds like fun. I only wish there was more for me to do.'

'You'll probably be getting a call later this afternoon. It will refer to the issuing of an identification card in the name of Donald Bowles. You okay it. Then I'll be out of town for three or four days. You won't hear from me.'

'And I'm not to ask where you're going. Or why.'

'I'll call when it's over. I'll tell you where to meet me and when. You have your passport?'

'Yes.'

'It'll work out well. There's nothing for you to worry about.' He drew her to him and kissed her lightly.

'Is that goodbye?' she said.

'I said three or four days.'

'I'd be a good thief,' she said, 'and a good partner. But you do things alone. I can feel it. That's the kind of man you are.'

'Is that what you were thinking before I came up, when you were looking at the water?'

'I'm tired of it here,' she said. 'I've got some friends in Denver. We can tool around, camp out until there's enough snow to ski.'

'You'll need some money.'

'I thought you'd never get around to that.'

'You're a tough kid, is that it?'

'You think I ought to be sweeter?' she said. 'Wear my heart on my sleeve? The fare to Denver is two hundred dollars. Another hundred while I look around.'

He counted out the money and gave it to her, four fifties and two hundreds.

'I never knew a real thief that wasn't a sport,' she said.

He held her face between his hands; there were no tears.

113

She wasn't one to cry.

'You stay around until the end of the week,' he said.

'I'm to stay next to the phone and wait for my old man to call. Is that it? I need more than that. I need you to open the door a crack, let me have a peek inside.' She held two fingers half an inch apart. 'Just a crack, Jean-Claude.'

'My name is Jack,' he said, for the first time without his accent. 'Jack Sullivan.'

'And you're not a thief,' she said. 'At least not an ordinary one.'

'You did say just a crack,' he said.

'This is Monday,' she said. 'I'll stay to the end of the week.'

They left the park separately.

He chose the subway, rather than a taxi, and rode as far as Grand Central. At the north end of the upper level of the station, he used the escalators to the lobby of the Pan Am building. From the building directory, he located a public stenographer. Janice had provided him with a dozen letter-size sheets of company stationery and as many envelopes. He bought a lined yellow legal pad from a stationer on the mezzanine floor, and using a phone booth with a small shelf as a desk, composed four brief letters. Three of them were to persons whose names and business addresses he invented at random; the fourth was to Mr Fred Morris, printer and engraver, on West Forty-third Street.

He found the public stenographer in one of several small offices on the twenty-third floor. Her name was Alice Palm, a woman of about seventy, small and quite frail, as if recuperating from a serious illness. Her make-up was heavy, although carefully applied, and her clothes and jewellery were expensive, but old-fashioned and eccentric. She had a raspy voice, from too much liquor and cigarettes, a cranky, independent, and tough old woman, who'd once been pretty, but had buried all of the men who remembered the way she'd been.

She told Sullivan she was busy and couldn't get to his letters until the following day. He offered to pay twice her regular rate, but she was adamant.

Time was essential to him. He needed to put his plan into

effect at once, but could do nothing until the letters were typed professionally. He couldn't afford the delay or risk involved in approaching a second stenographer.

So he let her see his most engaging smile, presenting himself in his most charming manner. He admired the large pearl brooch that she wore over her left breast. She was reminded that he was a man and she was a woman.

In the end she relented and promised to forgo her lunch and type his letters. He gave her all four, and told her his name was Shank. The letters would be ready in an hour.

He had lunch in the Oyster Bar on the lower level, a dozen little necks, a draught beer, and a salad.

By the time he'd finished and returned to the twenty-third floor, the letters were neatly typed, an addressed envelope pinned to each.

For the four letters Alice Palm charged him twenty-five dollars, which he paid in cash. When she started to make out a receipt, he told her he didn't need it. He wanted to leave no paper trail. But she insisted: that was the way Alice Palm did business, and nothing on earth could make her change. He saw that she'd typed out the receipt with a carbon and kept the copy for her files. It was made out in the name of Shank, the same name he'd had her type at the bottom of each of the letters.

He went to a men's room on the same floor to sign one of the letters and put it, folded, in the inside pocket of his jacket. The other three letters he tore into small pieces and flushed down the toilet. He then wet his hair, washed off the Go Bronze, parted and combed it in the style of Donald Bowles.

He left the Pan Am building by way of the Vanderbilt Avenue exit, across from the Yale Club, and walked west to Sixth Avenue, then downtown to Forty-third Street. He entered a tiny shop, no more than four or five feet wide, but rather long, and crammed with duplicating and printing equipment. The walls were covered with pegboards, which supported display cards of novelty key rings, pocket knives, and ball-point pens. At the rear of the store a small blonde woman worked at a jeweller's bench; from a radio beside her came the voice of Barbra Streisand.

The proprietor was a fat man of about sixty, with badly dyed hair and an unhealthy complexion. This was Fred Morris.

Sullivan introduced himself as Donald Bowles and asked to have an identification card printed in his name.

'What type of ID are we talking about?'

'My company. Computer Data Leasing. There's a problem in one of the lines, and they've just flown me in from California.' He sounded proud of it. 'I'm known as the starting quarterback on the Six-twenty Computer,' Sullivan said.

'And my grandfather was the head rabbi of Lodz.' Fred Morris was having trouble catching his breath, twice today he'd slid a nitro tablet under his tongue. 'If he walked in here and asked for Computer Data Leasing ID, I'd ask first for a letter of authorization.'

Sullivan gave him the letter Alice Palm had typed. Fred Morris put on his glasses to read it. He made one telephone call, reading the number from the letterhead. Whatever Janice had said satisfied him; he brought out a large presentation book with pages of sample ID cards mounted behind sheets of transparent plastic. He turned the pages, breathing heavily, until he found the Computer Data Leasing card; it was white with a broad green stripe, the photograph went on the upper-right corner, name and signature on the lower left.

He used an early-model Polaroid camera for Sullivan's photograph, trimmed, pressed, and glued it to the card. Then he typed the name Donald Bowles on it and Sullivan signed it in that name. Finally he ran the completed card through a laminating machine.

Fred Morris charged three and a half dollars and gave no receipt.

Sullivan returned to his hotel room, where he unlocked his suitcase, hung out the grey Brooks Brothers suit, selected a blue shirt with a button-down collar and a striped tie, dusted his wing-tip shoes with the waxed tissue provided by the hotel. He showered and shaved for the second time that day. He dressed in the American clothes after burning Jean-Claude Morvan's driver's licence and flushing the ashes down the toilet.

He neatly folded and packed his French clothes, locked the

suitcase, and rather than wait for a bellhop, carried the bag to the lobby. He retrieved his leather pouch from the hotel safe, and checked out, using cash to pay his bill.

He had the doorman hail a cab, tipped him, and only when inside the cab with the door and window closed so as not to be overheard, did he give the driver an address on Gramercy Park.

He stood for several minutes on the south-west corner of the park, the suitcase between his legs, his vision unobscured for a block in each direction. When he was certain no one had followed him, he hailed a second cab, directing the driver to take him to Park Avenue and Forty-sixth Street.

He carried his bag into the Nederlandsche Middenstands-bank of Curaçao. At a small writing table he worked the combination lock of his leather pouch, withdrew a cheque-book, and wrote a cheque to cash in the amount of two thousand dollars. He signed it J. Sullivan.

He gave the cheque to a teller and waited while she checked it against his signature card and then read his account balance from the computer print-outs. It took three minutes and when she returned it was to ask the number of his account.

'Two seven eight, stroke two.'

'What denomination bills would you like?'

'Ten hundreds, please. The rest in twenties.'

He watched her count the two thousand dollars, and when she'd finished he asked for an envelope, which he put in the inside pocket of his jacket.

He hailed a cab on Park Avenue and asked to be taken to La Guardia Airport. He sat on the far left of the cab, beyond the driver's rear-view mirror, and transferred the leather pouch and envelope of cash to the suitcase, which he locked.

It was two-fifteen when he arrived at the airport. By quarter of three he was on the American shuttle to Chicago, the locked carry-on suitcase under his seat between his legs.

From O'Hare Airport, he used a pay telephone to call station-to-station a number in Gary, Indiana. The conversation was brief. After he hung up, he went to the Hertz counter and rented a Ford Granada. He drove east on Inter-state 94, and then south across the state line into Indiana. He left the highway near Kosciusko Park and took Calumet Road to the outskirts of Gary. The drive took just over an hour.

It took him nearly as long to find the place he was looking for, a one-storey, unmarked factory warehouse, one of several such buildings built around the turn of the century. Between them were empty lots, overgrown with weeds and littered with rusting junk, the wreckage of old cars and machinery, all of it set beside an abandoned stretch of track, a feeder line of the old Southern Illinois and Central Railroad.

He parked and locked the Granada and walked around to a side door of the building. It was nearly dark, barely enough light for him to locate the bell over the door. He had to ring twice, which set a dog barking; the door was finally opened by a short, burly man with a nose which had long ago been smashed flat and cleaved in two, leaving a pale depressed scar which began at the corner of one eyebrow and ran the length of his nose to his upper lip.

He stood in the centre of the doorway, barring the way, an ugly greyish dog yapping at his side. He was a formidable man, with short brutal arms and powerful chest and shoulders. His expression was at first hostile and suspicious, but then he recognized Sullivan and relaxed. He even smiled. His teeth were broken and stained and the hideous scar in the centre of his face flushed deep red. He was an ugly man, remarkably so, with one handsome feature: his eyes were beautiful and framed by long curling black lashes. His name was Werner Lau.

He grabbed hold of Sullivan and hugged him with those brutal arms.

'Seven years, isn't it?' he said. 'Nearly eight. You look better. Younger. Well, maybe not younger, but better.'

'You don't change, Werner.'

'I'm fatter.'

'And another dog.'

'The last one drank himself to death.'

He led Sullivan into a large, well-lit, and elaborately equipped machine shop. Above the odours made by machinery, steel shavings and lubricating oils was one of food cooking.

'When you called I put a chicken in the pot.' He stirred the contents of a cast-iron pot simmering on an electric hot-plate. 'Your coming gives me the excuse to open a bottle of good wine.'

'I won't be staying for dinner.'

'Of course you will.' He smiled. There was a hint of coquetry in his lovely blue eyes, but at the same time he was serious, he was laying down the law. 'You must stay.' He was a stubborn, eccentric man, one of those mutilated by a nightmarish past. Perhaps he wasn't mad, but neither was he altogether sane. Once he got something in his head, it was there to stay. One did things his way or went elsewhere. But he was loyal, he could be trusted, and he was the best armourer Sullivan knew.

He'd learned his trade from his father, who'd turned hunting weapons by hand for the German aristocracy before the war. Werner had seen him assaulted on the street by a gang of Brown Shirt toughs, humiliated and beaten half to death; he was with him when he died some time later of a combination of shame, shock, and internal injuries.

Werner's mother was French, and she fled with Werner and his younger brother as far as Karlsruhe, on the French border. Her plan was to take both children to France and to live with her sister in Lyons. But the Gestapo detained Werner and his brother, who were German, and the French notified Werner's mother that, even if she were able to get them out of Germany, they wouldn't be let into France. As a French-woman, however, she would be admitted.

Werner's father had been a prosperous man, his gun shop known throughout Europe, but most of his property had been seized by the Nazis. The rest was sold at desperation prices. A few pieces of jewellery, some gold coins, and a few hundred Swiss francs were all that remained. War with France was said to be imminent. The borders would be closed. As a penniless Frenchwoman, the wife of a Jew, there was no saying what the Germans might do. Werner woke in the middle of the night in a little inn in Karlsruhe to find his mother gone. The hotel bill had been paid and she'd left them a few marks, enough to buy food for two days. After that Werner and his brother lived in the street and foraged in garbage cans. Eventually, they were arrested and shuttled from camp to camp, arriving finally at Ausch-witz. Werner's brother died there. In time Werner came to understand his mother, at least he said he did, and he never spoke out against her. Perhaps he even forgave her.

119

'I was surprised when you called,' Werner said. 'Not a peep, not a word in all these years. Then out of a clear blue sky.' He paused to glance at himself in a mirror hung on a long nail driven into the wall of the machine shop. 'I'm an ugly man, don't you agree?'

'There's nothing one can do about that.'

'That's easy enough for you to say.' Werner let the light dance in his blue eyes. 'Have you ever been really happy with a woman?'

'I never expected to be.' Sullivan was in no mood for this kind of talk; but Werner was a man who lived alone with his dog and brooded on things. He had to be humoured. 'I wonder what kind of man it is who stays with a woman because he thinks she'll make him happy,' Sullivan said.

'I wish I weren't so ugly,' Werner said.

'You never used to worry about that.'

'I just kept it more to myself,' Werner said. 'Secretly, I dreamed of being handsome. Robert Taylor was my idol.'

'I think it has to do with your mother leaving you.'

'She was a young woman then,' Werner said. 'Thirty-seven, and she was pretty. She wanted to live.' He closed his eyes for a moment, and took a deep breath, a long, grieving sigh. Sullivan saw him as a plump little boy, waking in that room in Karlsruhe. 'D'you suppose she suffered terribly for what she did?' Werner said.

'Probably not.'

'She wasn't a bad woman. I remember many good things about her. She was quite a loving mother. That makes it worse. If she'd been a monster from the first, there'd be no sense of loss. No ache, you see.'

Sullivan thought: I've only come to buy a gun. But he said, 'You did have your father. You certainly loved him.'

Werner shook his head, as if trying to rid himself of a painful memory. 'He was such a dear.'

Sullivan touched Werner's arm and said, 'We had fun in Guatemala. And Mexico City. You liked the whores there, didn't you, Werner?'

'We even had fun in La Paz,' Werner said.

'You kibitzing the beached Nazis in Yiddish.'

Werner laughed and said, 'I was glad when I heard you'd retired from the Agency. Glad you got out with your skin, and I even thought you might have a normal life. You could do that. You're the odd case. In this line of work we're all freaks. All but you, Jack.'

'It seems you're wrong,' Sullivan said.

'I saw you with the Frenchwoman. That friend of Roper's. What was her name?'

'She went back to Roper.'

'Lorraine. That was it. She was with the Good Shepherd. He brought her around, but that was years ago. Before Roper. She was a beautiful thing then.'

'Did the Good Shepherd tell you I was in love with her?'

'He didn't have to tell me. I saw the way you were with her. I liked the Good Shepherd. He knew wines, the Good Shepherd. He was from Alsace. We had some good meals together.'

'Where is he now?'

'Dead,' Werner said. 'He killed himself.'

'The Good Shepherd did?'

'Yes. And the odd thing was he took poison. Here's a man who lived all his life with guns, knew all there was to know about them, and then he goes and kills himself with poison.'

'Lorraine never told me.'

'Maybe it was a personal thing with her. The Good Shepherd always spoke well of her. Said she was the salt of the earth. So was he, for that matter. I can't figure why he did it. He'd just bought some vineyard near Volnay. A little run-down, but good growing land. He was full of plans to modernize the place. He had the money. And he yearned to see his name on a wine label.'

Werner brought out glasses and plates, set an old card table for dinner, and opened the wine. 'Why did he have to go and kill himself?' he said.

The food and wine soon raised Werner's spirits, and Sullivan got around to the reason he'd come; he wanted a gun, a weapon without a history, a cold piece, and it had to be a PPK.

'I know what you want. You and your Walther PPK. Is there no other gun for you?'

'I'm a faithful man.'

'Superstitious is more like it.'

'It's you that's my good luck, Werner. Not the damn gun.'

'I wonder what he'd do if I killed myself,' Werner spoke to the dog, who lay at his feet under the table, its nose twitching at the smell of the food. He fed the dog a scrap of meat and tenderly patted its head. 'What would you do if you heard I'd killed myself?'

'I'd grieve for you,' Sullivan said.

'Because you'd have to go elsewhere for your Frau Walther. I wouldn't take poison,' Werner said. 'Not a chance. Not me. I have one of my father's custom twelves, and I'd use that to blow my head off.'

'You're alone too much,' Sullivan said. 'It's affecting your sanity.'

'Very likely,' Werner said. 'Go tell me what else you need while I'm still able to function.'

'A silencer to fit the PPK. It's got to be right. That's why I've come all this way.'

Werner seemed not to be listening. 'Did I tell you it was me who gave the Good Shepherd his start?' he said. 'He'd got hold of a shipment of Kalashnikov AK-47s, must be twenty years ago now. They'd not been kept well and he needed someone to put them right. This is back when I had my shop in Corsica. Well, a couple of hundred cocked-up Kalashnikovs need a damn factory. But the Good Shepherd had a buyer, he always had a buyer, the old fox. Some African, Kenyatta or one of them. He had the guns and a boat to ship them to the African, but otherwise he hadn't a pot. Set them right on credit, he says. On the come. I trusted him, and he stood up. The African paid him and he paid me. Every quarter.'

Werner swirled the wine in his glass, sniffed, and filled his mouth, and held it a few seconds before swallowing. Then he nodded, in tribute to the Good Shepherd or the wine, Sullivan couldn't be sure.

'Have you the gun?' Sullivan said.

'I can get it.'

'And the silencer.'

'It'll cost you.'

'How much?'

'Drink your wine.'

Sullivan said, 'You've got to be careful you don't go off the deep end.'

'I have the gun in another place. The silencer will take a bit. It must be made from scratch.'

'I've a long drive ahead of me.'

'I wish you'd stayed retired,' Werner said.

'And what about you?' Sullivan said. 'You've got the money. Buy yourself a suit of clothes, for God's sake have a bath, and then buy yourself a vineyard in Provence.'

'The wines of Provence are second-rate.'

'Buy it anywhere you want. Close this dump down. Get out of the life. Nothing's fated. Nothing is predetermined. Not for you or me. Not for the Good Shepherd either.'

After dinner Werner insisted on going alone for the PPK. His ordnance was hidden in another warehouse and he wasn't about to share its location with Sullivan.

'You'd better let me have the keys to your car,' he said.

'I wouldn't follow you.'

'Just the same.'

Sullivan laughed and tossed him the keys.

'There's a bottle of cognac to keep you company,' Werner said.

Although a blustery wind had come up and it had turned cold and raw, Werner didn't bother with a jacket. He wore only a T-shirt, one of those hard, fat men who seem impervious to cold. He drove a battered Dodge pickup; the dog sat on the seat beside him.

Sullivan swirled a bit of the wine left in his glass and put it down untouched. He wanted no more to drink. The image of Werner and the dog on the front seat of the battered pickup stayed with him. The man slept alone on a folding cot behind a packing case in a corner of a machine shop in Gary, Indiana. After twenty-five years in the illegal gun business, he had all the money a man could need. It was sure to be in cash, dollars, Swiss francs, or Deutschemarks, all of it resting in numbered accounts. Werner would know how to handle that. The money lay in bank vaults and he lived with his dog and trusted no one. He sold more guns and made more money and drank his wine alone.

Sullivan looked out at an empty lot overgrown with weeds and littered with rusty junk. He had re-entered the desolate underground world of men like Werner.

123

CHAPTER NINE

The Vice-President trusted Mark Wells and was certain of his loyalty. Wells was his protégé whom he treated more like a son than an aide. Wells's father had owned a hardware store in Anaheim, and later a franchised coin-operated laundromat near the Farmer's Market in Los Angeles. Wells was an honours student at UCLA and one of the two white starting players on the championship basketball team. He always helped out financially at home, working summers as a ranger in Yosemite National Park, later as a guide. After UCLA he went to Harvard Law School, and from there to the legal department of the biggest theatrical agency. It was there that the Vice-President, who maintained close ties to the entertainment industry, discovered him.

The Vice-President admired Wells and came to rely on him. He was clever, and a good lawyer, and the Vice-President rarely made a decision without first consulting him. He saw something of himself in Wells, of the young man he'd been. But he also recognized that Wells had qualities he'd always lacked. Wells was the luxury model. Luckily the Vice-President was one of those rare men capable of admiration without envy. He was able to learn from his betters, use their talents, and not despise them afterwards for the inadequacy in himself, which made him turn to them in the first place. The Vice-President wasn't a coward and he wasn't a bully. He had no need to be surrounded by inferiors. Knowledge of his own limitations in no way diminished his self-love. His ego was gleaming hard, made of stainless steel.

He admired the surety of Wells's political instincts and the quickness of his mind. His ruthlessness made the older man feel at home. Wells was well educated. He'd been a fine athlete. He was handsome and debonair. He was a cocksman. He was graceful. He played wonderful tennis. He could dance and play the guitar. His pin-stripe suits were cut well and the collars of his shirts fitted. His socks stayed up, and he never wore shoes with laces.

The Vice-President understood the immense importance of the way a man moved, spoke, and dressed. A long career in public life had taught him that a man was, truly, what he seemed. He wasn't less, and he certainly wasn't more; a man was what people believed him to be. If he was believed to be smart, then he was smart. If he was believed to be honest, then he was honest. If people changed their minds, if a man thought to be honest came to be thought of as a crook, then he was a crook. Truth was word of mouth. There simply was no other yardstick.

The Vice-President confided thoughts of this kind to Mark Wells. He had told him the name of every woman he slept with, and even where some of his money was hidden. He opened his heart to the younger man.

That morning the Vice-President had acquired a piece of information which was potentially the most important of his life. The implications for him and the country were enormous, but he couldn't bring himself to discuss it with Wells. He wanted to. They were alone in the Vice-President's office, sharing a working lunch, and he was sorely tempted. This was a secret to make his tongue itch. But he controlled himself. His political instinct told him he must play this one totally alone.

He cautiously brought the conversation around to the Sullivan matter. He wanted to know if Wells had spoken to Ash Morgan. Had Morgan made contact with Sullivan?

'I think he's dragging his feet on this one,' Wells said. 'He was slow getting back to me on a couple of calls. When I finally did reach him, he said he was working on it, but had nothing specific to report.'

'Sullivan can't have vanished into thin air. There must be a way to find him.'

'We have to move quietly,' Wells said. 'No calling out the troops on this one. We don't want something like this leaking.'

'That's the last thing we want.'

'I don't think Morgan is levelling with us. Something tells me he's not giving this his best shot. He and Sullivan were friends. They may have worked something out between them.'

'Morgan has a lot of personal problems, doesn't he? Millie told me he's banging his secretary. And that girl-friend of his is apparently giving him a bad time. And the wife in the institution must be costing him a fortune.'

'He could certainly be in need of money.'

'The girl-friend is a Jap, isn't she?'

'Eleanor Harmon, sir. Thai and English mixture.'

'They turn out some beauts,' the Vice-President said. 'I was in Bangkok last year for the water festival. The women wear this thing they call a *parsin*. My God, Mark, I thought I died and went to heaven.' The Vice-President chewed slowly on a stewed prune, spit the pit into his spoon, and said, 'What about setting up an alternative route to Sullivan? This guy who works for the Senator. Lemoyne. He's got better contacts in New York than we do. That cop, what's his name?'

'Reese.'

'If we asked that donkey, he'd push his mother out of a window.' The Vice-President ate another prune, his third. He ate six every day. 'Something big has come up, Mark. Very big. But it's best I keep you in the dark for a day or two, until I've double-checked and am absolutely sure.' The Vice-President hesitated, locked eyes with Wells across the desk, and said: 'All I can tell you is it's the whole banana stand.'

Wells said, 'Then we've got to be doubly sure all our fences are mended.' He was a bright boy. No need to spell things out for Mark Wells. 'I'll fly up to New York this afternoon and take personal charge of this investigation.'

The Vice-President chewed his fourth prune; only two more to go. 'We've an area of real vulnerability there, Mark.'

'I'll close it down, sir,' Mark Wells said.

From his office, Wells called Lemoyne in New York and had him set up two meetings. The first was with Ash Morgan, the second with Sergeant Reese. Neither man was to know that Wells had contacted the other.

Wells then instructed his secretary to arrange for a priority seat on the three o'clock shuttle to New York, and a White House limousine to the airport. She was also to pack a clean shirt and a pair of socks in his attaché case. Wells kept a supply of haberdashery in his office, which his secretary was obliged to send to the laundry regularly.

At two-thirty, he telephoned his wife at their tennis club and told her that he would be in New York overnight. She reminded him that that evening they were expected for dinner at the home of friends. He explained that the trip was unavoidable; he'd been ordered to New York on urgent business by the Vice-President himself. Wells's wife was annoyed and disappointed. She'd been looking forward to the dinner party. Wells apologized and promised to make it up to her later in the month by taking her with him on a trip to California, where they'd spend a long weekend as guests of the management at La Costa.

Wells's third phone call was to a girl named Clare Wheaton, an artist and illustrator who lived on Leroy Street in Greenwich Village. She had been Wells's wife's room-mate at Sarah Lawrence and she and Wells had been lovers for more than a year.

He told her he'd be in New York and asked her to have dinner with him. She already had a date, and was offended that he hadn't given her more notice. He told her how busy he'd been, and that this trip to New York was something which had come up at the last minute. And then Mark Wells couldn't resist showing off for his girl. 'I'm on something urgent for the VP,' he said. 'An ex-CIA agent with the keys to the mint has disappeared. The boys in New York have been dragging their feet.'

Clare Wheaton was impressed. She allowed herself to be persuaded to have dinner with Wells.

After she hung up on Wells, Clare called the man with whom she had the prior date. He was an old friend, and while they occasionally slept together, he knew all about her affair with Wells, that she was in love with him, and she told him the true reason she was breaking their date. He frequently confided the details of his own romances to her. It was that kind of friendship. He was an Assistant US Attorney named Sheffield.

After Clare Wheaton told him what Wells had said, Sheffield couldn't wait to get off the phone with her so that he could call Lemoyne.

Sheffield had been digging into the connection between

Roper and the administration for the past year. He'd cultivated his friendship with Clare Wheaton because of her intimacy with Wells. While he'd turned up one or two interesting items – payoffs in return for political favours, money sent out of the country, washed clean, and brought back – he had so far come up with nothing hard, nothing with which to go public. He knew that Jack Sullivan was a central figure with the information he needed. But Sullivan had disappeared. Sheffield reasoned that Lemoyne and Ash Morgan either knew where he was or were also trying to find him. Morgan wouldn't trade; Lemoyne would.

Sheffield therefore called Lemoyne and arranged a meeting in a coffee shop around the corner from Lemoyne's office. They met while Wells was in the air between Washington and New York.

Sheffield told Lemoyne about his interest in Sullivan, and then he told him what he knew of Wells's affair with Clare Wheaton.

Lemoyne liked information of that sort. It gave him just the edge he might one day need in his dealings with Wells, an added bit of protection for his client, the Senator.

Lemoyne admitted to Sheffield that a search was on for Sullivan, that it had to be kept hush-hush, and he would let him know when he was found.

From the coffee shop, Lemoyne went by taxi to the East Side helicopter pad at Sixtieth Street. Ash Morgan was already there and they flew to La Guardia. Wells's plane was caught in a holding pattern, and while they waited in the Eastern lounge Lemoyne said, 'Ash, I sense a growing distance between us. This is distressing to me because I remember a time we used to trust each other.'

'I still trust you, Arnold.'

'What have you turned up on Sullivan?'

'Nothing. Not a goddamn thing.'

'With all due respect,' Lemoyne said, 'I think you're being less than truthful with me.'

'Then go talk to your pal Reese.'

When Wells landed, the three men boarded the same helicopter for the return flight to Manhattan. They were buckled into their seats when the attendant informed them that the flight would be delayed ten minutes to accommodate the in-

128

coming Boston shuttle. Wells glanced around the empty heli-copter and asked Ash if he had anything new on Sullivan's whereabouts. Ash shook his head, and Lemoyne quickly said, 'It's a cold trail. But we're trying as hard as we possibly can.'

'The Vice-President wants action. He wants something done. And he wants it done quickly.'

'He could call out the FBI,' Ash said.

'Christ, no. That's the last thing he'd do. I thought you understood this is definitely a low-profile matter.'

'We haven't found a trace of him,' Ash said.

'We've been around to all his old haunts,' Lemoyne said. 'Checked his habits. Called around. Not a trace.'

'Does that strike you as odd?'

Leaning over the back of his seat, the afternoon sun pouring through the window above him, Ash detected an idea glowing like a light bulb above Wells's head.

Wells said, 'Has it occurred to you that he might have decided to disappear for good? I mean he's packed up and gone to Australia, the Amazon, God knows where.'

'And swallow what he knows?' Lemoyne said. 'Gone, forgotten, out of our hair?'

'It's an interesting theory,' Ash said.

'It doesn't quite sound like Sullivan,' Lemoyne said.

'It does to me,' Wells said. 'I think he's decided to kiss us all goodbye. You know what I think? He was bluffing. And when we didn't throw in our cards, he took off. He's probably skimmed enough money over the past eight years to live comfortably. A man like that would know how to change his identity, wouldn't he?'

'He would,' Lemoyne said. 'And as for the money, it wouldn't surprise me. He was in a position to acquire a serious amount of money.'

'It's the kind of theory that solves a lot of problems,' Ash said. 'It certainly has that to recommend it.'

'The more I think about it, the more logical it seems,' Wells said. 'It explains why you haven't found him. He's gone deep. I'm convinced we'll hear no more from Jack Sullivan.'

And later that evening, meeting with Sergeant Reese in his room at the St Regis, Wells expounded the same theory.

Sullivan had gone deep. They'd hear no more from him.

Wells kept his date with Clare Wheaton in good spirits. He'd convinced himself that Sullivan was probably now at the other end of the world.

CHAPTER TEN

Sullivan drove through the night, stopping once at a Holiday Inn on US 80, south of Youngstown. He slept until mid-morning, showered, shaved, and had breakfast in the coffee shop. By eleven o'clock he was on the road. He carried with him an unused PPK from which all identifying marks had been obliterated, a soft holster that lay flat against his side under his armpit, a silencer that Werner had fitted precisely to the barrel of the gun, and a hundred rounds of 9 mm super vel hollow-point cartridges. None of this could be carried safely through airline security. Spot checks were also done on baggage checked through. The drive was boring, but more private and comfortable than a bus.

It was early evening when he arrived in New York. He deposited the Granada at the Hertz office on East Sixty-fourth Street, paid in cash, and went by taxi to the Summit Hotel on Lexington Avenue, where he checked in as Donald Bowles. He gave his grey Brooks Brothers suit to the valet to be pressed, had dinner and newspapers sent up, read and watched television for an hour or two, and was asleep by ten.

The next morning, he dressed in the freshly pressed suit, a white button-down shirt, and striped tie. He packed carefully and checked out of the hotel, using cash to settle the bill, and went by taxi to a luggage shop on Madison Avenue, where he bought an inexpensive canvas shoulder bag. He took a second taxi to the Penn Terminal Hotel across from Madison Square Garden, where he again registered as Donald Bowles.

In his room, he transferred the pistol, silencer and holster to the shoulder bag, locked his suitcase, and, as usual, deposited the pouch in the hotel safe.

Carrying the shoulder bag, he walked to the Camera Barn

on Herald Square across from Macy's. He bought a Pentax single-lens reflex with a flash attachment, three rolls of thirty-six exposure Tri-X Pan film, and a lightweight folding tripod. He paid cash and walked east for several blocks on Thirty-fourth Street, losing himself in the dense lunch-hour crowd. At Second Avenue, he hailed a taxi to a medical-supply store near Beth Israel Hospital, where he bought a pair of surgical gloves, a roll of tape, and a four-ounce aerosol can of ethyl chloride. Finally he stopped for lunch at a small Chinese restaurant. In the men's toilet, he transferred all of his purchases to the shoulder bag.

After ordering lunch, he reviewed all he'd done, ticked off each of his purchases, and satisfied himself that he was perfectly well prepared for the night's work. Then he ordered a bottle of beer, ate his lunch, smoked a cigar with a second bottle of beer, and spent the rest of the afternoon in a movie.

At four minutes to six he joined two men and a young girl crowding into the revolving door leading to the lobby of the Roper Building on Park Avenue. The party, laughing over some office joke, crossed the lobby and presented themselves at the desk of the security guard. Each flashed an identification badge with a broad green stripe and signed the dated time sheet. Sullivan signed last, as Donald Bowles. The others were known by sight and the security guard waved them in.

Sullivan's was the only unfamiliar face. The guard had a close look at the identity card. He was an older man, tall and stooped, a retired cop by the look of him, the loose skin under his chin raked by an old-fashioned safety razor.

'You one of the Computer Data Leasing people?'

'Yes.'

He waved Sullivan to the elevator.

It was now past six o'clock and only the master elevator was working. Sullivan spent the next hour and a half in the bank's main computer room on the sixth floor. He was familiar with the system, a somewhat out-of-date workhouse; there was one like it in Langley and another that'd been palmed off on the Israelis. It was useful, relatively easy to maintain, and was the most dependable of the series.

He pretended to tinker with it for an hour and a half,

managing to look busy and important, so that no one spoke to him or even looked his way.

At eight o'clock, he secured an outside line and called Swissair flight information. Their Geneva flight was on time. When he called again at eight-thirty, it had just touched down, the passengers preparing to disembark.

The pouch from Roper's Geneva office was the responsibility of the head steward; on landing, he handed it directly to the bonded courier. There was no baggage or customs delay. The courier travelled by motor cycle, his time from Kennedy Airport never less than twenty-five minutes nor more than forty.

At eight-thirty-five, the canvas bag slung over his shoulder, Sullivan slipped out of the computer room and walked quickly down the corridor to the master elevator. He pressed the up button and waited twenty seconds. The elevator doors opened on an elderly black man pushing a portable canteen, a basketball game blaring from a tiny radio near the coffee urn.

Sullivan rode the elevator to the twenty-ninth floor, one above the Roper offices. He reached up, slid the latch on the hatch of the car, and lifted himself through the open hatch on to the roof. He quickly closed the hatch and scampered across the roof of the car on to the steel safety ladder that ran the length of the elevator shaft.

He glanced at the illuminated dial of his watch: eight-forty-one. He had only to cling to the steel ladder until the courier arrived.

Euston Petty was the guard on duty at the security desk of the Roper offices. This was his week to work the first night shift, from 6 p.m. to 2 a.m. Petty was new at his job; he'd been in security work for only three months. He was twenty-six years old. He was an army veteran, trained infantryman, who did thirteen months in Vietnam. He saw a lot of combat, many of his friends were wounded and some were killed. He had his own close calls, although, miraculously, he was never so much as scratched.

He was reading a paperback novel when the phone on his desk rang. He answered as he'd been instructed to,

'Twenty-eighth floor. Officer Petty speaking.'

'Hi, Officer Petty. I want to know, how's my baby's cold?'

It was Sally, the woman Euston Petty lived with. She was a fine, loving woman with a good job in the billing department at Ma Bell, twenty-three years old with a six-year-old daughter from a first marriage. Maybe she wasn't the most beautiful girl Euston Petty had even seen, but then – he almost laughed out loud – neither am I the handsomest man.

'What's happening, baby?' he said.

'Sitting here thinking about you.'

'Thinking what?'

'You come here I'll show you. Man, what you think I'm thinking?'

'You're supposed to be a respectable woman. Respectable women don't talk like that.'

'Say who?'

'I'll tell you what you do, girl. You get into bed.'

'I'm in bed.'

'You put on something silky.'

'Then what?'

'Then you get yourself a good book and you read it.'

'Euston, I'm lonely.'

'Save me a warm spot. Two o'clock, I get off.'

'I'm listening to Stevie.'

'I can hear.'

'Oh, he's good.'

'Sure he's good.'

'Not so good as my man.'

'Your man has got a cold. Maybe a fever.'

'Drink liquids.' Her voice had changed, reminding him of his mother. 'Fruit juice and hot tea. You got the tea bags I gave you with your sandwich? Get some hot water and make yourself some tea.'

Euston hung up just as the elevator door opened and the Swissair courier stepped out, carrying the Geneva mail pouch.

Sullivan clung to the steel ladder inside the elevator shaft. The Swissair courier had arrived and just as Sullivan had begun his descent, someone on a floor above his had rung for the elevator car; it had passed within inches of him.

He'd measured the space between the steel ladder and the elevator car on one of the lower floors, forgetting the fire code, which mandated a narrowing of the shaft on the upper floors of the newer skyscrapers to reduce draught in the event of fire. It was very nearly a fatal oversight; were the car four inches wider, he would have been crushed to death. He'd saved himself by twisting around behind the ladder, flattening himself between it and the wall of the shaft. In that way the ladder stood between him and the body of the car.

Once he was down on the twenty-eighth floor he had to flatten himself again as the car streaked by with a breath-taking rush of air, the vacuum created by its passing almost sucking him from the ladder.

He clung to the ladder at the twenty-eighth floor for several seconds, catching his breath until the car reached the lobby at the bottom of the shaft well. He then opened the control panel and sprayed the Thermal Touch System console with the aerosol can of ethyl chloride. He sprayed until the can was empty and the control frozen. Twenty-eight floors below, the one car in operation was now im-mobilized. Short of climbing the twenty-eight flights of stairs, or summoning the elevator-maintenance people to re-activate the subordinate elevators, there was no way of reaching the offices of Roper International.

Sullivan drew and cocked the PPK. The silencer was already in place. He released the bolt and sprung the latch on the door from the elevator shaft to the corridor.

He stepped out, the PPK at the ready; the security desk was unoccupied, the guard was in the mailroom, sorting and locking away the contents of the Swissair pouch.

Sullivan walked quickly across the corridor and used his key to open the glass door to the Roper offices. Once inside he crouched behind a desk, his back to the rear wall of the secretarial pool. He waited there, the PPK in his hand, until the security guard returned and took his place at the desk just inside the locked glass door.

Sullivan had an unobstructed view of the back of his head. He was new to him, a tall young black with a moderate Afro. He could easily have killed him then, one silent shot of the super vel 9 mm and the young man would never have known

134

what hit him. Sullivan had planned it that way. But at the last moment, he found he'd lost his stomach for that sort of killing. He would have to open the security cabinet in a riskier way. He lowered his gun and silently made his way through the maze of corridors behind the secretarial pool, arriving at last at the door to Ash Morgan's office. The cabinet stood in the near corner of the office, to the right of the door.

He went to work on it with the stethoscope, as George Knapp had taught him.

Euston Petty's cold was worse. His limbs were heavy, he felt feverish and his throat was dry and hurt each time he swallowed. His head might have been stuffed with cotton.

He needed a cup of tea. In order to get it, he would have to fill his cup from the hot-water dispenser behind the secretarial pool. Strictly speaking, he wasn't supposed to leave his desk unattended. But they'd given him the task of sorting and locking away the mail, for which he had to leave the desk. And of course more than once during his shift he had to use the toilet. It was, properly, a job for two men. But they were too cheap to pay two men.

Much better, Euston Petty thought, to hire one man to do the job of two.

He took his mug from a drawer, lifted the receiver from his phone, unlocked the office door, and walked through the secretarial pool to the hot-water dispenser.

Euston Petty was at the dispenser when he heard something, the click of metal against metal. But he wasn't sure. He held his breath and listened. He heard nothing. But he felt something. A familiar tension ran along his spine. It wasn't exactly fear, more a tightening of nerve ends. All of his senses were heightened; he heard his own breathing, his eyes were sharp, and even his sense of smell was heightened, so that, despite his cold, odours reached his nose which he hadn't noticed before. He'd had the same feeling more than once in Vietnam, a sense of armed men waiting somewhere in the dark. Those without this sense were killed.

He put down the mug and walked along the corridor to the executive offices. He was confident, expecting to find no one. It was routine. He began to hum.

He was still humming when he saw the man at the file-cabinet safe. He was about thirty feet away, a file folder in his hand; the light was poor, and it took Euston Petty a second or two to see the pistol in his other hand.

When he saw it, he froze. He neither went for his gun nor tried to duck. He opened his mouth but made no sound. He watched the pistol, saw it pointed at his chest, and still he neither moved nor cried out.

He thought: No!

Finally, he reached for his holster, and at the same instant felt a terrible blow in the centre of his chest; he felt himself split open and break into pieces. And then he felt nothing. He was cold, and the darkness came up like a sheet over his eyes.

CHAPTER ELEVEN

The afternoon following the burglary of Ash's office, the Vice-President called a meeting. The Senator was present. Ash and Lemoyne took an early shuttle from New York, and Mark Wells, who had spent the night in the apartment of Clare Wheaton on Leroy Street and couldn't be located until his secretary arrived for work with the number, took a later flight and was the last to arrive.

The Vice-President sat at his desk, everyone else on chairs grouped around it. It was a handsome room, done in pale blue and beige. There were flags and emblems, a painting by Frederic Remington, and several signed photographs of heads of state; the Shah of Iran's picture was on the desk in silver frame. And there was one of the President of the United States in shirt sleeves on a deck chair, sunning himself on the fantail of an American warship. The President was smiling and squinting into the sun, and behind him, in soft focus, were the flags of the line feathered by a stiff sea wind. Other photographs were of actors and sports figures, one of the Vice-President and Arnold Palmer clowning together at Burning Tree, the Vice-President kneeling to place a ball on a tee for Palmer.

But that was a happier time; at the moment the Vice-President's mood was grim, and he began the meeting with a series of pointed remarks directed at Ash Morgan.

'I want to know what happened last night,' he said. 'Some-one has been fucking up by the numbers. I want to know how and why. I've just got off the phone with Walt Roper in Geneva, and he's as upset as I am. He wants to know what's going on. Unless he finds out damn quick he's going to cut some people off at the knees.'

The Vice-President had spoken directly to Ash, glowering at him across his great desk.

'I spoke to Roper an hour after the burglary,' Ash said. 'And a second time just before I left New York. He knows all I know. And I suspect that at the moment that's more than anyone else does.'

'Are you telling me he's satisfied with the way you've handled this?'

'Roper is an intelligent man and a practical one.' Ash spoke slowly and clearly, his voice under control. 'The bur-glary is a fact. Unfortunate, but there it is. At the moment Roper is less interested in threats and pointless recriminations than in how best to cut our losses.'

There was a long moment of tense silence; the Vice-President's face had flushed deep red. He looked on the verge of leaping across the desk and grabbing Ash by the throat. Ash watched him steadily, his face without expression. Mark Wells started to speak, but the Vice-President cut him off. He'd taken the measure of Ash Morgan and deter-mined that brow-beating wouldn't work. Slowly, he re-gained his composure.

'Was it only your office that was burgled?' His voice was uncharacteristically husky, as if he'd been shouting into the wind. He cleared his throat and said, 'That was my im-pression from Mark's initial report.'

His manner was now cordial, and Ash answered similarly: 'Actually, nothing was touched but the security file. The lock was manipulated, and very skilfully.'

'Were all the Astra documents taken?'

'Those I had in my possession,' Ash said.

The Senator was reaming the bowl of his pipe with a tiny silver implement shaped like a spade. 'Have you read the

Astra file?' he said.

'No. It was given to me sealed.'

The Senator and the Vice-President exchanged glances. 'Was anything else taken?' the Vice-President said.

'Nothing. There was some cash in the cabinet. Eleven hundred dollars. That wasn't touched. And more than two hundred thousand dollars in bearer's bonds. Also untouched. A pistol registered to me. Nothing was taken but the file.'

'Are you sure it was Sullivan?'

'I'm sure.'

'Was the security guard able to make an identification of any kind before he died?'

'He was shot in the chest by a nine-millimetre gun. Death was undoubtedly instantaneous.'

'Split him open like a watermelon,' Lemoyne said.

The deep flush returned to the Vice-President's face. 'Two hundred thousand in bearer's bonds. The whole damn Astra file. What was it doing in a cabinet in your office?'

Ash waited several seconds and then said, coolly, 'The bonds needed laundering. They were to go to Geneva. As for the file – where would you have put it?'

'In a safe-deposit box in a bank vault.'

'Where it's subject to subpoena?'

The Senator said, 'I don't like recriminations. They're fruitless. All that matters now is that the file is gone and presumably Sullivan has it. All the original documents, not Xerox copies, which we can get out from under.'

Mark Wells spoke for the first time: 'When I heard the news of the burglary, I called Reese.' He looked directly at Ash; Wells served only the Vice-President, and had decided that his own interests were served by challenging Ash in the presence of his boss and bringing Ash's dealings with Reese into the open. 'Now that we know Sullivan is in New York, Reese promises me he'll find him in forty-eight hours.'

'I want no agencies involved in this,' the Vice-President said. 'Federal, state, municipal. None of those back-biting sons-of-bitches. That's an order.'

'I made that perfectly clear to Reese, sir,' Wells said. 'He intends to use only a few trusted men. I believe he'll rely for the most part on his underworld contacts.'

'That's the ticket,' the Vice-President said. 'Set a thief to catch a thief. That's the way it should've been handled in the first place.'

Ash watched the tobacco curl from the bowl of the Senator's pipe. He had a sudden urge for tobacco, a pipe or a good cigar. He took a deep breath, and said, 'I spoke to Sullivan this morning.'

Lemoyne looked up from admiring his shoeshine.

'He called me just after midnight,' Ash said. 'He described the contents of the safe, so there could be no doubt that it was he who'd taken the file. He's living on West Forty-fourth Street. He's given me a number, and he's expecting a call. He's got what he wants, so he's come in.'

'And now the ball is in our court,' Wells said.

'Did he say what he wanted?'

'What he's always wanted,' Ash said. 'The money. The subpoena quashed. And then he disappears. We never hear from him again.'

The Senator said, 'What is your advice, Ash?'

'What it's been from the beginning,' Ash said. 'Give him what he wants.'

'And if we don't?'

'I don't see that we have a choice,' Ash said.

The Vice-President opened his mouth to speak, but caught himself. For a second or two he stared at Ash with his mouth open. He'd remembered something which he dared not say. His small hard eyes darted to the left, and then to the ceiling before returning to Ash's face. In those few seconds he'd made a decision. His glance now held something crafty and menacing.

Wells said, 'It might be time to go to our back-up position. We've worked on the assumption that with enough pressure, enough of the stick and the carrot, Sullivan would be persuaded to step forward, take the blame and that would be it.'

'What are you getting at?' the Senator said. 'Get to the point.'

'He's talking about somebody else taking the fall.' Lemoyne's voice was shrill. Ash watched the muscles under his eyes twitch. 'Back-up position! He means to throw somebody else to the wolves.'

The Senator laid a restraining hand on Lemoyne's arm. 'I

don't think it's come to that,' he said.

'If it's not Sullivan,' the Vice-President said, 'then it will have to be somebody else. Somebody with knowledge, somebody credible, who we can sell to the public.'

'And who would that be?' Lemoyne said.

The Vice-President slowly shook his head and stood up, ending the meeting. Everyone filed out except the Senator. He and the Vice-President needed a word or two alone.

The Vice-President used a key to open the refrigerator bar that stood behind his desk. He made each of them a tall, cold drink. Then he took off his jacket and loosened his tie, complaining of the heat.

'Bob, you and I have been close for more than twenty years,' the Vice-President said. 'We come from different parts of this country, and our backgrounds are almost totally different. I'm a Baptist, Bob, and you're a Hebrew. My father was poor and yours was rich. You graduated from one of our finest universities and went on to Oxford and even Heidelberg in Germany. My formal education consisted of four years at Cow-Shit Tech.'

The Vice-President was inclined to be long-winded, particularly when he got around to his humble origins, and the Senator moved gracefully to cut him off. There was a plane he wanted to catch. He'd weighed in that morning a pound and a half heavy, and needed to be in New York in time for a workout with Jimmy Burke. 'I think you've got something on your mind, Ernest,' he said. 'And I'm very anxious to hear what that is.'

But the Vice-President wasn't quite ready to come to the point. 'You and I have had our disagreements,' he said, 'but they've been for the most part over tactics, not goals. I think we want the same things for ourselves and for our country as well.'

The Senator said, 'While there's nothing I enjoy more than sitting around with you and chewing the fat, I do have rather urgent business in New York.'

'I apologize for coming at this ass-ways,' the Vice-President said. 'But there aren't six people in the whole country that know what I'm about to confide in you. I've played for big numbers in my time, as you well know. But this makes even me a little nervous. So I ask you to bear with me.'

The Senator decided to have one of his aides call Jimmy Burke and have him wait.

'Have I ever bullshitted you?' the Vice-President said.

The Senator smiled and said, 'Not to my knowledge, Ernest.'

The Vice-President appreciated that. 'Fair enough,' he said, but then began pacing the room. He was restless and uneasy. He opened a door hidden in the wooden panelling to the left of his desk and stepped into his private bathroom. He ran the zipper of his fly and began to urinate, the door open between them.

'You understand that what I'm about to tell you must remain between us. Do I have your word on that?'

'Of course.'

The Vice-President's back was to the Senator, his head lowered, observing his water cascade into the centre of the bowl.

'Come a little closer and tell me what you see?' he said.

The Senator came alongside of the Vice-President. 'I see reaffirmed the ancient truth that in this great country all men are indeed created equal.'

'That's fine, Bob. You're a witty man, with a wonderful and expensive education, but at the moment I'm very serious. Please don't think me discourteous, but I'd appreciate you having a closer look at my urine.'

'It's clear as spring water,' the Senator said.

'Has it an unpleasant odour?'

'No.'

'Has it any odour at all?'

'Christ, Ernest. It smells like piss.'

'Exactly.' The Vice-President shook himself and zipped up his fly. After he'd washed his hands, he said, 'It doesn't smell of decaying fruit, does it?'

'No.'

'Dead flowers, or anything of that nature?'

The Senator shook his head and the Vice-President continued: 'Having observed me, would you say I find urinating a pleasurable act, one free from all pain and discomfort?'

'I would.'

'Would you further say that if one's urine is clear and free of unnatural odours, and if one experiences no discomfort in the passing of it, one's urinary tract is likely to be in good condition?'

'Yes, I would.'

'And likewise, if one's urine is unclear and malodorous, if the act is painful, that it raises the possibility of a health problem in the urinary tract?'

The Senator had begun to see the point. 'I certainly would,' he said.

'And if one has had a past history of serious urogenital problems?'

The Senator said, 'You were with him in Maryland.'

'There was blood in it,' the Vice-President said. 'The pain was excruciating. Had I not caught him, he would have fainted. Those weren't polyps last year, Bob. The President is a very sick man.'

The Senator hadn't touched the drink made by the Vice-President. He disliked liquor, always had; and had never once even been tipsy. But he rarely refused a drink, fearing that if he did, it would soon be passed around that he was a reformed drunk. So he accepted drinks but left them untouched, pouring them down johns and into flowerpots.

But he was shocked and somewhat awed by what the Vice-President had just told him. He saw at once that the Vice-President wouldn't have told him if he hadn't something specific in mind. The Senator grasped the significance for his own career. *We come from different parts of this country,* the Vice-President had said, *'and our backgrounds are totally different.'*

The Vice-President's meaning was unmistakable. The Senator's hand began to shake. He saw himself about to take a giant step towards the realization of his life-long ambition. He put down the protective whisky, aware that the Vice-President was looking at him closely. Just to have something to do, he began to rummage in the Vice-President's refrigerator until he found a carton of Tropicana orange juice, just starting to go bad.

'I'm sorry, Bob,' the Vice-President said, 'I hadn't realized

142

how very fond of the Chief you are.'

'He's a great man.'

'And this is a very grave moment.'

'I assume there's no danger of us being recorded or over-heard.' The Senator held the situation up to the light, swiftly calculating the dangers and possible advantages to himself. The workout with Jimmy Burke was forgotten. But a vague uneasiness remained. And he still held the carton of sour orange juice. 'There's not to be a record of this conversation,' he said.

'I have my own people sweep every morning,' the Vice-President said.

'How sick is he?' the Senator said.

'They did the cystoscopic last week,' the Vice-President said. 'The White House dispensary was fitted up. They flew that Jap specialist in from New York.'

'Hikama,' the Senator said. 'I had a problem two years ago. Thank God, it was just a strain.'

'All of this takes Secret Service,' the Vice-President said. 'Naturally, I've got some close friends over there. Hikama took tissue samples. They were sent to his lab under a phony name.'

The Senator said, 'What was the finding?'

'Malignant. They took more tests, and apparently it's metastasized. Bob, the President is a dead duck.'

'Will there be an announcement?'

'Only that he's going into Columbia Presbyterian for minor surgery. That's Hikama's hospital. He's got his crew there and he won't operate anywhere else. They screamed for Bethesda, but Hikama wouldn't go along.'

'He's tough. Presidential prostate or Joe Doaks's, it's all the same to him.'

'He's going to have to resign,' the Vice-President said.

'You'll be President, Ernest. President of the United States.'

'You can bet your ass on it.'

'The one fly in the ointment is the Astra file,' the Senator said. 'That can ruin us. It must be shut down.'

'We don't dare go around quashing federal indictments,' the Vice-President said.

'Or tossing around huge amounts of cash. No matter how skilfully done, there's always a chance of that leaving a trail.'

'I'm going to lay this in your lap, Bob. I'm going to rely on you. I'm going to say to you, "Bob, go out and do it. Don't tell me how or when. Just close it down." And I know you appreciate what's involved, and that you'll do the job for me.'

'I understand what has to be done.'

'Anything comes up, you talk to Wells. You understand? I'm going to have to be out of it from now on.'

'You put it out of your mind,' the Senator said. 'From now on you'll have quite enough to think about. You have to prepare yourself for the months ahead.'

'I'm going to want you for my Vice-President.'

The Senator set down his glass of sour orange juice. 'I'm honoured,' he said. 'And I'm confident we'll make a great team.'

CHAPTER TWELVE

The operation was called Bodybuilder. Wells had named it and was in charge, directing from Washington. Lemoyne was on the spot; the Vice-President and the Senator stayed in the shadows, severed from the evidential chain, protected by Wells and Lemoyne.

The Senator told Lemoyne only that they were now playing in a very fast league, that the stakes were high, and they must play to win. The Senator tended to use the vocabulary of sports and gambling when he spoke to Lemoyne. It was a way of patronizing him, which Lemoyne either didn't notice or didn't mind.

The Senator made it clear that Sullivan must be shut down. He didn't come out and say so, not in so many words, but Lemoyne knew what the Senator wanted without being told; his value came from this shadowy ability to grasp what dared not be said. Sullivan stood between them and the goal line. He would have to be taken out of the ball game.

Lemoyne understood: Sullivan needed to be killed.

Lemoyne respected Sullivan. The man made him nervous, perhaps afraid. But it wasn't a duel, not to Lemoyne, who was without honour. He would do it but he wasn't sure how. He needed help, and went to Ash Morgan.

Ash advised him to forget it. Lemoyne said he had a plan: it involved a wirer, a top man. Reese had recommended him.

'I told you to forget it,' Ash said. 'I don't care what the plan is, it'll go wrong. You'll only make matters worse. He'll beat you, and once he's done that you'll have made him sore, and he'll raise his price. He's an odd duck. I promise he'll try to stick it to the lot of you.'

'What the hell is he?' Lemoyne said. 'He's flesh and blood.'

'So are we.'

'Are you afraid of him?'

'I am if we play his kind of game.'

'They won't bargain with him,' Lemoyne said. 'They're already talking about another scapegoat.'

'They're stupid,' Ash said. 'Worse, they're arrogant.'

'Let me tell you my plan.'

'I don't want to hear it.'

'Just the part about the wirer. His name is Elias. A Greek, something like that. Reese says he's the best.'

'I never heard of him.'

'Most of his work has been done in Europe.'

'If Reese knows him it must be through the wise guys,' Ash said. 'He'd have a speciality. Car ignitions? TV? I knew one who wired the electric toaster. Start your day off with a bang. If the wise guys use him, it's to make things go boom.'

'He wires the telephone,' Lemoyne said.

'I knew one who wired an electric toothbrush,' Ash said. 'They're creative people, wirers.'

'You ought to take this more seriously,' Lemoyne said. 'And don't stand around on your high horse. You draw a fat salary from Roper. Sweet Jesus, you're no little sunbeam. I need your help to make Sullivan come out from under the covers. Elias then brings his kit, he hooks up to Sullivan's phone while you've got him out of the house making a bargain.'

'I won't be a part of killing Sullivan,' Ash said.

Lemoyne let it go. He would have to do without Ash, but when it was over he would see that Ash was cut out. There'd be a time to pay him back. The Senator would carry the tale to Roper.

Lemoyne went back to Reese and arranged for surveillance of Sullivan. Reese put his best men to work on their own time. Wells carried the cash to pay them from Washington in a Mark Cross case. They staked out Forty-fourth Street, waiting for Sullivan to leave his apartment. He did so only once every forty-eight hours, walking to the bodega on the corner. He bought two bags of groceries and returned to the apartment. Total time in the air: twenty-eight minutes.

Elias, the wirer, was kept on tap, tinkering with his equipment in a garage on Tenth Avenue. Lemoyne had to spend time with him, keep him amused. He was high-strung and temperamental, a prima donna. Lemoyne had to lose to him at gin. He'd expected someone older, more sophisticated. Wirers usually ran to middle-age, men who'd slowed and lost their taste for gunplay. Wiring was a second trade, the fundamentals learned in prison workshops.

But Elias was in his twenties and wore his hair long, with something about it that wasn't quite right, as if it were dyed or a wig. He was short and broad, powerfully put together, with a rugged brutal face. An ugly, hairy man, but vain, with the funny hair and fingernails professionally trimmed and polished. Wiremen were sour and scholarly; this one had the nasty, kinky look of the younger shooters; he killed for money, and spent the money on gaudy clothes, dope, and spreeing with women one could knock around.

Lemoyne was with him in the garage on Tenth Avenue when the call came that Sullivan had finally gone out. One of Reese's men had rented an apartment across from Sullivan's. Another followed him in a car with a transceiver.

Sullivan had returned to the bodega, this time to use the phone. Reese had said he used his phone to receive calls, never to make them.

Elias waited against a Ford panel truck, a portable electrician's case between his legs. He wore a collection of trinkets on a gold chain around his neck, odd bits and pieces of brightly coloured metal made to catch the eye, like a mobile swaying above a baby's crib.

Lemoyne told him to start the truck. They'd drive to Forty-fourth Street and keep in touch with Sullivan's tail by radio receiver; perhaps this time he'd be out of his apartment long enough for Elias to do his wiring.

Sullivan plucked a small reddish banana from a bin near the phone. The Colombian woman smiled and returned his wink; he peeled the banana, the receiver of the phone tucked between his ear and shoulder. Black Irish, his mother had called him, her beautiful son, her rogue.

'I'll meet you at noon,' he said into the phone. 'D'you know Tout Va Bien?' The banana was ripe and sweet. 'I'll be at the bar. We have to make plans,' he said.

The Colombian woman refused to accept anything for the banana Sullivan had eaten. He'd noticed her when he'd been in earlier for his shopping. They'd spoken Spanish together. Now they were alone in the bodega, near the bins of ripening fruit. She was a woman to live with simply, in a warm and languid climate. Sullivan felt his sexuality that morning, felt it heavily against his leg.

'Are you French?' she said. 'I don't understand the French language, but I had a man in Bogotá who spoke French to me. When he spoke Spanish to me, it sounded like you.'

Sullivan said, 'Under what circumstances did he speak to you in French?'

Although her teeth were good, she covered her mouth with her hand when she laughed. 'When he wanted me to be nice to him.'

'And were you nice to him?'

'He was a handsome man, too.'

'And a lucky one.'

'I was lucky too.' She smacked Sullivan playfully on the arm. 'Now that I remember, he looked a little like you. Maybe taller, but not with such beautiful eyes.'

Sullivan asked for a quart of orange juice, which he opened and drank from the carton. It was a cool day, but she wore a blouse with short sleeves; there were two large vaccination scars on her upper arm and a tuft of jet black hair in her armpit which had been shaved and had grown back. When he put down the juice, he drew close to her and inhaled gently, sniffing her as he would a glass of wine; she

147

gave off a faint salty-damp smell; it was his morning to take pleasure in the odours of women.

'Your Spanish is like they speak around Panama, somewhere near there.'

'Yes, in Panama.'

'We speak better Spanish in Colombia.'

He had drunk half the carton of juice. She watched him with her head cocked to one side, her odd golden eyes fixed on his face. 'You're not an American,' she said. 'Not a Frenchman either. I can't decide about you. I'll bet you work in a restaurant. With so many languages, a head waiter.'

'How did you know?'

'Or maybe a ship?'

'Yes, I worked on a ship.'

After he'd paid for the juice and left, she wondered about him. He was a handsome man, but a dangerous one. Next time she'd ask how his front tooth had been broken. She liked his eyes, but behind them she detected a dark secret. He hadn't spoken truthfully to her, but simply agreed to everything she said. He was a head waiter, his Spanish was learned in Panama, and he'd worked on a ship. She knew none of it was true.

Next time she would ask why there were men out looking for him, why one had come in with a photograph, and others followed in cars.

Sullivan knew he was under surveillance. He'd spotted the unadorned blue Plymouth just a few seconds after leaving the bodega. He'd been waiting for them to come down on him and expected that as soon as he went out they'd be inside his apartment, bugging his phone and searching for the file. They'd find nothing, learn nothing. It was a minor inconvenience in the form of a ritual, like being stranded in a Catholic country on Good Friday.

The Plymouth trailed him to Tout Va Bien, and parked across the street when he went in.

It was just before noon and Janice hadn't arrived. There were no other patrons. A long rectangular table in the rear was occupied by the waitresses and kitchen staff, chattering and smoking over the last of their lunch like members of the same family; the chef in a white apron and toque sat at the

148

head of the table, smoking a curved pipe over a glass of beer.

Sullivan ordered a bottle of Perrier and, a few minutes past noon, Janice walked in. She wore a short russet jacket and a long, loose tweed skirt over reddish boots. Sullivan had noticed several girls wearing boots, but those Janice wore were the real thing, the kind that cost a few hundred dollars in Hermès, and he wondered if they were a gift of the same man who'd bought her membership in the nude swimming club.

She didn't kiss him or even offer her hand, but took the stool next to him at the bar, and began to talk nervously while avoiding his eyes. He was also jumpy and his heart began to pound. It wasn't at all what he expected. He hadn't planned to call her or even thought much about her. Now his feelings came in a rush and he was caught off guard.

The conversation came awkwardly, in fits and starts; she also drank Perrier. Much remained unspoken between them, undeclared, as much from her side as his, and he began to examine her closely as she spoke, and to realize that she was different from he remembered, older and perhaps not as pretty. He saw that her face was longer and thinner and that she had great luminous eyes on which nothing was ever lost. He sensed a more sharply defined personality, one who managed well and saw things clearly; he now saw that she'd had a complicated and difficult past. Fierce loves were hidden there. He'd been blind not to have seen all of this before.

He caught the barman's eyes and ordered two glasses of white wine with a dash of cassis. It was called *kir*. For a moment he hadn't been able to think of the word.

He thought of her as a lover. He knew her to be greedy, calculating, and sensual. She was a woman eager to take from her lover, to exploit him, and yet she gave something back, true passion, honesty when making love, and a certain sympathy when, in that part of his life which was not sensual, the man faltered; and he felt that the material things she took were passed on to someone else whom she loved. This was the secret which she held back. Sullivan had seen the same trait in the daughters of refugees, particularly in Vietnam.

But how had he missed all this? He should have seen it all before, when they were drowsy or playful. He remembered that they'd been on the verge of confiding in each other.

She said, 'I never thought you'd call. Not for a minute. When I saw you walk away in the park, I thought – that's it, I'll never see him again.' She turned her eyes on him and said, 'Why did you call?'

'It was something that built up in me,' he said. 'I hadn't expected to.'

'And it's caught you by surprise, is that it?' She was smiling, as if she knew something he didn't. 'Is that the way it is?'

'I've been ambushed,' he said.

She said, 'I know why you really wanted the stationery.' The smile had faded. 'That part of it's over, isn't it?'

'Not quite.'

'I read about the robbery in the paper. A burglary at Roper International. The story seemed to have been played down, and the details were fuzzy, as if something were being held back. A guard was killed. Was it you who did it?'

'Yes. He pulled a gun. I waited as long as I could.'

'Then why haven't you run?'

'I told you, it's not finished. There are loose ends.'

'Am I one of the loose ends?'

'No. A man told me I wasn't a solitary. "You're not a freak," he said. When I do run, I want you to come with me.'

He paid the bar bill and tipped the captain to give them a corner table where they'd be able to talk.

They ordered lunch. Men in business suits presented themselves at the door, smiling and rubbing their hands in anticipation of lunch. The captain glided back and forth escorting them to tables. Waitresses followed with drinks on small plastic bar trays with cork bottoms. A single busboy scurried around with wicker baskets of slices of bread and little dishes of butter patties laid on ice.

While they ate, Sullivan told her everything, the killings he'd done in South America, Europe and Vietnam. He needed to start fresh, and he emptied his soul to her.

And all of this was at a corner table in a small, busy

French restaurant, while all around them people were having lunch.

Sullivan even joked about it; they were a man and woman to whisper their deepest secrets not in bedrooms but in restaurants.

'I've loved other men,' she said. 'I thought I did. No, I truly did. I had to love them so as not to be a whore. You understand.' She laid her hands on his. 'I have much more to tell you. One thing that can't wait.'

'Sexual things? Your other men? Women? Whatever. None of that matters a damn to me.'

'Nor to me. This is something deeper,' she said. 'Will we have to run?'

'Until we find a place. There'll be money. We'll live as long and as well as we can.'

'Just like the rest of the world,' she said.

'Just like that.'

'I have a family,' she said. 'It's not all the way I told you. My brother who went into the navy is dead. And the other isn't married and he isn't a lawyer in Richmond. He's here in New York, living with my mother.'

'I thought she was dead.'

'Another lie.'

'And they depend on you?'

'My brother is paralysed.'

'Will you be able to leave them?'

'No one else knows about him,' she said. 'He and my mother are my true life. They're a secret.'

He repeated his question. 'Will you be able to leave them?'

'Yes. If it's to go with you,' she said.

She wanted him to meet her mother and brother. He called for the check, and while they waited for it to be brought, he warned her that he was being followed; she was to leave first, and he would watch through the window of the restaurant to see if she was followed. She gave him an address on Eighty-fourth Street. He would be there in an hour.

She left the restaurant and Sullivan sat at the bar, looking through the window at the blue Plymouth. It didn't move. He could see the driver clearly. He was middle-aged and overweight, a cop by the look of him, one of those who liked mixed drinks and red meat, a bored hack and not worth a damn. Janice had come alone, left alone, and so he never even so much as glanced at her.

Sullivan hailed a cab and told the driver to take him to Sixth Avenue and Central Park South. The Plymouth followed. Sullivan left the cab in front of the St Moritz, crossed Central Park South, and entered the park. The fat cop tried following him on foot. Sullivan drew him deeper into the park before turning off on a footpath leading up from the lake, and broke into a run in the direction of the zoo. He lost the cop in the afternoon crowd near the bear pit.

He left the park on Fifth Avenue, walked to Madison Avenue, and hailed a cab. There was no sign of the cop or the blue Plymouth. Just to be sure, he left the cab on Eighty-first Street and walked to the address on Eighty-fourth Street that Janice had given him. It turned out to be a high-rise with a small circular driveway near an elaborate fountain built around massive blocks of granite which made him think of Stonehenge. He was announced by a spiffy doorman and directed to an apartment on the eleventh floor. Janice let him in. Her mother had gone to market and Sullivan had a chance to glance around the apartment.

It was a modest place, two bedrooms, one closed at the moment, her brother was asleep. There was a small living-room, a dining alcove, a kitchen, and two baths. The furniture was heavy, old-fashioned, substantial, good pieces acquired one at a time over the years. All of it had been bought for larger quarters, a sprawling suburban house, and then squeezed into these cramped New York City rooms. Everything was spotless and neat as a pin, a widow's apartment, one who had passed through better times; still, it was the home of a woman with a firm grip on her life and possessions, a person of order. Were Sullivan's mother alive, she would have made such an apartment for herself.

Janice gave him a mug of coffee and a few minutes later her mother returned, carrying a neatly tied white box from Dumas, an expensive French bakery.

As they shook hands, she looked directly at Sullivan. Janice's eyes were very much like hers, almost the exact colour and shape and the lowering angle at the corner of the

152

upper lid was also the same. He was fascinated. She held him with her level glance.

Otherwise she was very different from Janice, smaller and darker, with a figure which had once been good but was now plump. Certainly she was attractive, but never had she been a beauty, not anything in her daughter's class. By the look of the apartment neither did she share Janice's taste for the high life. He saw that Janice was one of those children who create themselves, who baffle and exceed their parents. They seem to grasp the secret desires of one or another parent and base their lives on making it come true. But this is a dark secret forever unknown to both sides. They grow up to flourish in a world of which the parents know nothing. Childhood is quickly put aside by such people. All that remains of it is loyalty and a fiercely protective love.

Mrs Blackmur served the chocolate cake she'd bought, and without a word replaced the coffee mug with an elegant china service. She was good at small talk and had a sweet tooth. Sullivan had become a stranger to family situations, but was made to feel at ease. He began to enjoy himself, and saw that Janice was smiling and relieved. She'd kept her two lives apart and was surprised how little it cost her to bring them together.

She brought a framed photograph from her mother's room. It was of her father; a gaunt, intense face with a large, well-formed and sensual mouth, the one feature Janice had inherited. His eyes were large, heavy, grave. They stared directly at the camera lens, brooding and intelligent. Sullivan saw suffering in them, disappointment and bitterness, hopes turned to ashes. It was an old photograph.

'My husband died in nineteen seventy-one,' Mrs Blackmur said.

'He looks like an unusual man.'

'He had strong convictions.'

'Of a political kind?'

'No. His early training was for the ministry. He never completed his studies and went into business. He was also interested for a time in art.'

'He was a painter,' Janice said.

'There were some people who said he was good.'

'He *was* good,' Janice said.

'Have you any of his paintings?'

'I've rolled them all up and put them away.'

Just then a bell jingled, sounding as if it were amplified; it came from the closed bedroom. The women exchanged a quick glance and both rose. But Janice restrained her mother by taking hold of her arm, and went quickly out of the room. Sullivan heard the bedroom door open and close.

He was alone with Janice's mother.

She studied him for a few seconds and then said, 'Have you a family of your own?'

'No. They're all dead.'

She nodded her head, as though this confirmed a notion she had of him. 'D'you smoke, Mr Sullivan?'

'No. I'm sorry.'

'I don't either. I only meant if you do, please do so.'

'My mother and father died within a year of each other,' he said.

'Were you a close family?'

'My brother and I were. That is when we were young. My father was away much of the time. My brother and I loved my mother.'

'Would you like another piece of cake?'

'I don't think so.'

'I'd like one, but I won't have it.' When she smiled the resemblance between her and Janice was strongest. 'You're not used to conversations with nosy old women, are you? But you see, you're the first of Janice's friends I've met.'

'Then it's natural,' he said.

'She keeps us quite apart from her other life, sheltered and wrapped in cotton wool. You're the first who's been allowed to cross over.' She expected him to answer that, perhaps with something reassuring. But he had little talent for such things, and the patience to endure awkward silences.

'I don't know what Janice has told you about her brother,' she said. 'There's only two years between them, but she was always very much the big sister. Since his accident, they've grown even closer. He's come to depend on her. I'm afraid we both have.'

'You'll still be able to depend on her,' Sullivan said.

'She told me you'll be taking her away. She said you were

154

a businessman. That you'd sold your business and wanted to travel.'

'Nothing will change,' he said. 'Listen to what I say: you will be able to depend on her. Even more now than before.'

She leaned forward in her chair until her knees came within inches of his, her eyes fixed on his face. Finally, she smiled and said, 'I'll bet you were the younger son, and that your mother adored you.'

'The first year my brother was away at school,' he said, 'my father was off at the other end of the world, and there were just the two of us at home. We lived in San Diego, on a forty-foot boat, just my mother and I.'

'That must've been wonderful.'

'It was.'

'I've always wanted to live near the water,' she said.

A few minutes later he met Raymond. The resemblance between him and Janice was striking. They might've been twins, the same clear skin and fair hair. Of the two he was the better-looking, although less healthy, leaner, the skin of his face stretched against the sharp bones of his jaw. His eyes were clear and frank, of a darker blue than either Janice's or their mother's, and without their probing wariness. The hand he offered Sullivan was fine-boned, but cool, hard, and strong. His neck and upper body were powerfully developed; an elaborate system of pulleys and springs had been rigged above his bed for him to exercise his arms and shoulders. He met Sullivan in a wheelchair, a blanket covering his useless legs.

Most of his time was spent painting. He'd studied it as a boy, when his father was alive, and then given it up, and began again only after his accident.

Janice explained it. It was she who did most of the talking, Raymond for the most part was silent. But it was a friendly silence. He didn't scrutinize Sullivan, he didn't judge him or look at him as a rival, a man with good legs come to take his sister from him. Sullivan saw that he was simply content to let others talk. There was about him an air of sweetness. One was in the presence of someone rare, whom suffering had made more gentle and patient. Janice kept smoothing his

155

hair, or touching his hand, and her loving eyes never left his face. He was adored by both mother and sister, but this family intimacy did nothing to exclude Sullivan. Quite the opposite, he found himself drawn into it.

Part of Raymond's room had been converted into a studio, the walls covered with his work. He painted seascapes, gulls swooping over a tranquil bay, sailing ships, and waves crashing against glistening rocks. He painted the Mediterranean sky and sun. One picture, which caught Sullivan's eye, was of a strip of golden beach, the sand made wet by the receding ocean, a small white house set among palmettos in the foreground, while far down the beach, drawing together the lines of perspective, a man ran on the edge of the water.

Sullivan said, 'It looks like a place I know in Greece. One of the islands.'

'You mean there are still places like this?'

'Yes. A few. There's a comfortable hotel and a few small villas, like the house in your picture. The boat comes once a week, twice in summer. The fishing is good.'

'I like to fish,' Raymond said, smiling. 'I'm able to.'

'There's a baker on the island,' Sullivan said. 'And a goatherd who makes his own cheese.'

'Can you grow vegetables?'

'You'd have to scratch for it. It's pretty rocky, but you could grow some things.'

'And we could learn Greek,' Janice said.

'Yes. That would be a wonderful thing to do,' Raymond said.

'Then we'll do it,' Sullivan said. 'It may take a little time, and we must all be patient.'

'I've learned all about that,' Raymond said.

'Six months,' Sullivan said. 'At the most, a year.'

Later Sullivan and Janice walked together in Carl Schurz Park beside the East River.

'I wanted you to meet him,' she said. 'To see how he is. He's had so much pain, and of course never being able to walk again or have a normal life . . . But there's no bitterness in him, no resentment.' She spoke with great intensity, her eyes reflecting the darkening sky above the river. 'He's one of those who come through hell and are then at peace. Nothing more can be done to them.'

Sullivan said, 'Most come out of hell worse than when they went in.'

'Yes. But not him. He was spoiled and wild, egotistical. A brat, really. Of course I adored him, but even I admitted he was shallow and selfish.'

'How was he hurt?'

'He raced stockcar. He wouldn't go to school, wouldn't do anything he was supposed to. Just racing wasn't exciting enough, or maybe he wasn't really very good. He had to take crazy risks. So he cracked up and broke his spine. Now he paints, like my father.'

'Tell me about your father.'

She acted as if she'd not heard him. 'Is it possible, the house on a Greek island? Or was it something you just said to make Raymond happy?'

'I meant it,' he said. 'Greece would probably work. If not there, somewhere else. Yugoslavia is good right now. We'll find a place and send for them.'

'Why would you do that?'

'I don't know. I just want to live that way, on an island, with a boat and a family.'

'You are more than you seem,' she said. 'Man of secrets. Secret loyalties, I'll bet. Secret loves, too.'

'Look who's talking.'

'Tell me about the skeletons in the closet,' she said. 'Did you work for the government? Were you a spy? An agent, something like that?'

'I retired some time ago and went to work for a man named Roper.'

'The burglary.'

'I was about to be canned. There was a small pension. Very small, and a term of penal servitude, not quite so small.'

'What kind of man is Roper?'

'He's become a vegetarian.'

'I know a girl who did a turn on one of his yachts,' she said. 'She told me the food was delicious, the pay was good, and nobody even screwed her.'

'I wasn't quite that lucky.'

'Is he really a vegetarian?'

'He's one of those who eat fish. In fact he eats a lot of fish. Fish and kinky sex and money. He's worth about a billion, give or take. He believes in money, in its magical properties. There is a spirit which lives in money. It's like the air, the earth, fire, and fresh water. The money spirit. Roper's not a simple-minded tycoon. He's got a mystical side. One of his grandmothers was a Choctaw Indian. They tried to bring all of that out in the *Playboy* interview.'

'My friend said he went around bare-ass and made everyone else do the same. He said it was healthy, and also good for the soul.'

'Well, there you are, I told you there was a mystical side to Roper.'

'D'you also believe taking down your pants is good for the soul?'

'As good as anything else.'

'I think it's time we went home,' she said.

CHAPTER THIRTEEN

While Elias traced the telephone wires from the instrument to the terminal box, Lemoyne hooked the transceiver to his belt and set about examining Sullivan's apartment. He noticed, first, the neatness of the place, its cleanliness and the military precision with which objects were aligned, everything in its place, centred and at right angles. The few odd pieces of furniture were worn and looked as if they'd been picked up secondhand. Lemoyne sensed no connection between them and Sullivan and was sure they'd come with the apartment. He found no television set or clock. There was a bedside radio and next to it, in a soft leather case, a Pentax single-lens reflex camera. He examined a small old-fashioned desk, its drawers unlocked, but opening them one at a time, he found each empty. He'd not expected to find anything of value, certainly none of the Astra documents would be left lying around, but there wasn't even blank paper or pens, no old letters or postage stamps. Not a rubber band or paper clip, just a few dry grains of tobacco in the seams of one drawer. Lemoyne couldn't remember if Sullivan smoked.

Lemoyne parted the venetian blinds and looked down at

the street; children played on an abandoned mattress and an old man smoking a pipe led a tan mongrel dog along the kerb. Everything seemed as it was; and then Lemoyne noticed the figure in the green Volkswagen parked at the eastern end of the street. He couldn't remember if the Volkswagen had been there when they'd driven up.

Elias had removed the plate covering the terminal box and was working with the wire connections. Lemoyne considered asking Elias if he'd seen the Volkswagen, but decided against it.

He said, 'How is it going?'

'No problem at all,' Elias said. 'Should be another ten minutes. Fifteen at the most.'

'He's still in the restaurant,' Lemoyne said.

He continued his tour of the apartment. The tiny kitchen was spotless, every cup and dish, all the cutlery stowed away like a ship's galley. The refrigerator held a single carton of milk and a jar of honey. A bowl of fruit caught the sun on the window sill. There were cartons of breakfast cereal, the kind without sugar or preservatives, and a canister filled with raw cashew nuts. The bathroom was also immaculate. He slid back the mirrored panel of the cabinet above the sink. It contained only the barest necessities: a toothbrush and a tube of Colgate toothpaste, the bottom neatly rolled, cap securely in place; a Gillette Trac II razor and plastic dispenser of blades. He could find no stubble in the crevices of the razor, no dried shaving cream. There was a bottle of aftershave that smelled faintly of lemon; a cake of soap and a small bottle of Listerine mouthwash; a comb which had been picked clean of lint.

He'd hoped for something more intimate, a medication or device to expose a secret of Sullivan's. His own medicine chest contained sleeping pills and hair dye, aspirin, vitamins, and salve to soothe his haemorrhoids. Sullivan's bathroom held nothing of that order. Lemoyne was disappointed.

The bedroom was much like the rest of the apartment. The blanket which covered the bed was folded and tucked under the mattress and drawn taut as a drumskin. Lemoyne had served as an enlisted man in Korea and remembered a regular army first sergeant bouncing a quarter on his blanket to test its tightness.

159

Lemoyne went through the bureau one drawer at a time, searching in the stacks of Sullivan's shirts, his underwear and socks, careful to leave everything as he'd found it. Nothing was old or worn, and nothing brand-new. The shirts were white or pale blue, the ties conservative. Lemoyne guessed everything had been bought the same afternoon, and likely as not picked out by a woman, a secretary or girl-friend. The more Lemoyne thought of it, the more certain he became that Sullivan had his clothes picked for him by a woman. It was an odd thought for Lemoyne to have had. Odder still, he envied Sullivan for it. No woman had ever offered to pick out Lemoyne's clothes.

Lemoyne checked his watch: they'd been in the apartment eleven minutes. Six since his last call from the man in the car across from the restaurant where Sullivan was having his lunch.

He used the transceiver to contact the stakeout in the apartment across the street; he'd also noticed the man in the green Volkswagen.

'I'd like a better look at him,' he said. 'He's illegally parked. We could hassle him on that.'

'Let it alone,' Lemoyne said. 'I don't want him stirred up.'

Elias had replaced the terminal plate and was at work on the wiring on the base of the telephone. He'd be another five minutes.

Lemoyne wanted a look at the closet in Sullivan's bedroom. He went methodically through the pockets of his suits, but found nothing, not a matchbook, ticket stub, not a scrap of paper. The suits were of good quality but off the peg; Sullivan wasn't a man to spend his time before a tailor's mirror.

A row of four shelves had been built into one wall of the closet. Sullivan had laid out his shoes on these. Lemoyne ran his hand along the underside of each of the shelves. He knew what he was doing; on the bottom shelf, just a few inches from the floor, taped to the underside and completely out of sight, he found a heavy-duty plastic bag. Lemoyne lay flat on the floor and carefully peeled back the tape. The plastic bag contained a Walther PPK. It had recently been cleaned and oiled and was fully loaded. There was a silencer,

160

a box of cartridges, and an envelope. The envelope was un-sealed.

Lemoyne hadn't known what exactly he'd been searching for. But with the contents of the envelope in his hand, for the first time he realized what he'd been after: he wanted something close to Sullivan, some bit that opened on to his life, something intimate.

It was a family photograph. Four people standing on what seemed to be the shore of a large lake. A motorboat was moored close by and in the background, trailing off into the distance, was a range of mountains. It seemed to be some place out West. Lemoyne supposed the mountains were the Rockies.

Lemoyne switched on a bedside lamp and examined the photograph more closely. He recognized Sullivan at once, although he appeared to be no more than fifteen or sixteen. The features were the same, particularly around the jaw and eyes, frowning slightly into the sun. The smiling, hand-some boy next to him would be his brother, two or three years older. The brother resembled their father, and was taller and broader than Sullivan. It was he and his mother who looked alike, and it was in front of his mother that he stood, her hand resting naturally on his shoulder. From just this one snapshot, Lemoyne felt the closeness of the mother and younger son, the unity of these two people standing slightly apart from the other two males.

Lemoyne switched off the light and stood for a moment in the semi-darkness, the photograph in his hands. An un-natural stillness had fallen upon him. He'd found what he'd come for.

He replaced the plastic bag with the pistol and cartridges and slipped the photograph in his pocket.

Elias had prised the earpiece from the telephone receiver and from his electrician's satchel brought a round steel case, the size and thickness of a pocket watch, with two protruding wires. He snipped a wire inside the receiver, peeled back the plastic insulation, and twisted the wires from the steel device to both ends. He fitted the steel device inside the receiver and replaced the plastic cover before returning the receiver to the phone cradle.

'It's a beautiful little thing,' he said. 'Japanese terrorists developed it. They got their training courtesy of Sony. Clever little nips.' Elias smiled broadly, squinting for comic effect, like a Japanese in a World War II movie. At the same time, he was a specialist with pride in his work. 'The detonator, which by the way is no bigger than a contact lens, works on DC current, less than forty-eight volts. The phone rings with one-oh-five AC, but when the receiver is lifted, the contact is broken. There's an automatic switch-over to forty-eight volts of DC. The instant you pick up the receiver it goes pop.'

'And it's all in that little disc?'

'It'll blow anything within five feet.'

Elias then checked to be certain he'd left behind no bits of snipped wire or paint chipped from the terminal box screws. Lemoyne preceded him through the door and reset the locks, using magnetized tungsten wire to slide the upper plate on the Fox lock. They walked quickly and silently down the three flights of stairs to the street. Lemoyne opened the front door and glanced west; the green Volkswagen hadn't moved, the man behind the wheel still waited.

Lemoyne touched Elias's arm. 'It was a telephone tap,' he said. 'Not a word about the bomb.'

Elias shrugged; it was all the same to him. Lemoyne left him at the garage on Tenth Avenue and walked farther west to the river. Now that it was over he realized how frightened he'd been. If someone had tripped up and Sullivan had come unexpectedly into the apartment, he might have been killed himself. Sullivan was capable of anything. He worked miracles and Lemoyne feared him. Only when he reached the Hudson River and inhaled deeply of the breeze coming off the water did he begin to relax.

He found a phone booth and called the stakeout across from Sullivan's apartment.

'The guy in the Volkswagen had a clear look at you and the wirer,' the stakeout said. 'When you came out, he wrote something down. That's what it looked like.'

'Let him alone,' Lemoyne said. 'Trace the licence plate and let me know. I'll be in Ponte's with Ash Morgan. Call me there.'

Ponte's was a restaurant on Desbrosses Street, downtown, two blocks west of Canal. Men who ate two meals a day in restaurants, who never looked at prices, said Ponte's served the best meat in New York. Sports people used it, judges and people with the city and the courts, which were a few blocks away, and of course a lot of mob men. The Senator ordered a veal chop whenever he was in town.

Lemoyne arrived before Ash, and ran into an old friend at the bar. They were just shaking hands when Ash came in.

'Ash, I wonder if you know Marty Pearl,' Lemoyne said. 'Ash Morgan.'

'I never had the pleasure,' Marty Pearl said. 'Only heard of you by word of mouth. And only good things, Mr Morgan. Only the best.'

'Marty's a dear old friend, I haven't seen in what? Five years? It is five years, isn't it, Marty?'

'More like seven, eight. But I'm a regular bad penny.' He held out a large tanned hand, with age spots on the back, hard as wood. He was white-haired and courtly, with the nose of a Roman senator, wearing a powder-blue leisure suit and a gold star of David around his neck. 'I haven't been East in seven years,' he said. 'Not since I moved to Phoenix.'

'Marty built a magnificent villa in Phoenix,' Lemoyne said.

'It's a nice place.'

'Tennis courts, a swimming pool. The Senator loved it.'

'D'you know Frank Lloyd Wright?' Marty Pearl said. 'Well, one of his students built it for me. Tell you the truth, it's for my grandchildren. I got six momsers. I give them a good time, maybe they'll remember Grandpa.'

The captain had a table for Lemoyne, who invited Marty Pearl to join them for a drink.

Once they were seated and the drinks ordered, Marty Pearl began to talk about Arizona. It was Paradise. God's country. He was happy there in the Great American south-west, for the first time in his life he was at peace. Every morning he raised the American flag and thanked God for the blessings of his life. That's what Marty Pearl said. But his eyes were never still when he spoke, darting around the room, and he perched on the edge of his chair, both hands on his knees, as if ready to leap to his feet.

'D'you like horses?' he said to Ash. 'We got wonderful horseback riding. Take a ride on horseback through the desert, you'll know what I'm talking about. By the way, how old d'you take me for, Mr Morgan?'

Ash thought him about seventy, but diplomatically took five years off.

'Seventy-eight,' he said. 'New York is full of memories for me. Some good, some bad. D'you like sports, Mr Morgan?'

'Ash is a lover.'

'Thank God, I'm past all that,' Marty Pearl said. 'Baseball, horses, and the fights. Old fighters are a weakness. I grew up a few blocks east of here, Rivington Street. Fighters were our heroes. I've seen them all, from Dempsey, Harry Greb, down to Louis and Robinson, and all the other great coloured fighters.'

'Tell me who was the best you ever saw,' Lemoyne said.

'Benny Leonard,' he said.

'You said that very fast,' Lemoyne said.

'Benny was the best,' Marty Pearl said. 'Benjamin Leiber, God rest his soul.'

'D'you say that just because he was a Jew-boy?' Lemoyne said.

'There's some of that in it,' Marty Pearl said. 'But Benny could've been a Chinaman, he was still the cleverest ever to lace on a glove.'

'If he was a Chinaman would you have paid a hundred dollars to see him fight?'

'I would,' he said, 'but only because I care for the sport of it.'

Marty Pearl said this with a heavy, self-conscious dignity, and abruptly stood up. 'Benny was a wonderful man, and there were others. Lindbergh, Lucky Lindy, Al Jolson, and in politics you had Al Smith and Roosevelt. FDR. He was a saint. Better times all around. But I'm an old man, and I can see I'm boring the pants off you gentlemen.' He held out his hand. 'A pleasure to have met you, Mr Morgan.'

'Please sit down and have a bite with us, Marty,' Lemoyne said.

'Another time,' he said. 'Come to Phoenix, I'll show you a good time.'

He walked to the other end of the restaurant and stood at the bar.

'Who is he?' Ash said.

'He was with Bugsy Siegel and Lepke when they ran the protection rackets in the garment centre,' Lemoyne said. 'The Lower East Side boys. Your Jewish gangsters. After the war, he set up in Dallas. He handled all the big southwestern loan-sharking. There's a story about Marty.' Lemoyne smiled and leaned closer to Ash. 'Jack Ruby owed him a hundred thousand dollars.' Lemoyne paused, still smiling, and then said, 'After Ruby shot Oswald, Marty tore up his marker.'

'Why did he do that?'

Lemoyne's smile grew wider. 'I never asked him. Patriotism, probably. Marty came here as a little kid. He was a newsboy. He never went to school and today he's a very rich man. He loves America.'

'So does the Senator,' Ash said. 'So does the Vice-President, you, and me. We all love America.'

'Sullivan, too,' Lemoyne said. 'He's crazy about America.'

'You wired his apartment today,' Ash said.

'You know that from Reese,' Lemoyne said. 'He talks too much, he really does.'

'Did you do a hot wire?'

'It's done,' Lemoyne said. 'Over, finished. You had nothing to do with it.' Lemoyne spoke soothingly. He understood Ash and was sympathetic; Ash had a conscience. Lemoyne had certainly heard of such things. He watched Ash's struggle from a distance, with a faintly condescending smile. Conscience was an impairment to the way one saw reality. But Ash was his friend, and Lemoyne would do what he could to ease him around a hard place.

'Sullivan has to be taken off,' he said. 'There's no other way.' He looked with imploring eyes at Ash, he spread his palms and asked him in the name of reason: 'You can see there's no other way, Ash. It's not personal. Nobody hates the guy. But they were getting ready to throw someone else to the wolves. It could've been you. It could've been me. Now we pin it on a dead man.' He glanced at his watch. 'And besides it could be over by now.'

'How was it done?'

'A thingamajig on the phone,' Lemoyne said. 'That's where the kid was so impressive. He knew just what he was doing. The thing is inside the receiver, about as big as a silver dollar. The phone rings, he picks it up, and boom. All he does is come home and get a call and that's it.'

Ash thought of Eleanor and then of his son. Murder separated him from them. He watched Marty Pearl squeeze himself into a phone booth next to the cloakroom at the head of the bar. He dialled a number and then began to speak into the receiver.

Lemoyne brought an envelope from the inside pocket of his jacket and laid it on the table in front of Ash. In it was the photograph he'd taken from under the shelf in the closet of Sullivan's apartment.

Ash studied it.

Lemoyne said, 'Did you know his family?'

'Sullivan never talked about them. Once, his brother. I had the feeling he was closest to him. We were in Washington and he went to Arlington to visit his grave.'

'Sullivan did?'

'Yes. There was that side of him.' Ash studied the photograph. All were dead but Sullivan and now they'd set him up. 'Why did you take it?' he said angrily. 'You're going to kill him, why d'you need a keepsake? You want a piece of him, is that it?'

Then Ash put the photograph in his pocket.

The front door of the restaurant opened and the Senator walked in. At almost the same instant Marty Pearl stepped out of the phone booth. With a gasp of surprise, they pounded each other on the back.

They chatted for a minute or two before the Senator walked across the room, waving to people and shaking hands, and finally joined Lemoyne and Ash.

The captain appeared at the Senator's elbow and took his order for a drink, the veal chop and a salad. The Senator was hungry, he'd just finished sparring with Jimmy Burke. He'd swum his dozen laps. His face bloomed with health and good spirits. He talked about sporting events, the pennant race in the National League, a fishing trip he planned to Alaska. He'd been reading a book about Harry Truman and he talked about that. He had one or two personal memories of the former President. Ash watched to see if any signal passed between the Senator and Lemoyne, any indication that he'd known in advance what had been done that afternoon in Sullivan's apartment.

No sign passed between the two men. Not a word was said. Lemoyne had acted on his own authority; the Senator, his interests served, had been protected from the beginning.

Lemoyne suddenly looked at his watch and, with a quick glance at Ash, excused himself to make a phone call.

Ash watched him through the glass door of the booth, taking change from his pocket, dialling a number.

The Senator said, 'There's a meeting in Washington next week. Roper's man is flying in for it. The Englishman, I forget his name.'

'Nugent.'

'Yes. I couldn't think of it for a minute. There was a girl I knew years ago named Maureen Woodstock. I was in law school in New Haven and she lived on Nugent Street. I'll think of her and then I'll remember the Englishman's name. I've trained myself to remember names that way, by association.'

Lemoyne dialled seven digits. Ash counted them; he watched him listening to the ringing of the phone on the other end.

The Senator said, 'Has Nugent called you?'

'I've been out of my office.'

'He'll want you there.'

Ash caught Lemoyne's eye; Ash knew he was calling Sullivan. He held the receiver several seconds longer before abruptly hanging up.

'What day next week?' Ash said.

'Tuesday. The Vice-President's office.'

Lemoyne returned to the table. A waiter brought the Senator's chop and salad, and the captain came by to be sure everything was just so. Lemoyne gave Ash no indication whether or not Sullivan had answered his phone.

CHAPTER FOURTEEN

Sullivan's mother collected china vases, urns, and miniature figurines. It was a passion of hers, begun in China in the early 1930s, when she'd gone out on her honeymoon with his father, who'd been military attaché.

Janice murmured something but he couldn't make out the words. She'd wakened him with her fingertips, her warm breath raising the hairs on his belly. They'd come back to his apartment, made love, and dropped off to sleep.

'Lie still,' she whispered. Now her long hair swept his genitals. He lay flat on his back and parted his legs. 'Don't move,' she murmured. 'Do nothing.'

The china figures were both animal and human. One he remembered in particular was an Oriental woman, a reclining nude, with a body of iridescent white, and red lips and hair lacquered black. A lascivious, beautifully detailed figurine; he'd run his fingers along the moulded belly, the tiny navel, the delicately raised triangle where the legs joined.

The piece had been broken. His mother was in tears, it was her favourite. His brother had broken it, although he'd denied it. Sullivan kept his secret, and was given the job of gluing it back together. He was known to be skilful with his hands and his mother had come to him, with tears in her eyes, like a child, to restore her precious figurine.

It had taken place on a rainy afternoon in December. He heard the rain tapping on the window of his room as he bent over his desk, the broken figure spread on a newspaper before him. He smelled the glue, his fingers sticky with it. With great patience, he fitted the pieces together and held them tenderly until the glue dried.

'You'll be a surgeon,' his mother said. When she leaned over his shoulder to admire the job he'd done, her hair brushed the back of his neck. She patted his cheek.

'You're a marvel,' she said. 'My marvellous boy.'

Janice brought him an exquisite, unendurable pleasure. The moment went on, he was tautly balanced on it, tottering, and then it gave way, rose up, and rushed from him with great force.

He dozed again. When he awoke, the room was dark. He saw a glow of street lamps through a crack in the bedroom curtain. Janice was awake, curled under his arm.

'I have a secret,' she said. 'A thing I know, a rare bit of knowledge. D'you know how it is with something true, you know it always, but then there comes a time when you say it to yourself?'

He knew just what she meant: one has all there is of truth early; later, one finds the words for it.

'It's about love,' she said. 'And so it's about you.'

He thought it was a game she was playing, that they were simply teasing and toying with each other after making love, but then he felt her tears on his skin, and he realized he'd underestimated her feelings, and his own, and the solemn, enduring intimacy of this moment.

'With love you're always close to tears,' she said.

'Tell me your secret.'

'I've had two lives, one as a child, loving my father and brother. Then a time with strangers. That meant nothing and seems never to have existed. And now I'm with you. I've come back again to the earliest life. I love you in the same way I love my father and brother.' She raised her head, her eyes glistening with tears. He tasted those tears and made her smile. 'I loved them,' she said. 'And the secret is that I feel for you, and do with you, what I didn't dare do with them.'

She lay under his arm, the soft full weight of her breast on his chest; he loved the tender life beating beside him, the smell of her hair and skin.

The telephone rang.

It jarred them both; in his arms, he felt her flinch.

The room quivered with the sound of the phone. It rang on and on. He held her tight and let it ring.

'It's one of my friends.' He put his finger over his lips and switched on the bedside radio, fiddling with the dial until he found something he liked. He listened a few seconds; it was a Brandenburg. He turned the volume up.

'I'd guess the phone has been bugged by now,' he said. 'The apartment as well.' He'd begun to whisper. 'We have plans to make.'

'Is everything we've said on tape? Roper, the President, or whoever, will they sit around and listen in on us?'

'Every word. Every dear sound.'

'I hate them!' she shouted above the concerto. 'Them and their damn fucking tape.'

'We're part of the library in Langley now,' he said. 'The permanent record. You and me and Bach. All immortal.'

'What can we do about it?' she said.

'We can eat dinner,' he said. 'A couple of large steaks, and a bottle of wine. Two bottles.' He climbed out of bed and began to dress. 'While I'm gone play the radio, use up their tape. But don't open the door and don't answer the phone.'

'I want to tell you about my father,' she said.

'Later.'

'We have so much to talk about.'

'And things for a salad.'

'Will it be all right?'

'There's nothing they can do,' he said. 'Two months from now we'll all be living in a large house on the beach. We'll need a boat. Boats are one thing my father taught me.'

'Bring some garlic and onions,' she said. 'There's a sauce I do for the steak.'

Just outside the front door of his house, from the top of the stairs leading to the street, Sullivan spotted the tail. A quick movement at the periphery of his vision, a figure stirring in the front seat of a car. Sullivan pretended to fumble with his keys. The car was a Volkswagen. Sullivan walked in the direction of Eighth Avenue; the tail hauled himself out of the tiny car and followed.

Next to the bodega, the butcher was still open. Sullivan bought two steaks and a pound of bacon. The tail waited in a doorway halfway down the block. He found a bottle of Rémy Martin in the small liquor store, and settled for a California wine since he found no French wine which he knew.

In the bodega he bought milk, eggs, butter and orange juice, things for salad, a hand of bananas. He took his time, picking boxes from the shelves, onions, garlic, and vegetables from the open bins. Finally, the tail passed, glanced in, and continued along Eighth Avenue.

He was young, with long fair hair and a wispy beard, inconspicuously dressed for the West Side of Manhattan:

jeans, sneakers, and a knit shirt, a small canvas bag slung over his shoulder. He might've been an actor, or a homosexual cruising. But Sullivan knew he was neither, somewhere he'd seen him, but couldn't quite place him. He made him a solo and a poor one. He wondered who it was had sent him such a lamb. He wondered, too, what might be in the canvas bag.

He gave the Colombian woman a twenty-dollar bill and smiled as she handed him his change.

She spoke to him in Spanish. 'How did you break your tooth?' she said.

'It happened when I took a big bite of a duck,' he said. 'There was something hard in it.'

'A lead pellet where it had been shot?'

'No, a pearl.'

'Pearls are in oysters, not in ducks.'

'This duck had eaten an oyster.'

'I like you, Frenchie,' she said. 'The world is full of men, but not many cockeyed enough to make a woman laugh. I'm going to close up now. Come upstairs with me and I'll give you a glass of something. Also you'll never break a tooth on any duck of mine.'

'Could it be another night?' he said. 'You're a beautiful woman, but I have business.'

'I saw the business you brought home,' she said.

'What else have you seen?'

'You're no sailor off a ship, Frenchie,' she said. 'Tell me what you are.'

'I just owe people money,' Sullivan said. 'Did you see the boy up the block, the one with the bag on his shoulder?'

'Him. And two others in a truck. Another came in here with a picture of you. He was a police.'

'You have a sharp eye.'

'It passes the time.'

Janice wore an old bathrobe of his and had gone to work straightening the apartment. She had made the bed and set the small table in the kitchen for dinner. He had only a few unmatched plates and dime-store cutlery, meagre things which had come with the apartment. Only now did Sullivan think of flowers and regretted that he'd brought none. He opened the brandy and the Californian wine and while she prepared dinner he went over the apartment. He did it unobtrusively, so as not to alarm her. He saw fresh scratches on the screws closing the telephone terminal box and concluded that a bug had been installed. It was best to ignore it. The furniture, closets, and drawers, everything was as he'd left it, but he could nevertheless feel that someone had been through his things. The back of his neck prickled. It was a sense he had. Only when he ran his hand under the bottom shelf in the closet and felt his gun, was he certain. The gun had been taken out and put back, and the family photograph was missing.

He sat on the bed and checked to see that the PPK hadn't been tampered with. He took the theft of the photograph to be a message. They wanted him to know they'd been through his things. They wanted him to know how easy it was to take the thing closest to him.

It was meant to warn him; he put the pistol in his belt, under his shirt.

Janice had managed to light the ancient broiler. She'd melted butter and rubbed fresh garlic on the steaks. She was washing the lettuce. He looked round at the mean little kitchen, the chipped crockery.

'We won't be living like this,' he said. 'There'll be money. I can provide for all of us. This apartment was a whim. One of my smaller eccentricities. We'll have peace and be comfortable.'

'Not one of those places where the rich live like lords and the poor beg in streets.'

'No beggars in the streets.'

'And a boat for you,' she said.

'Yes. I'd forgotten how much I'd enjoyed that. Once I went out on the Gulf Stream with my father and brother. We were out for a week, not seeing another soul. I thought we'd sail to the end of the world, and that not another soul existed. I still dream about it, the empty sea.'

'How old were you then?'

'Twelve. My brother was fourteen. And my father was about my age now.'

'Oh, my darling,' she said.

After they'd eaten and drunk the wine and some of the

cognac, and made love again, he told her that he would be leaving first thing in the morning. He needed to make certain arrangements.

'They may be getting desperate, scared, and a little reckless. We're going to have to run first and make the deal afterwards. I want to be out of America. That way the odds favour us.'

She sat up and poured out more of the brandy. 'Will they try to kill you?' she said.

'That would be stupid,' he said. 'They don't know what I've done with the goods, or what arrangements I've made for them to be taken public if I die. They're bunglers, but I don't think they're as stupid as all that.'

She looked at him thoughtfully a second or two and then said, 'Running is much harder for two than for one, isn't it?'

'I told you it can be done.'

'You've got me around your neck. My family, too. If I hadn't popped up you'd be long gone.'

'Without you I'd have no reason to go,' he said. 'And no place to go to.'

'I'm afraid of you,' she said. 'I know you killed the guard. I love you but –'

'But you don't know if you can trust me.'

He walked to the closet and took a blank envelope from the inside pocket of his jacket. In it was a signature card for a safe-deposit box.

'The box is in the name of Corbett. Mr and Mrs. The full name is printed on the top. You sign it and you'll have access. I'm going to get you a passport in that name.'

He removed a safe-deposit key from his ring and gave that to her. He kept one and returned the ring to his pocket.

'What's in the safe-deposit box?' she said.

'All they're looking for. My life insurance. If anything happens, it's yours.'

'A sign of trust.'

'It's all I've got.'

'My mother is going to ask questions. What're we doing in Greece? It's a long way to go with a crippled boy.'

'Tell her we're getting married there and they're invited to the wedding.'

'That'll persuade her,' she said. 'Me, too. I've always wanted to be married in Greece.'

And later he said, 'There's no need to fear the people on the other side. They're not as dangerous as they used to be, not nearly as skilful. First of all, there's too many of them, so they fall all over themselves.' He was feeling good, not in the least drunk from the wine and brandy. 'It's that the great war is over,' he said. 'The war between good and evil. Evil won. It was a good, tight game for a while, timely hits and fielding gems, a pitcher's battle. But now that it's over there's been a natural let-down in efficiency on the winning side.'

Towards morning, he told her what she must do. 'I'll be gone twenty-four hours, no more. You stay in the apartment. Don't answer the door or the phone unless it rings three times and stops. Then wait sixty seconds for it to ring twice and stop. When it rings after another sixty seconds, just lift it off the hook and drop it. Don't lift it to your ear. It'll be me. One hour after I call, you look for me in Grand Central station. I'll be on the OTB line.'

'Will I need other clothes?'

'We'll buy them on the way.'

'And my family?'

'You'll be able to contact them.'

A drab grey light came through the curtain. The room was cold. He sat on the edge of the bed, pulling on a sock. She moved under the covers until she was against his back.

'You can call it off,' he said.

'No. I want to be with you.'

'You'll only have to wait twenty-four hours,' he said.

She sank back on the bed, the sheets drawn up to her chin.

'I'm going to spend most of it asleep,' she said. 'When I wake up, I'll do my nails and my hair. Don't worry about me, I'll have a fine time.'

'Not quite yet,' he said. 'First you're to have your picture taken.'

He threaded the Pentax with a twenty-exposure roll of Tri-X Pan. He posed her between two lamps and quickly ran the complete roll, which he dropped in his pocket.

174

He put the PPK and the silencer along with a clean shirt and his shaving gear in an overnight bag, kissed her again, and was at the door when she ran after him wearing only a shirt of his. When he held her she felt small and fragile, and she had scrubbed her face, ridding it of the make-up she'd needed for the photographs. She seemed a child, and like a child she clung to him, anxious and afraid of being alone.

'You'll be safe,' he said. 'Morgan is running the show and he doesn't hurt little girls.'

'And you?'

'I'll be okay.'

'Go quickly,' she said and turned away from him.

It was a raw, cold rainy morning, and he put up the collar of his coat. He'd worn a hat. The early dog walkers were out, a bakery truck, a pair of old winos, sleeping together in a doorway, clinging to each other for warmth. He wrote the name and address of the bank on the envelope with the signature card and mailed it.

He'd walked two blocks and crossed Broadway, before he saw, reflected in the window of a Florsheim shoe store, the wispy beard and long fair hair of the tail he'd spotted the night before.

Sullivan continued uptown on Seventh Avenue, leading the tail into the lobby of the Hilton. He took an elevator to the seventh floor; there, he took a second car to the tenth floor. He had his room key in his pocket. He laid his shaving things out in the bathroom, rumpled the bed to make it look slept in, left the locked bag with the PPK and took the elevator to the lobby.

The tail was sitting in a chair near the coffee shop reading *The New York Times*.

Sullivan went straight up to him. 'D'you know what Nixon said when he first saw the Great Wall of China?'

'He said this is a great wall.'

'You think that was Nixon being funny?'

'I did at the time,' Sheffield said.

'It was Nixon being profound,' Sullivan said. 'We can talk over breakfast.'

They found a booth in the coffee shop. Sullivan ordered juice and coffee; Sheffield wanted pancakes and a double order of sausage.

'I had no dinner,' he said.

'Did you spend all night in the Volkswagen?'

'Most of it.'

'Who're you with?'

'Justice,' Sheffield said.

'You poor lamb.'

'With a very small private income.'

Sullivan drank his juice and said, 'You've a knowing smile, Sheffield. Tell me, what is it you know?'

'I've a hunch you're a man I can talk to. Of all of them, you're the one to understand.'

'You want to nail Roper? Is that it? Make a career exposing the sinister doings between Roper and the military brass, Senators, Congressmen, the Vice-President, maybe the President himself. They've all been conspiring for years to loot the country, duck their taxes, and steal the rest of us blind. Is that what you want?'

'That's the general idea.'

'It'd be a hell of a story, Sheffield.'

'Wouldn't it, though.'

'It'd make you famous.'

'I'm a different kind of blockhead,' Sheffield said. 'I'm not in this for fame.'

'For what then?'

'For truth,' Sheffield said. 'I'm queer for truth.'

Sullivan plucked Sheffield's arm and squeezed his bicep, which he found puny. He was near-sighted and anaemic, and either brave as a lion or a great fool.

'There's more to this than love of truth,' Sullivan said, gleefully. 'Come, don't be modest. You've a mission. You're out to save the country.'

'I said you were the one with the gift of understanding.'

'You won't let America slip down the drain.'

'Not Eddie Sheffield. Not while there's a breath in my body.'

'And that's why you're laying up in a Volkswagen across from my apartment?'

'To talk to you.'

'They're a powerful bunch. Big money's at stake. International reputations. You're menacing men of lofty principle and high honour. Great men, Sheffield, and you nothing more than a little Justice Department turd.'

'Why have you quit Roper?'

'Who says I have?'

'I do.'

The waitress brought breakfast. Sheffield peeled the paper from three pats of butter and spread it thickly on his pancakes. Then he drenched them with two jugs of syrup and cut the pancakes into bite-sized pieces before he began to eat. Sullivan watched him while sipping black coffee.

'You may have read of the robbery at Roper International,' Sheffield said with his mouth full. 'The story is that the burglar was surprised by a security guard. He killed the guard and took off without stealing a thing.'

'And you don't believe that?'

'I believe Roper's people think you had something to do with the burglary.'

'Why's that?'

'Because late yesterday afternoon they wired your place.'

The waitress refilled Sullivan's coffee cup. When she'd gone, he said, 'What school did you go to?'

'Yale.'

'And your father, how did he make his money?'

'Simulated leather. It was used on furniture and to cover the seats of automobiles.'

'D'you play tennis?'

'Nope.'

'Ski?'

'Whenever I have the chance.'

'Well, there you are.'

'Is it a game with you, Mr Sullivan? Your life doesn't mean a damn? What about the girl in your apartment? What about her life?'

'Tell me what you saw yesterday afternoon.'

'A man named Lemoyne. He's the Senator's financial aide and all-purpose scumbag.'

'He's not a wirer.'

'Two men went in. A third with a transceiver spotted from a parked car. The one who went in with Lemoyne was a little guy about twenty-five, wearing trick-or-treat clothes. Gold bangles around the neck and a face like a rat. A lot of hair. He carried one of those electricians' black boxes.'

The man who'd recruited Sullivan had known Molotov. Molotov never made a sound when he laughed and stammered when he spoke. For some reason Sullivan thought of that, and the afternoon twenty years before in Riverside Park, when he'd been invited to join the Agency.

He said, 'Tell me why wiring my place means the story they put out about the burglary is false.'

'If nothing was taken, then there's nothing to look for. They broke into your place to see what's there, to learn what you know.'

He'd been gobbling the pancakes while they spoke. He ate the last piece and mopped up the syrup left on his plate. When he'd finished, he lit a cigarette, flicking the ashes on the sticky plate, his feet up on the seat next to Sullivan.

'Let's talk frankly,' he said. 'That burglary at Roper International was your de-luxe model Langley special. Right out of the spook handbook. The guard had been dead a minimum of two hours when they found him. He was shot with a nine-millimetre automatic using a silencer. Whoever did it didn't panic and run off. He stayed and got what he came for.'

'And what is that?'

'Documentation. Proof of conspiracy. The kind of hard evidence that would hold up in court. My guess is it's big stuff. Shenanigans between Roper and the people at the very top.'

'And you want it for your day in court?'

'Our day in court.'

'It's you who's queer for the truth, Sheffield. Not me.'

'What about money? Insurance. Without it, they'll shoot your ass full of holes.'

Sullivan lifted the check and stood up. 'I'm going to buy you breakfast,' he said. 'Now don't try to follow me. I'm not where your truth is.'

'Will you help me?'

Sullivan shook his head. 'You've got the wrong man,' he said.

CHAPTER FIFTEEN

Sullivan occupied a window seat in the coach section of the American Airlines noon flight to San Francisco, drinking a small bottle of red wine with his lunch. After leaving Sheffield he'd been busy, first making sure he wasn't followed, and then there'd been a stop at the Nederlandsche Midden-standsbank, where he withdrew fifteen thousand dollars in cash, and then the hotel safe for the leather pouch with his British passport blank.

Now on the plane there was time to reflect and to run Sheffield's description of the wirer through his memory. Small, about twenty-five, trendy clothes, lots of hair, rat-faced. Sullivan sipped his wine. A stewardess took away his lunch tray and asked if he wanted to rent a headset for the sound-track of the in-flight movie. Robert Mitchum was playing a detective. Sullivan paid for the headset and asked if he might have another bottle of wine.

He had the name of the wirer: Elias.

He was one of the best, talented and ingenious, an outside party used by the Service here and in the Middle East. He was closer to thirty-five than twenty-five, but worked at looking younger. Elias liked young girls, was himself a former street urchin, a graduate of the Greek Cypriot assassination teams. He was a Jew, second-generation terrorist with a father who'd helped blow the King David Hotel for the Irgun. The mother had died in the holocaust, and when the British shot his father dead, Elias was shipped to Cyprus to live with an uncle. For a time he ran wild, living by his wits in the streets of Nicosia, until the Mossad, the Israeli Secret Service, plucked him from a youth detention camp and gave him a scholarship. Before he was twenty, he commanded the team which wired the Syrian Embassy in Athens. He was that clever. But there was too much of the wise urchin in him, he was too much the thief. He liked money. He was a showboat. The Israelis put a tail on him and found out he was moonlighting for the Di

Bennato Corsican syndicate. When the Mossad threw him out, he went straight to kill for pay. The Mossad hated him, and given the chance, they'd sever his right hand, one of their own gone sour.

For the rest of the flight, Sullivan watched the movie and sipped his wine. If they'd brought in Elias, it was to wire explosives. He weighed the possibility that they'd set out to kill him. It was stupid, an act of panic. It didn't sound like Ash, who knew more than that, who was better. But what if Ash were outside, what if they'd gone around him because he wasn't ready to have killing done for him by scum like Elias?

But Ash hadn't called him. Why was that? Had he in fact been left out, or hadn't he called because he was in on the killing?

A slow dread built in Sullivan. Before leaving Janice, he should have swept the apartment clean. He had a pang of self-doubt. He'd been outside for eight years and the technology moved fast. Elias could wire a bomb to an electric toothbrush or a light bulb. He prayed Janice would be safe, that she'd do just as he said. At any rate, there was nothing he could do now.

When the plane landed in San Francisco, he used a public telephone in the airport to call the British Consulate and was put through to his old pal Ruddy, who'd just returned from lunch.

It was three-twenty. Ruddy lunched long and well. He was known as an authority on food and wine, with special emphasis on the dishes of South-East Asia. Ruddy wrote and lectured on the subject, and from time to time appeared on television.

On the phone, Sullivan impersonated an old friend passing through town between planes. Mention was made of an extended world tour. Quite impossible to touch down without a peck on the cheek.

Ruddy picked up on that; he wouldn't let an old dear friend pass through without a drink.

'Nothing exotic,' Sullivan said. 'It has to be tea. Green tea.'

Ruddy understood. Green tea had changed hands before, in Saigon; but things had changed.

'Your brand has become terribly hard to come by,' Ruddy said.

'I count on you to manage.'

'And on such short notice.'

'Why not take a couple of hours to put things together?' Sullivan said. 'Say around six.'

Ruddy naturally insisted on setting the place. 'Joseph's, on Taylor Street,' he said.

That gave Sullivan time to drop in on Loo Sim, who lived at the bottom of an alley off Grant Street, two floors above an importer of bric-à-brac from mainland China. The importer was a niece of old Loo Sim, related by blood or tradition, perhaps mistress or merely business partner.

Loo Sim was seventy, but had been seventy for as long as Sullivan had dealt with him, now more than a decade. He was ageless, like imperial jade, a stocky yellow-brown man in carpet slippers, with two gold teeth and a cigarette dangling always between his lips. He spoke English well enough, although with a singsong Cantonese accent. He was an artist and engraver, a collector of classic Chinese pornography, and one of the three or four best forgers in North America.

From his leather envelope Sullivan took the blank British passport and the roll of undeveloped film, the photographs he'd taken of Janice earlier in his apartment.

'I'm sorry to have come without first giving you greater notice,' Sullivan said. 'It's a great discourtesy.'

'You're not a discourteous man, Sullivan,' Loo Sim said. 'Therefore, there must be good reason.'

'There is, but I won't burden you with it,' Sullivan said. 'I need to have something made at once.'

'I'm very busy.'

'A few hours of your time.'

'There are others.'

'Not with your skill.'

'That parchment you brought me,' Loo Sim said. 'The one with the swan. Where did you get that?'

'From a friend.'

'You are a devil, Sullivan.'

'Two British passports. I will pay fifteen hundred dollars each.'

'My mother has died,' Loo Sim said. 'I only heard from Hong Kong last week.'

'She must've been very old.'

'Oh, very old. Yes, remarkably old.'

Sullivan said, 'Thirty-five hundred for the two.'

'But only one is here.'

'I'm going for the other. In the meantime, you begin. Develop the film. The name on both will be Corbett. Husband and wife. Woman, Maria Porter. Born London, May third, nineteen fifty. I shall be Richard Howard. Manchester, born nineteen thirty-four.'

Loo Sim had written it all down. 'What date of issue?'

'Fourteen months back, that way you'll have no problem with the serial numbers.'

'Never a problem with numbers on British passports. But date and place of entry to States?'

'New York, two months ago. Zurich before that. The Corbetts are skiers. If you've West German entrance and exit, use that. The Scandinavian countries as well. It's always best to weather a passport.'

Loo Sim demanded a thousand dollars before he'd begin and Sullivan paid him in cash. The old Chinese went into his darkroom to develop the film, and Sullivan left to keep his appointment with Ruddy.

Joseph's was an authentic saloon, which might well have survived the earthquake. The proprietor was a former boxer, now a promoter and manager of boxers with a vast collection of old boxing films which were screened by request on the rear wall of the place.

There were a dozen or so people at the bar when Sullivan arrived. Ruddy was alone in a booth, drinking a Whitbread ale from the tap, Willard and Jack Johnson flickering on the wall behind him.

He was several inches above six feet tall with a soft round face and a mane of silver hair worn long. The kind of man to seek out restaurants that flew turbot from France and served Whitbread draught. He was sure to have grown fatter and more red-faced each time one saw him; a glib, flamboyant man, he wore a blue shirt with a white collar and cuffs and a flowing mauve tie.

He began by telling Sullivan about the hotel he'd bought

and was remodelling in Sardinia, planning his retirement from the British Foreign Service, and produced a four-colour brochure printed on slick paper. 'It's actually a series of small villas,' he said. 'Much better than one great building. Each quite independent, with its own kitchen and patio, since in Sardinia one eats alfresco ten months of the year. The pool is Gunite, ninety thousand gallons, and costs the absolute earth. Two tennis courts and next year your cohabitational sauna for the gay young crowd.'

'And you the perfect patron,' Sullivan said. 'Whitehall accent and chequered past. We'll gown you in white, espadrilles against a tanned foot, and perhaps a touch of your favourite mauve at the throat.'

'I shall be splendid.'

'Yes, you shall.'

'You are the most sympathetic man I have ever known.' Ruddy spoke with great feeling. 'To be perfect you needed only to have been born homosexual.'

Sullivan appeared moved, and said, 'Have the start-up costs in Sardinia left you on the balls of your ass?'

'Dump cost a bloody fortune.'

'Bit off more than you can chew?'

Ruddy shrugged. 'I have always thought on the grand scale.'

'So you need money?'

'I shall have to charge you seventy-five hundred dollars.'

'Is it like the other one?'

'Direct from Her Majesty's Printing Office. Good as gold, not a mark. *Tabula rasa*, love. Do with it as you will.'

'I can give you six.'

'I'd ask why you need the second one, but I suppose it's none of my business.'

'No, it's not.'

'I think of you as a friend. Truly, I do. I'm a sentimental old queen. Seven and you've a deal.'

'We'll do it at six thousand seven hundred and fifty,' Sullivan said.

'Of course we will,' Ruddy said.

Sullivan left Ruddy at the table and went to the men's room, where he counted the money and wrapped it in a paper towel. When he returned to the table, Ruddy had ordered fresh glasses of ale.

Sullivan gave him the money and Ruddy handed him the British passport blank in a manila envelope. No one in the bar noticed; Willard had just knocked down Johnson, who lay on his back and seemed to be shielding his eyes from the Havana sun.

'I hope you've time for another drink,' Ruddy said.

'Another time.'

'Perhaps in Sardinia,' Ruddy said. 'It's a discreet place. I expect a few old friends will drop in from time to time. Those of us who haven't yet drunk ourselves to death all seem to be retiring at the same time. Our generation –' He left his sentence unfinished, drank off half his ale. 'I don't get to keep the money,' he said. 'Not all of it. It's rotten. I've never liked it, not really. When I began in the Service, I expected something better.'

Sullivan put the blank passport in his pocket.

'Thirty years ago next March,' Ruddy said. 'Stars in my eyes, the bloom still on the rose, I knew nothing of corruption in high places. Mum never told me. Sullivan, I truly thought it was a better government I served.'

'You'll be happy in Sardinia.'

'D'you think so? I've made a million friends, you know. I won't be lonely.'

'You're a good queen.' Sullivan patted Ruddy's large pink hand.

'God knows I've tried hard,' he said. 'And I'm sorry to soak you for the passport. My end is the same, it's the big cheeses want more. Greed. It's all greed. I'll bet there's a share goes straight to the bloody Queen.'

'She's a good Queen, too,' Sullivan said.

'I expect she does the best she can.'

Sullivan drank the last of his ale.

'Stay and have another,' Ruddy said.

'I'm afraid I've got to be going.'

'You watch yourself,' Ruddy said. 'I don't want to hear bad news. You're the old school, chum. I don't hold it against you that you're not queer. D'you believe that, Jack?'

'Of course I do.'

'I'm not one of those who want everyone on their side of the aisle.'

'I'll come and see you in Sardinia,' Sullivan said.

'You do it,' Ruddy said. 'I'll take care of you. I swear I will. If you've a friend, bring her. I'll see you'll be able to take your shoes off.'

After he left Ruddy, Sullivan found an all-night barber shop where he had his hair cropped close and dyed black. On his way to Loo Sim's, he stopped at a pharmacy and bought a tube of Estée Lauder's Go Bronze.

By the time he arrived at Grant Street, Loo Sim had finished Janice's passport. Sullivan darkened his skin with the Estée Lauder and put on brown contact lenses to change his eyes for the black-and-white passport photograph for which the Chinese used an early-model Polaroid camera.

He worked on the second passport for the better part of two hours, but when he'd finished it was perfect. Sullivan now had two undetectable and untraceable British passports. He paid Loo Sim the remaining twenty-five hundred dollars, and after a light meal of shrimp grilled with ginger and a plate of sautéed pea pods, he went by taxi to the airport. He was in time for the TWA midnight flight to New York.

In the first twenty hours that Janice was alone in the apartment the phone rang four times. She followed Sullivan's instructions and never answered. The last time it rang once, stopped, and after an interval of just over a minute, rang again. It was deep into the night, she'd been reading and dozed off with the book open on her chest. But with the first ring she was instantly awake, her heart pounding, certain it was, at last, Sullivan calling. She actually felt his presence, joined to her by the telephone line.

The phone rang again. And then the tiny bedroom was unnaturally still and she felt a fleeting second of panic, of confusion in which ghostly dreams whirled around her head until the phone rang again, shattering the silence.

The ringing continued. Sullivan said he would ring and disconnect twice. She was to pick up only on the first ring of the third series. This was not his signal. She knew to follow his instructions precisely, to do just as he said; he would make no mistakes, and she must make none.

She must trust him, and she did, absolutely, without second thoughts.

The phone continued to ring, eight, nine, ten times; she was careful to count the rings. She had a sense of an angry and frustrated caller. The ringing went on. She felt herself engaged in a battle of wills with the person on the other end of the line. Finally, she used a pillow to close her ears to the ringing. Eventually, it stopped.

Sleep was impossible. She lay awake in the shallow light from the bedside lamp, the book open on her chest, and gazing vacantly into the shadows at the corners of the room, drifted in the ebb and flow of memory, and dreamed what life would be for her brother and mother, and for her and Sullivan on the island he would find for them.

Her love for Sullivan was a miracle. That she'd permitted herself to be swept away by it astonished her. There'd been men she'd wanted. Loves undertaken for pleasure, for curiosity, for the way the hair grew at the back of the neck, for a mournful expression around the eyes, for whim or exuberance, for old times.

But she'd surrendered to no one. Perhaps she'd loved no one. Even in rapture something was held back, some tattered scrap of consciousness, of identity, of calculation. She had habitually contrived to turn even rapture to advantage.

But not with Sullivan. He was, surely, different. He was her love, certainly the first, perhaps the last of her life. As she'd always held back, now she wanted only to yield, to surrender again in love that last scrap of identity. She'd known that ecstasy and there was no turning back. Love had come upon her as an absolute. She vibrated to the idea, was thrilled to discover this talent, and could barely believe herself capable of it. She remembered falling into the water as a child and discovering she could swim. That was also miraculous, an achievement quite beyond self-esteem or simple happiness. Now she discovered that she could love, and that, too, was a miracle.

Eventually, she got out of bed, and looking for a way to pass the time, decided to cook something elaborate. She carried the radio to the kitchen and found an FM station playing something romantic and rather lilting. She thought it was Tchaikovsky, but wasn't sure.

She had a look inside the refrigerator and then emptied the cabinets until she found what she needed to bake a cake. She wondered if she might bring it with her when she went to meet Sullivan. It amused her to think that she would be the first to go underground carrying a cake.

She turned up the volume of the radio. It was still an hour or two before dawn. She mixed the flour and milk and broke half a dozen eggs, melted the butter and was soon absorbed in the music and mixing the batter.

Sullivan slept for most of the flight and was awakened only when the 707 began its descent and banked into the approach to Kennedy Airport.

But he'd slept fitfully, his legs cramped in the coach seat, aware of snatches of conversation, the passage of stewardesses along the aisle, the odour of painted plastic.

The 707 landed with a little jolt and taxied slowly to a gate at the southern end of the field. He used the lavatory to wash the sleep from his face and contrived to be the last passenger out of the plane. He walked alone through the covered mobile ramp, confident that his arrival was unobserved. He carried his bag and hailed a cab from the line waiting at the Arrivals building. The sky had just begun to lighten and the traffic built slowly along the expressway and on the approaches to the city. He switched cabs at the East Side Terminal. It was morning when he pulled up at the Hilton.

He went first to the hotel safe and carried the contents of his box to his room, where he locked the door and spread everything on the bed and took careful inventory: the two British passports in the name of Corbett – he was satisfied with these. They were untraceable, a fresh identity to be found on no list. His Swiss bankbook showed a balance of one hundred and twenty-two thousand Swiss francs. Another sixty-three hundred dollars in cash. The PPK and silencer.

He packed all of it in his attaché case, locked it, undressed, and stepped into the shower.

He'd call Janice only after he'd showered and shaved. He was anxious to call, to assure her that all had gone well, that within an hour they'd be on their way. It was, however, much like him to delay certain pleasures once they were in his grasp.

As he relaxed under the hot spray, he decided that they'd

not fly out of Kennedy. He'd rent a car and drive to New Orleans. He knew people in one or another end of the profession who shipped in and out of New Orleans and Galveston. He thought they'd ease their way slowly by boat to South America. Roper and the rest of them could wait, and wonder what his next move would be. South America suited him. He knew people who had retired to Ecuador, Venezuela and Peru. He'd always liked Peru. Lima was a good city: although the climate wasn't the best, it would be fine for a few weeks. Cuzco was a fascinating place.

He finished his shower and wrapped himself in a large yellow towel. He shaved slowly, with great care, enjoying the scent of the cream and the lotion he splashed afterwards on his face. Although he'd slept poorly, he wasn't at all tired. He was eager and energetic. For the first time in years he looked forward to the future.

It was time to telephone Janice. She'd like Cuzco. It was a fascinating place, the ancient dead city of the Inca.

The first ring startled Janice. She had put the cake in the oven, packed the things she'd worn, and dressed in those Sullivan had bought her, and was making coffee when it rang.

She held her breath waiting for the second ring, then the third. After a minute of silence it rang again twice. Now she was certain it was Sullivan. The final-minute interval seemed to go on forever. She mentally counted the seconds.

Her thoughts came in a rush. Vivid pictures of people and places: her brother and mother; an apple orchard seen through the dormitory window of a school to which she'd been sent as a child. Her father. A friend with whom she'd shared a tiny apartment in Los Angeles. Such a dear friend, she'd married and named her first daughter Janice.

The sixty seconds passed. A moment or two and the phone rang again, the third in the series of three. As she reached to lift the receiver, certain it was Sullivan, relieved that he was safe, Janice was happy.

CHAPTER SIXTEEN

Ash was told it wasn't a farewell lunch. He wasn't to think of it in such terms. Eleanor insisted. Farewells were sad and their lunch must be gay.

'What will we call it?' he said.

'We'll call it lunch, darling.' Since she'd bought the airline tickets for Hong Kong, nearly every remark was made to end with an endearment.

'Pass the butter, darling.' She called him darling, just as one cuddled an old pet on the last drive to the veterinarian to be gassed. But even as he said it to himself, he knew it wasn't being fair. It was just her way of being decent, of being civilized and kind. That was the way they played in her world. There were rules for the way in which a love affair ended. There was an etiquette. Alan Bedford would know how it was done. He could be depended on to act exquisitely. Hadn't he sent a case of Taittinger to the stateroom of a famous model when she sailed on the *QE II* with another man?

'I wonder if he was right to have sent champagne,' Ash said.

'The man was thirty years older,' Eleanor said. 'I told Alan to send a backgammon set.'

'He should've just kept his big nose out of it,' Ash said.

'Send nothing? That would've been equivocal. If he'd sent nothing, they'd never have known what he felt.'

'They might even have forgotten about him,' Ash said. 'But old lovers don't want to be forgotten. Particularly Alan, whose life's work is to build his own legend. The Oscar Wilde of the jewellery business. I can hear it now: when Alan Bedford's mistress left him for an ageing certified public accountant with the North American distribution rights for Loch Ness Scotch Whisky –'

'You're drunk,' she said.

'I am in a pig's eye.'

'You're ruining our lunch.'

'Pass the butter, darling. In the name of God, pass the fucking butter.'

'I'm going to walk out,' she said.

But just then one of the captains brought an ice bucket, carrying it in front of his chest between both hands, like a basketball. The slender green neck of a bottle of Dom Pérignon rose from the icy water. Both watched the captain twirl the bottle, lift it dripping from the bucket and lay it in a napkin before twisting off the cork as though wringing the neck of a chicken.

In spite of the fanfare, it was delicious. 'With the exception of freshly squeezed orange juice, champagne is the finest cold drink on the face of the earth,' Ash said.

'You taught me to mix the two for breakfast,' she said. 'That was something, those three days in Monte Carlo.' They clicked glasses and drank to good times.

'What shall we call this lunch?' he said.

'Why call it anything? As Tarzan called his son simply Boy, we'll call this simply lunch.'

'I like bon voyage,' he said. 'It's gay.' Lutèce was the place they chose when there was something to celebrate. 'A hundred-dollar lunch needs a proper name.'

'You're a great sport,' she said. 'Connoisseur of food and wine, and a superlative lover.'

'You've said that before,' he said. 'Once more and I'll begin to doubt it.'

'Once more, darling,' she said, 'and I'll never leave.'

'I owe it to you,' he said. 'You've civilized me. Food, wine and foreign movies. A gracious and generous view of life. More than my mother, you've made me what I am today.'

'What about the superlative-lover part?'

He paused, took her hand, and then said solemnly, 'There is not one second of our many intimacies that I will ever forget.'

'Not one second?'

'No.'

'Not the time with the aerosol shaving-cream can in the shower of our room in the Dorchester?'

'Without the clowning,' he said. 'You can call this a

bon-voyage party, call it anything, but the truth is, it's goodbye.'

'You're going to ruin everything,' she said. 'Why not keep it gay? A celebration. I've a great new job. Hong Kong is a fascinating and exciting city. Darling, I want this to be a happy lunch.'

'You want me and you want Hong Kong. You want love and you want freedom. You want too damn much.'

'Don't be angry,' she said. 'I thought you understood my taking the job. You knew from the beginning I was ambitious. You've nothing to be angry about.' Her eyes were misty, but she fought to hold back the tears. 'I've been straight with you. I've been faithful. I know what you think about me and Alan, but it's not true.'

'I never asked you about Alan,' he said.

'You didn't have to.'

'The point is – I never did.'

'And you never would,' she said. 'They could break you on the rack, you wouldn't say a word. But I've seen that look in your eyes. That cop's look. I know what you've been thinking and it's not true.' She dug in her bag for a pair of dark glasses, which she put on to hide the tears. 'Why not pack up and get out?' she said. 'You hate Roper and the rest of them. You told me so. After what they did to Sullivan's girl, tried to kill her.'

'It was Sullivan they tried to kill.'

'What's the difference? It's the girl who's in the hospital.'

'It's not for Roper that I'm staying here,' he said. 'Not for my job or the money. I just won't trot after you to Hong Kong. I won't do that.'

'It's your pride,' she said. 'Stupid, rock-hearted pride. You'll break both our hearts, make us both miserable, and for nothing.'

'What about your pride?' he said. 'So damn tough and independent. Well, be independent. Be tough.'

'Don't beat up on me, Ash,' she said. 'You know how it was with me. Ambition and having to prove myself and all the rest of it. The chip on the shoulder. My mother one place, father another. Bloody half-breed wog. I've never whined about it, have I? But I did tell you. I opened up to

191

you, and you did the same to me. Were we truthful to each other?'

'We were.'

'And we did love each other, didn't we?'

'We still do.'

'Then why are we throwing it away?'

'We don't have to. My wife's illness is incurable. I can divorce her and we can get married. All you have to do is give up Hong Kong.'

'We don't have to get married,' she said.

'It wouldn't make any difference.'

'It would to me. You want me bound hand and foot.' She was able to mimic him, the way he walked, and now the way he spoke. 'Boys, I want you to meet the little woman. The better half.'

'Sensational,' he said. 'I've never heard a better Howard Cosell.'

'The little lady. The missus. Oh, Ash, darling, shit in your hat.'

It was just past two-thirty when they finished lunch. Her plane left at four, but her bags were already locked in the trunk of Ash's car. He drove her to the airport, parked his car in the public lot, and stayed with her while she checked in and had her baggage ticketed. He brought her an armful of magazines and they sat together until it was time for her to board.

'I want to be with you,' she said. 'There's no one else.'

He felt his throat tighten, but that passed. There was another moment in which he wanted her to go, for this to be over. He saw himself in their empty apartment, walking from room to room and turning on the lights, a can of beer in his hand.

'There's nothing final in this,' he said.

'I just want to try Hong Kong,' she said. 'It's not over with us.'

'Of course not,' he said. 'Nothing like this ever ends.'

He left her when she joined the boarding line and walked quickly out of the terminal. He might miss her later, and even panic and chase after her to Hong Kong, but it didn't seem so to him at that moment. He couldn't separate or identify his feelings. As a boy he'd been hit on the forehead by a baseball, and he now felt much of the same painless distance from the scene around him. But he was relieved to have her gone. He loved her, and he was glad to be alone. He was a man; he thought of all that was possible for him.

He had to look for his car in the airport parking lot. He'd locked it, and it took a few seconds before he found his key and opened the door. He'd just started the engine when he felt the muzzle of the pistol against the base of his skull.

It took him several seconds to recognize the face reflected in the rear-view mirror.

'What've you done to yourself?' Ash said. 'I could've passed you in the street without knowing you.'

Sullivan increased the pressure of the pistol.

'Were you with them, Ash?'

'No.'

'Were you asked?'

'Yes.'

'Then you knew about it.'

'I was told about it only after it was done. I was against it from the beginning. It was stupid.'

The pressure let up. 'Turn off the ignition and open the front passenger door. Use the automatic lock release.'

Sullivan went around to the front and climbed in beside Ash, the pistol under his coat pointed at Ash.

'I've been watching you,' Sullivan said. 'You and your woman. Is it over between you?'

'I don't know.'

'How old are you, Ash?'

'Fifty-three in July.'

'You carry it well.'

'It's still fifty-three.'

'We'll drive back together.'

Ash started the car and followed the exit signs to the pay booth. Ash said, 'I have to reach in my inside pocket for the parking card.' He handed the card and a dollar to the attendant; the electrically operated wooden barricade lowered and they drove through the airport in the direction of the Van Wyck Expressway.

'The hospital report is that Janice's condition is fair,' Sullivan said. 'What does that mean?'

'That she'll recover. There were fragments in her arm and shoulder. They had to remove them surgically, but that went well. There were no bones broken, no muscle damage. But there was severe concussion. At the moment there's eighty-per-cent loss of hearing in the right ear. That's temporary. The worst is the shock.'

'Is she disfigured?'

'No.'

'Take the Queensboro Bridge. I'll get off at the other end.'

'I've told them to give you what you've asked for,' Ash said. 'I've told them it's the only way.'

'They have to throw someone else to the wolves.'

'They'll find someone,' Ash said. 'You leave that to them.'

'Did you know the wirer?' Sullivan said.

'No.'

'His name is Elias.'

'What're you going to do?'

'There were two of them,' Sullivan said. 'Lemoyne was the other.'

'If you love the girl, wait for her to come around, and then go.'

'Is that what you'd do?'

'Of course I would. It's the only thing to do.'

'Tell them not to bother looking for me or the goods. I'll kill whoever comes, and the goods are where they can't touch them. You tell them I have the originals. No copies, nothing they can fudge in court. The paper is the right age, so's the ink. By the balls, Ash. Tell them that.'

'Are your terms the same?'

'The same, and I'm taking her with me,' Sullivan said. 'How soon before she can be moved?'

'Four, five days. Maybe a week.'

'The KLM flight to Amsterdam. One week from today. You bring her to the airport. Bring the money. And come alone. I'll meet you at the KLM desk.'

'I'll be there,' Ash said. 'Just the girl and me.'

CHAPTER SEVENTEEN

To find Elias, Sullivan went to see a man named Severo Freire, who owned a small electric-appliance repair shop on the Upper West Side of Manhattan. Freire was a Cuban, first under contract to the Agency during the Batista regime in the early 1950s. He'd been used to penetrate the July Twenty-sixth Movement, a clandestine terrorist group, which supported the revolution against Batista from the cities while Fidel Castro was still in the Sierra Maestra. Freire left Cuba in 1960, settled for a time in Miami, where he recruited anti-Castro refugees to train in amphibious landing and assault techniques in Guatemala. He returned to Cuba with Assault Brigade 2506 at the landing on the Bay of Pigs. He lost a leg there, spent six months in prison on the Isle of Pines before being ransomed with the other survivors.

The Agency rewarded him with seven thousand dollars in back pay and severance, an artificial leg, and one hundred dollars a month for life. He was now nearly sixty years old, a bitter, ill, and crippled old man, who despised the United States Government even more than he did Fidel Castro.

His shop was used by most of the wirers operating in the North-east and it was there that Sullivan went seeking information on Elias, knowing that Freire would help if he could.

Sullivan had helped the older man when the Agency had cut him loose.

The men of Brigade 2506 had been betrayed by the United States Government, which had kept none of the promises made to them, and their disappointment and fury were turned against the Agency. Freire, who was known to be an agent, was treated as a traitor by the men he'd recruited. None of his fellow prisoners would speak to him. For four months he ate alone and barely spoke a word, a skeleton of a man with one leg, sick and weak with dysentery. Only he knew that he'd acted in good faith, that the Americans had betrayed him as surely as the others. The support which had been promised never came. In the end the Americans lost their nerve. The mighty American Air Force and Navy stayed in Florida. The 2506th Brigade was left to die on the beach. It was shameful.

Freire kept silent. He never asked for a hearing with the prisoner courts, never sought out the leaders to explain that he had also been duped, that the Americans had welched and that he'd been double-crossed with the rest. He was a stubborn man, intensely proud. He'd always been a secretive sort, and perhaps he was convinced he'd not be believed.

As for the Agency, it merely paid him off and tossed him out. After the Bay of Pigs they had no use for him. The whole affair had been a fiasco and he had become an embarrassment. His own people hated him and he became one of those people without a place to stand.

He was a tough old man, not one to sell himself or take his own life. If he despaired no one knew of it. He simply had his monthly cheque mailed to a PO box and dropped out of sight.

Sullivan, of course, knew the truth, knew how shabbily Freire had been treated; he had traced him through the PO box and gone to see him. He lived in a slum in San Juan, in a tiny room with a bed and desk. There was no electricity or running water. He cooked his meals over a can of Sterno. Stacks of books in Spanish and English spilled over the desk on to the floor. The tiny room was filled with books and old newspapers. He seemed to be writing a book of his own on an ancient Underwood typewriter. Sullivan saw a pile of manuscript a foot high. Freire went around with half a dozen ball-point pens clipped to the breast pocket of his shirt and his pockets stuffed with scraps of paper on which he was always scribbling notes.

He still suffered from the dysentery. Sullivan had paid a doctor to treat him. He had felt an obligation to this solitary old man and tried to help him. At first Freire would accept no favours and barely spoke.

One day Sullivan brought something he knew Freire wanted, something he would accept. In a plain white envelope he brought copies of high-level cables from the White House refusing air and naval cover to the 2506th; he brought proof that the administration had double-crossed the Agency as well as the 2506th. These cables vindicated Freire.

From then on they talked openly. They were alike in some ways and understood each other. For all his toughness, Freire was relieved to have someone with whom he could talk freely, someone who knew he'd dealt honestly with his own people and had not betrayed them.

Sullivan persuaded him to leave Puerto Rico and settle in New York. The seven thousand dollars the Agency had given him was long gone; Sullivan loaned him the money to open the electric-appliance repair shop.

It was a friendship, but an odd one; Freire had spent his life underground and had lost the habit of self-revelation. Perhaps he never had it, and chose his profession accordingly. At any rate, he never showed the cables to another soul and never let on what it was he was writing.

Sullivan asked Freire about Elias.

'What d'you want with him?' the older man said. 'Is it for the Agency?'

'No. It's personal.'

'I'd heard you weren't with them any more. But who knows?'

'I'm not with anybody. Like yourself, a solitary.'

'So is he. A cocaine user. I believe he chews it, like an Indian.' Freire made a face. 'Peacock clothes and cocaine. Every day the profession grows more repulsive. Are you hunting him?'

'You've become nosy in your old age.' Sullivan laughed when he said it, so as not to offend Freire and show him that he didn't mind his questions.

'He's a customer of mine,' Freire said. 'Cordite, tungsten. Also high-quality copper wire, tripping mechanisms. He does it all from scratch.' He unlocked a drawer of a steel desk and thumbed through a small loose-leaf book. 'He rents a loft and garage on Tenth Avenue.' Then he read the address to Sullivan. 'Will anyone be by to ask if I've seen you?'

'They may. I doubt it.'

'Be assured I'll answer none of their questions,' Freire said.

Later the same day Sullivan went to the address on Tenth Avenue given him by Freire. It was a corner building made of red bricks which looked to have been recently steam-cleaned. A small garage and body shop was on street level with four floors of lofts above it. There were no commercial signs and no names of any kind on the mailboxes. Sullivan looked inside the garage, which seemed deserted. Yet it was well organized and equipped. Whoever ran the place made a speciality of vintage English cars. Sullivan saw a Morgan, an MG-TD, and an E-Model Jaguar up on blocks, a right-hand drive Bentley, and even a pre-war Riley. Hidden away in a bay at the rear of the garage, behind a Rover in the last stages of cannibalization, was a blue Ford panel van, the very thing Sheffield had claimed to have seen when he'd staked out Sullivan's apartment.

Just then Sullivan heard a heavy footstep, and turned quickly around.

'You looking for something, fella?'

He was a squat, brown man in stained coveralls, a heavy double-head wrench worn through a loop on his hip and against his leg like a side arm. He had a lot of black curly hair, a full moustache, and a milky left eye, which went off at an angle and looked to be made of glass. He stood bent slightly forward at the waist, balanced on the balls of his feet, ready to throw a punch, a mean short-armed bruiser with murder in his good eye.

Sullivan moved slightly to the bruiser's right, in the direction of the blind eye, and felt the PPK in the holster under his left arm. The silencer was already fitted to it; this was a hitter and a brawl was out of the question.

'I'm a collector.' Sullivan could speak good Cambridge la-de-da. 'I was wondering if any of these cars were for sale.'

'I don't own them,' the bruiser said. 'I just do body work on them.'

'That MG-TD is a nice piece of work. Lovely restoration. I'd be interested in that.'

'It's not for sale.'

'I'm in the market for a panel van as well,' Sullivan said. 'Something like that. Possibly you know the owner?'

'It's closing time,' the bruiser said.

Sullivan showed him a fine dim-witted smile, and started to have a look at the plate number of the van. But the bruiser caught him by the arm, and Sullivan let himself be shown the door.

From a candy store across the street he bought a news-paper. There was a diner two doors farther along, and from the counter he was able to watch the garage and the door to the stairway which led to the lofts above it. He drank coffee and opened the paper. He dawdled over a second cup and then ordered scrambled eggs to justify his time at the counter. But then his luck turned; the eggs were still hot when the door to the building opened and Elias came out. He stopped briefly at the entrance to the garage and spoke briefly to the bruiser with the wrench. Both glanced in the direction of the diner. The bruiser went back to the garage and Elias swaggered across Tenth Avenue alone, a dapper figure in a short leather jacket. At the corner he hesitated, made a show of patting his pockets as if looking for some-thing, and then walked directly into the diner. Sullivan ate his eggs and read his paper.

Elias changed a dollar with the counterman, used the vending machine to buy a pack of cigarettes, had a good look at Sullivan and went out.

Sullivan finished his eggs, paid for them, and went after Elias without waiting for his change. He was fairly sure he'd not been recognized, but was obliged to follow Elias at a distance.

Elias went first to the post office in Rockefeller Center, where he had a letter registered, and then had his photo-graph taken in a shop on the arcade below the US Passport Office.

He walked north on Fifth Avenue as far as Fifty-ninth Street. There, he turned east, and Sullivan followed him into Bloomingdale's. It was Thursday, a late night for de-partment stores, and the place was jammed. Sullivan found it easy to keep several dozen people between himself and Elias.

Elias wandered through the street floor from west to east, pausing first at the men's toiletries bar. He sampled several brands of cologne, spraying his wrist from the sample atomizers on the counter. He spoke briefly to a salesman, and when the fellow turned his back, Sullivan watched Elias slip a silver tube of something in his pocket. It was sleight of hand, quick as a magician. Security could've stood next to him and not seen it.

He walked away from the toiletries bar without making a purchase and continued to the east end of the store, where he rode the escalator to the basement. Here were clothes of the latest style, leather jackets and denim trousers. Rock music blared over a public-address system as if at a party or disco. Elias joined half a dozen others – slender young men for the most part – picking over a heap of prewashed jeans thrown on a table.

At last he found a pair his size, held them against his waist, and carried them in the direction of the fitting rooms.

Sullivan picked a pair at random from the same pile and followed him. The fitting rooms were a series of cubicles, each with a brightly painted swinging door, some red and others bright yellow, none with a lock.

Sullivan paused before the one Elias had entered, and with his back to the room, swiftly drew the PPK, concealing it all the while under the jeans, which he'd hung over his arm.

He pushed against the swinging door and stepped inside the cubicle. Elias had his back to the door, his own slacks down around his ankles. To Sullivan's surprise, he wore no underwear.

Sullivan noticed a small plastic packet taped to his right buttock. But just then Elias turned and looked back over his shoulder. There was just a half-second in which he recognized Sullivan from the diner and saw the muzzle of the PPK before Sullivan shot him once in the centre of the forehead.

The report, muffled by the silencer, was lost in the blare of the rock music. Sullivan replaced the PPK in its holster and went out, returning the jeans before disappearing into the crowd which filled the store.

CHAPTER EIGHTEEN

Elias's body was discovered by an elderly woman, a widow named Florence Lang, an employee of Bloomingdale's. She'd begun three years ago, first as a temporary salesperson during the Christmas rush; her industry, good nature, and over-all competence had come to the attention of her department manager, who recommended she be retained on a permanent basis.

She'd taken the Christmas job as a lark, and because she was bored and, with her husband dead and her children grown, had come to feel suddenly old and useless. It was a common enough feeling among women her age, friends of hers, but while most did nothing about it, and spent their time and husbands' money pampering themselves, Florence plunged into her new job. Within a year she was promoted to department supervisor and put in charge of one of the most troublesome departments in the store: the Fifty-Nine Shop. Here it was that the young East Side crowd came for their denims, their leather jackets, and Cardin leisure suits. The pilferage rate was the highest in the store. The dressing stalls were trysting places for homosexuals.

Management had first thought to put its youngest people to supervising the Fifty-Nine Shop. When that failed they tried tough security types; sales plunged. Finally, someone had the brilliant idea of using an older woman, a sensible grandmotherly type, authoritative but not threatening.

Florence Lang was chosen, and she did a splendid job.

She was at first shocked by some of the goings-on, particularly the dishonesty of the affluent young people and the flaming homosexuality. But she quickly got used to it. Her attitude was both tolerant and firm. In the store she gathered under her wing several of the younger salespeople. She was calm and sensible.

So when she opened the door to the dressing stall and saw Elias dead on the floor with his pants down, she didn't panic. She didn't scream. She touched nothing, and planted herself in front of the door so that no one else could enter. Then she called one of her salespeople and told him to phone the police.

When he asked what was wrong, she spoke in a calm but firm voice, and told him only that there'd been a murder, to tell no one but the police, and to do it at once and without another word.

She was still at her post, guarding the door to the dressing stall, when Sergeant Reese arrived.

He had a quick look inside the stall, positioned two uniformed men to hold back the curious, and while a younger plainclothes detective named Duckworth examined the corpse, Reese and Florence got to know each other.

'By the way, Sergeant, I think it's only fair to tell you I have a son, a brilliant lawyer,' were her first words. 'Harvard Law School. At the moment a clerk for a federal judge.'

'Who might that be?'

'Judge Morris Bellair.'

'I'm glad you warned me.' Reese had a winning smile; his teeth were good and he wasn't a bad-looking man, particularly if he lost a few pounds. 'This way I won't give you the third degree.'

He stripped the cellophane from a cigar and fumbled for his Zippo lighter.

'D'you mind if I smoke?'

'Not if you don't mind my throwing up on your feet.'

'Is there a Mr Lang?'

'Not for four years.'

'You want to run away with me?'

'Do I have time to pack a bag?'

Detective Duckworth came up with a worn brown wallet engraved with a map of Jerusalem in faded gilt, the kind sold in souvenir shops.

Reese and Duckworth exchanged a glance; they needed to talk privately. But first the sergeant thought to question Florence Lang, particularly to learn if she'd known the victim or seen his killer.

'Every face is a blur,' she said. 'Particularly on Thursday night. The store is a mob scene.'

'He hadn't used a charge card? Nothing that would identify him?'

'He was just trying on the pants. He hadn't bought anything yet.'

'And you saw no one who looked out of place? No one hanging around, maybe dressed differently from the usual bunch?'

She shrugged. 'I get doctors, lawyers, businessmen. I get celebrities. These days the biggest people are into denim casual wear.'

Reese thanked her, asked if she'd be available later to make a statement, and went off to huddle in private with Duckworth.

'No question, a professional hit,' Duckworth said. 'Victim was Elias Garfinkle. The guy we recommended to Lemoyne. The wirer.'

'Are you sure? There's not much left of his face.'

'That's what his green card says. Also a couple of letters postmarked Athens. There's pocket litter in three, four names. Credit cards, the usual dreck. You can forget that. It's our friend Elias.'

'What's in the bag taped to his ass?'

'Cocaine.'

'I didn't know he was into that.'

'Then it's sugar. Elias Garfinkle went around with ounce bags of sugar taped to his ass.'

'Any cash?'

'Three hundred and ninety-two dollars. Three one-hundred-dollar bills numbered in sequence. They're unbelievable, your friends.'

'Give me the serial numbers off the hundreds and then put them away, they're ours. You give out it was a drug hit. Wrap it up. I got a call to make.'

'I know about your calls,' Duckworth said.

Reese had started to leave, but remembered something and turned back to Duckworth. 'Did you recover the slug?' he said.

'From the wall behind him.' He held it between his index finger and thumb. 'Beat up, but ballistics could probably do something with it. Nine millimetre, like the one that killed the guard at Roper International.'

Reese took the slug.

'I hope you remember your old pal when your friends

make you head of the FBI,' Duckworth said.

Lemoyne was in Palm Springs with the Senator and the Vice-President. He'd given Reese the unlisted phone number in the residence of the former Ambassador to France, where they were house guests.

It was late afternoon in Palm Springs and Lemoyne and the others were on the golf course. Reese's call was taken by a young secretary, who put it through to the Secret Service agent on duty in the communications room. Reese gave him the number of the pay phone in the bar on Lexington Avenue from which he was calling, and told him it was urgent; the agent used a transceiver to contact the senior agent with the Vice-Presidential party on the eleventh green.

Six minutes later Reese was drinking a bourbon and water and watching Tom Seaver pitch the opening inning of the Mets game when the phone rang. It was Lemoyne.

Reese described the killing to him and read the serial numbers of the bills. He also told him he had possession of the slug, which was almost certainly from the same gun which had killed the Roper guard.

Lemoyne said, 'Is there any way you can get hold of Sullivan?'

'Not without an all-out effort. Even then I wouldn't bet on it.'

Lemoyne had noted the slip in Reese's confidence; it had begun to seem to him that Ash was right; the only way to deal with Sullivan was to give him what he wanted.

'Talk to Ash,' he said. 'If anyone can get hold of Sullivan, he can. Tell him all the top people are meeting tonight. Wells is flying in for it. My guess is they're going to come up with a compromise. They'll give Sullivan more or less what he wants, but it has to be in a way they can live with. Have Ash tell him that. Put Sullivan on twenty-four-hour hold. He'll get what he wants. I'll be in New York tomorrow morning to put the cash together.'

Reese reached Ash at home and arranged to meet him at a bar on Second Avenue and Twenty-eighth Street, where neither was known and it was unlikely they'd run into anyone they knew.

They ordered drinks and Ash listened to all Reese had to say.

'I don't know where Sullivan is,' Ash said. 'I've spoken to him, and he's changed his terms. Now the girl is part of the package.'

'Call him. Tell him about the meeting.'

'I don't know how to reach him,' Ash said. 'And if I did, he wouldn't listen. He doesn't trust me. He doesn't trust any of us. We're all enemies. He's going to keep up the pressure. Hit us and play it alone. That's the way he'll think.'

'What's he want done with the girl?'

'I'm to bring her to Kennedy and put her on board the KLM flight to Amsterdam. Wednesday.'

'And what about him?'

'He's going with her.'

'You're kidding.'

'Don't be stupid. You bat an eye at him, the temple comes down. Kill him, everything he took out of my office goes public. Be certain he's taken out the proper insurance.'

At three the next afternoon, Ash received a call on the private line in his office. It was Sullivan.

Ash told him of the meeting in Palm Springs. 'They've decided to give you what you want. The hospital will release the girl. She'll be on the Wednesday Amsterdam flight. Your ticket will be at the KLM desk.'

'I want you to come alone with the money,' Sullivan said. 'It's to be in the form of US Treasury bills. They're to mature in no more than thirty days and be made out to the bearer. Denominations of twenty-five thousand dollars.'

'Lemoyne has a problem with the cash. He's in New York now trying to put it together, but it's not easy. He says he's got a way of getting it to you in Europe, but it'll take time.'

'Ask him how much time.'

'You can ask him yourself.'

'Which of you is being smart?' Sullivan said. 'Which is trying to finesse it?'

Ash knew at least that this phone wasn't tapped. 'It comes down to the money,' he said. 'It's stuck at the narrow end of the pipe.'

'Lemoyne has always been greedy,' Sullivan said. 'Greedy and crooked. It's not in him to do something straight.'

'He thinks of it as his commission,' Ash said. 'I'll see about it.'

'So will I.'

Sullivan decided to kill Lemoyne. He'd wanted to from the time of the bombing, planned for it, but held back. Elias was another matter, a necessary killing, both punishment and threat. The survivors were reminded that they were dealing with a killer. Notice was served to look sharp. They were to live fearfully, and never forget that he was loose and might be stalking any of them. None was safe. He stole their appetite, invaded their dreams, made them impotent.

There was passion in his killing of Elias; his motive was revenge. Elias had bombed Janice. He was a mercenary, a killer without ideals, acting simply for money. Sullivan had despised him. It was, he thought, a satisfying killing.

He felt none of this for Lemoyne. He went about planning his murder dispassionately, as an abstract problem.

Lemoyne lived in a modern high-rise apartment house on the corner of Fifty-seventh Street and Second Avenue. Rents here were among the highest in the city and security precautions were extensive: doormen round the clock, a security guard as a backup after six o'clock. The entrance through the garage monitored by closed-circuit television and locked after dark. No one but tenants admitted without first being announced.

At his office Lemoyne was accessible only by appointment, and each visitor was screened first by a receptionist and then a private secretary. He travelled mostly by private limousine, occasionally by cab, but he did frequently walk the two blocks from his office to Fiftieth Street to '21', where he regularly lunched.

It would be possible to kill him in the street or in the lobby of either of these buildings. But a street killing wasn't what Sullivan wanted. He needed to deliver a more terrifying message, and for that he would have to kill Lemoyne at home, where he felt most safe and secure.

The means to kill Lemoyne came to him in the room he'd taken in a run-down hotel on upper Broadway. He'd stopped shaving after his last meeting with Ash and dressed in jeans and a second-hand field jacket picked up from an open stall on Fourteenth Street. He'd even pierced his ear and fitted it with a narrow gold earring. He came and went easily in the wretched hotel, which catered for the most part to junkies, prostitutes and petty thieves.

He left the hotel early, bought a carton of orange juice and two freshly baked bran muffins from a bakery, and breakfasted on a bench in Central Park.

It was just after ten o'clock, and there were children in the park, toddlers and infants in carriages; the older ones were in school. There were dogs of nearly every breed, and old people, an occasional teenager idling away the morning with a portable radio. Sullivan fitted in; an unshaven man in a field jacket on a bench. He even plucked a *Wall Street Journal* from a trash basket.

Just before twelve he left the park by way of Fifth Avenue, walked east to Madison, and then continued downtown to Sherry-Lehmann, liquor and wine merchants. He paid two hundred and eighty-five dollars for a case of 1970 Château Pétrus, a gift for Arnold Lemoyne.

'To what address shall we send it?' The salesman wore a double-breasted blazer and a club tie against a shirt with a broadly striped bosom and white collar, gold half-glasses mid-way on an impressive nose. He didn't at all like the idea of a man dressed like Sullivan acquiring a wine like Pétrus.

'Home or office? Nobody tell me.'

His accent confirmed the salesman's judgement. 'Have you a number we can call?' he said.

Sullivan had him repeat that; his English was very bad. But at last he understood. The salesman was given Lemoyne's office number. He spoke to Lemoyne's secretary, who put him briefly on hold. When she came back to the line it was to ask if she could call Sherry-Lehmann back. Sullivan had expected Lemoyne to be cautious. But he also knew him for a greedy man, unwilling to look too closely at an expensive gift.

A case of wine was awkward to transport home from the office; when she called back the secretary gave instructions that it be sent that night to Lemoyne's apartment, and gave the salesman the address.

Sullivan then asked that the wine be brought up from the cellar. His English was getting worse. The salesman tried to explain that arrangements had been made for them to deliver it. Sullivan smiled stupidly and said he would take it over himself, that the smile on Mr Lemoyne's face when he saw the Pétrus was a pleasure he couldn't deny himself. By this time the salesman had no idea what Sullivan was talking about, except that he wanted to take possession of the wine for which he had paid in cash. The salesman could see no objection to that – besides which it was his lunch hour and he was sick of the whole business. The Pétrus was shortly brought up from the cellar, Sullivan hoisted it on his shoulder, shook hands warmly with the salesman, and hailed a cab. He returned to his hotel, locked the wine in his room, went out for a bite to eat, and returned for a nap. He awoke at seven-thirty, washed, checked the PPK and tucked it into his belt under the field jacket, and, carrying the wine, took a cab to within half a block of Lemoyne's apartment house. He carried the case into the lobby, where he told the concierge he had a delivery from Sherry-Lehmann for Mr Lemoyne.

The delivery was expected. Mr Lemoyne was in apartment 32-H.

The door of 32-H, like all of those in the building, was steel, fireproof, with a peephole in its centre. Before he rang Sullivan positioned himself so that the wooden case of wine on his shoulder partly hid his face.

Lemoyne opened the door and then stepped aside for Sullivan to enter. He had taken two steps into the apartment when Lemoyne bolted, sprinting at top speed for the bedroom. A second too late Sullivan saw the small gilt mirror on the wall opposite, his face behind the wooden wine case clearly reflected in it. He had only a glimpse of Lemoyne in trousers and an undershirt as he dashed into the bedroom. Sullivan dropped the case of wine, and went after him, the PPK in his right hand.

But Lemoyne had several seconds on him, just enough to have reached the .38 Smith and Wesson he kept in the drawer of the table next to his bed.

Sullivan dived through the open bedroom door, just as Lemoyne fired; the slug whizzed past his ear, burying itself in the wooden door frame.

But that was all the time Lemoyne had; from a prone position, Sullivan aimed and fired, striking Lemoyne in the centre of his chest. The impact of the high-velocity 9 mm slug knocked him backward across the width of the bed.

Sullivan lay for some seconds on the floor, getting himself together. Lemoyne's shot had missed him by inches. The sound of it still rang in his ear and the air in the bedroom was heavy with the acrid odour of cordite.

The windows were closed, which would muffle the report of the Smith and Wesson and make it sound like nothing more than the backfire of a car. Sullivan satisfied himself that Lemoyne was dead; he'd been shaving, a bit of dry lather still on his face. Lemoyne had a small faded tattoo, crossed anchors over a globe on his upper right arm. His upper body had the look of a man who worked regularly with weights. And there was a pair of dumb-bells in the corner, and next to them an incline board for sit-ups. A small sauna had been built into the bathroom. Lemoyne had taken good care of himself. Sullivan put the PPK back in its holster. Lemoyne had lived well. He certainly hadn't wanted to die. Sullivan left the apartment and took care that the door locked behind him.

After the shooting, Sullivan walked north on Third Avenue. He continued aimlessly, with no place in mind. Finally, on Eighty-fourth Street, he went into a place and ordered a beer. It was a bar and restaurant done up to look like an old-time saloon, with a long dark wood bar, the barman in shirtsleeves, and a couple of dozen small tables, each with a small brass lamp with a globe of green glass to shade the bulb. The menu was written in chalk on a large blackboard.

There were several people at the bar, but Sullivan managed to seat himself between two empty stools. It was instinctive.

Most of the men in the place were younger than he. The women looked like schoolgirls. All seemed to be having a good time and he felt generous towards them. He'd never been much of a man for easy good times. Something had always taken hold and driven him on. He'd gone about the world in secret. He thought about his life as if it were drawing to a close, a thing already in the past. Regret was too great an emotion. He was weary, and missed Janice. If it worked and he got away to Europe, they'd come after him there. If the end were near, he wanted her close.

There was laughter in the bar, good food being eaten. It seemed that people walked around him, steered clear, as if they knew the man he was. His beer glass was empty but the barman didn't ask if he wanted another.

He was left alone. The stools on either side of him remained empty. He had the look of a solitary, of someone dangerous.

He imagined himself locked in a tiny room with bare stone walls: a cell. He realized that he'd lived without learning to understand himself. There were puzzles, dead ends, blank spots. The image of the bare walls and the locked door returned. He belonged in that cell. It was for him an appropriate fate.

He asked himself if there were such a thing as a soul, and if it were immortal. It seemed certain there must be such a thing. He looked out at the young faces under the soft light from the green lamps. He knew Janice believed in God and the immortal soul. He must have Janice with him.

CHAPTER NINETEEN

Sergeant Reese parked his car, with its police department plates, in front of a fire hydrant, and entered the Blarney Stone Bar and Grill, just north of Fifty-third Street. He drank a bottle of Harp beer and smoked a Romeo y Julieta double corona. It was a marvellous cigar, rolled by hand in Cuba, and banned from the United States since the embargo of 1962.

Sergeant Reese had an unlimited supply, gifts from an old police crony, now an assistant to the director of the Enforcement Division of the Alcohol, Tobacco and Firearms Department of the Internal Revenue Service. Since the embargo, there naturally existed a lively black market in Cuban cigars so that vast amounts were run across the border from Canada and Mexico, and by American tourists and businessmen returning from trips abroad. Each year, thousands of boxes were confiscated and stored in a customs shed on South Fishkill Street in Galveston, Texas.

Several times a year, Reese's old police crony filled a truck with Cuban cigars, cognac, and Scotch whisky, which he either sold or gave as presents to friends in a position to reciprocate with favours or presents of their own. Over the years, he'd gathered a lovely nest egg, to put beside his pension, which, he'd confided to Reese, now led him to look with favour upon an early and graceful retirement.

Reese decided he wanted the job that his old crony would soon vacate and while he smoked his Cuban cigar he thought carefully what his next move should be.

Finally, he paid for his beer, took three dollars in silver, and used a pay phone on Third Avenue to call Mark Wells in Washington.

Wells already knew that Lemoyne had been killed, but as soon as Reese began to describe the details, Wells abruptly cut him off.

'Where are you calling from?'

'A phone booth on Third Avenue.'

'I'm going to call you back,' Wells said. 'An hour from now.'

'My office?'

'That won't do.'

Reese carried an address book in which he wrote, along with certain unlisted numbers, those of public phone booths in midtown Manhattan. He picked one on First Avenue and Seventy-third Street and read it to Wells.

Exactly an hour later he was in the phone booth to receive Wells's call.

'I've spoken to people here,' Wells said from Washington. 'It seems we have one or two matters to clarify. I'm going to be on the five-o'clock shuttle.'

'How's seven o'clock?' Reese said. 'Bryant Park.'

'Where's that?'

'Back of the main branch of the library. Forty-second Street and Sixth Avenue.'

Reese took care to arrive five minutes early in order to see if Wells came alone. He did, arriving in a taxi, an immaculately groomed and barbered figure in a pin-stripe suit and polished slip-ons with a tiny gold triangle sewn to the instep. It was a warm night and he'd flown up from Washington and ridden with his knees against his chest in the back of a filthy New York taxi, but Mark Wells hadn't a wrinkle in his suit, not a hair out of place; in Bryant Park, among the dopers, ragpickers and winos, he looked to have come fresh from a set of tennis, a shower, sauna, and five minutes with a hair blower.

Reese stayed out of sight and let Wells sniff the foul air of Bryant Park. He let him stew, let the winos bump him for quarters. Reese had picked Bryant Park because he wanted to go at the Vice-President's man off-balance, on unfamiliar ground. This kid from California treated Reese as if he ought to be left out for collection tied inside a plastic bag. Reese needed now and again to remind himself that he was not only tougher than men like Wells, he was also smarter.

When at last he showed himself, Wells didn't offer to shake hands. Instead he glanced pointedly at his watch. 'What made you pick this place?' he said.

Reese looked at him innocently. 'We won't run into anybody we know here,' he said.

'We may if we're patient.' Wells glanced with a thin smile at a ragged old man plucking at a trash can. 'But we'll have to wait until after the election.' Then in a more businesslike tone: 'Our friend Ash is to escort the girl and the money to the airport. He's to be alone, those are Bodybuilder's instructions.'

Reese stared at him blankly. Wells liked code names and it took Reese a moment to remember that Bodybuilder was Sullivan. But he said, 'When? What airline?'

'Wednesday night. The KLM to Amsterdam.'

Wells put his hands in his pockets and began to jingle his change. They walked a few steps, Wells looking straight ahead. Finally he said, 'We're going to have to do something about Bodybuilder. Say we meet his price, we strike a bargain, we have to be sure six months from now, or a year, or whatever, he doesn't come back and say that wasn't good enough.' Wells turned his pale-blue eyes on Reese. 'We have to be sure we put this thing behind us. We have to be damn sure.'

'You're going to have to tell me just what you want,' Reese said. 'Spell it out.'

'We want to be done with him,' Wells said. 'Somewhere down the road he will come back to haunt us. We don't want him starting an auction. You understand what I mean? I can't make it any plainer than that.'

'You can make it a lot plainer,' Reese said. 'You can even make it so plain that I know what the fuck you're talking about. Relax, Wells, I can show you people who'll swear I don't go around with a tape recorder up my ass.'

'Retire him,' Wells said. 'Put him down.'

'You mean kill him?'

Wells started to speak, caught himself and said nothing. Finally he nodded his head.

'What about the stuff he stole?' Reese said.

'First things first. This guy is trying to kill us all.'

'Okay, it can be done,' Reese said. 'Not easy, not by a long shot. But it can be done.'

'I don't think I really ought to know the specifics. I think my role in this is simply to indicate the nature of our problem, and then say, go on and deal with the matter in the way that seems best to you at the time.'

'That's fine,' Reese said. 'All of it, every word. You put it beautifully. As long as we understand that you're telling me to go and kill Jack Sullivan.'

Wells's eyes popped and he began to look around for a way out of Bryant Park.

'Except I want it clear that this is no piece of cake,' Reese said. 'That Sullivan is no virgin. So if I kill him for you, I'm going to want something back. And when I tell you what it is, you nod your head or blink your eyes. You could stamp your foot like a horse in the circus. Any way you want it, Mr Mark Wells, as long as we understand it's yes or no.'

'Go on.'

'Alcohol, Tobacco, and Firearms,' Reese said. 'Enforcement Division. It's part of the IRS. The assistant to the Director is retiring. I want to move over there.'

Wells nodded. 'On the other thing,' he said, 'I don't want to see you or hear from you until after it's done.'

213

CHAPTER TWENTY

Ash was to carry the Treasury bills to the airport. Wells had collected the cash from office safes and deposit boxes, large drafts sent out of the country and smaller ones sent back in to be converted to cash. Wells picked up the strings left dangling by Lemoyne's death. The others had run for cover. Wells was made to collect the cash and buy the negotiable bearer bills; Ash to carry them to the airport. Sullivan would meet no one else.

On the morning of the flight Wells came to Ash's office with the bills, two hundred and seventy-five thousand dollars' worth folded neatly into an ordinary white envelope.

'You'd better have protection,' Wells said. 'At least as far as the airport. You can go alone then.'

'I don't need protection,' Ash said. 'I just need you to keep your nose out.'

'Don't worry about that,' Wells said. 'I put the package together; that's as far as I go.'

'I'll call you when it's done.'

'It's a lot of money, isn't it?'

'It's a start in life.'

Wells sat on the edge of Ash's desk, a handsome man with a glowing, polished face and beautiful teeth. Ash wondered what he did to get them so white.

'I've been wondering about him,' Wells said. 'Sullivan, I mean. I met him once or twice, but I can't say he made much of an impression. What kind of man is he?'

'Good company,' Ash said. 'He tells a joke well and has a fine singing voice.'

'He's killed three men.'

'He was always a good shot.'

'Are you afraid?'

'No. Are you?'

'I won't be at the airport.' Wells glanced at his watch, which he wore with the face turned to the inside of his wrist.

'Around flight time I'll be in Cambridge, giving a little after-dinner talk at the Harvard School of Business.'

Check-in time for the KLM Amsterdam flight was seven-thirty. Ash arrived at Roosevelt Hospital just after six. Janice was out of bed, dressed, and in a wheelchair. She was pale and rather weak, but in good spirits. It was the first time Ash had seen her out of bed. He saw that she was a pretty girl, perhaps not a beauty. He wondered what about her had attracted Sullivan and made him choose her. One could know a man well, know him in the world with other men, but be totally unprepared for his women. The women were so often a surprise, and their appearance made Ash uneasy, as if he were about to be told a secret he didn't care to know.

She knew who Ash was. 'Jack has mentioned you,' she said.

'I was told he called.'

'Last night. He told me to do as you say. I know about the flight, and I'm ready for it.'

'We can go out in an ambulance if you like.'

'There's no need.'

'I didn't think you'd want one,' Ash said. 'I've got a car downstairs.' She wore no make-up, her lips were bluish, and her hands shook. 'There's nothing to be afraid of,' he said. 'It's all being done his way. He's won. You both have.'

'They were trying to kill Jack, weren't they?'

'It was stupid.'

'I thought I was going to die,' she said. 'I was conscious, you know, all through it. I knew what had happened to me, but there was nothing I could do. I couldn't move. I felt nothing, and I was so far away from it all. I thought I had died.'

'It's time to go.'

'Will you come with me?'

'Of course.'

'Jack said you weren't like the others,' she said. 'That you were better.'

'We were friends,' Ash said.

'He said you were just too far along to take a stand against them.'

'We'd better go.'

215

'He told me you had nothing to do with the bombing. That they had to go around you.'

'I could've done more to head it off,' Ash said.

'Jack said the same thing,' she said. 'He told me none of us is free of guilt.'

'You are,' Ash said. 'And you're the one who's been hurt.'

She smiled; a private joke. 'I was involved from the beginning. I put in with Jack knowing what he was. Suspecting, anyway.'

'It's time to go,' Ash said.

Ash saw to her release from the hospital. The bill had been settled earlier in the afternoon by means of a draft on a Swiss bank brought by a messenger. Ash signed the release, and wheeled her to the car. She was able to stand and get into the car herself.

Ash stood next to the car and had a look around the streets. He saw no men in parked cars, no stakeout on the roofs or in windows, no sign of surveillance. But he felt something, a tightening of the nerves along the spine and at the back of his neck. He sensed someone near, watching every move.

He slowly climbed in the back of the limousine and joined Janice.

'D'you feel it too?' she said.

'I feel something.'

'It's him.'

'Last night on the phone. What did he say?'

'Only what I told you. I was to do as you say. I was to take the flight. The rest was private, between him and me.'

During the drive to the airport she began to talk about dying.

'I thought of all the things I hadn't told Jack. Particularly about my father. He killed himself, you know. And I was ashamed of that, and terribly guilty, as if it were my fault.'

'You're a close family, aren't you?' For the first time he saw a spark in her eyes. It was an apprehensive look and he quickly said, 'Your mother and brother are safe. No one will bother them. Matter of fact, the others don't even know they exist. No one thought to dig deeply into your life.'

'Jack promised to take care of them.'

Ash smiled and said, 'He has a way of keeping his promises.'
They barely spoke the rest of the way.

Her ticket was filled out and waiting, paid for in cash that
morning by Louise Vernon. Ash pushed Janice as far as
Passport Control and located a flight attendant to look after
her the rest of the way.

'Will they let us go?' Janice said to Ash. 'Just leave us in
peace?'

'I don't know.'

'But you don't think they will.'

'I think they're afraid of Jack.'

'Which means what? That they'll stay clear or try to kill
him? We'll live as long and as well as we can.'

'I think he's found the right girl,' Ash said. Impulsively,
he bent and kissed her cheek. 'I wish you both luck,' he
said.

Ash returned alone to the KLM desk. The boarding notice
came on, but there was no sign of Sullivan.

The terminal had quickly filled; there were lines at each of
the ticket counters, masses of people with luggage piled all
around them, a babble of languages and the blare of the
public-address system. A porter pushing a luggage cart
almost knocked Ash down. He again heard the KLM boarding announcement; he looked around frantically for
Sullivan.

And then out of the corner of his eye, Ash saw what he
most dreaded, and what he'd convinced himself they were
not stupid enough to try. He saw Reese. And a second or two
later he saw Duckworth. He began to pick the cops out of
the airport crowd. He counted four of them. Four, plus
Duckworth and Reese. Six armed men ready to close in on
the KLM desk, ready to make a shooting gallery of the
International Terminal.

There was still no sign of Sullivan. But he must come. The
girl was on the plane, the envelope with the Treasury bills in
his pocket.

Ash started for the courtesy desk. He'd decided what to
do: he would have them make an announcement, warning
Sullivan off.

But just then the electrically operated door of the ter-

217

minal slid open and a young man in a wheelchair pushed by an older woman entered and went directly to the KLM counter.

Ash tensed; out of the corner of his eye, he saw Duckworth with his hand deep in his coat pocket move quickly towards the electronic door.

Ash looked closely at the man in the wheelchair: it wasn't Sullivan.

The family resemblance was strong. Ash knew at once who they were, and stood silently while Mrs Blackmur collected their prepaid tickets. He waited while their baggage was weighed and ticketed. She suddenly turned to him and smiled. 'Are you Mr Morgan?'

Duckworth broke into a heavy trot, picking up speed as he ran, digging at the pistol in his coat pocket. Reese had started towards them from the other end of the terminal.

'Mr Morgan?'

'Yes, Mrs Blackmur.'

'I have a message for you,' she said. 'Mr Sullivan won't be on this flight. He sends his apologies, and hopes he caused you no inconvenience.'

'None whatsoever.'

'He also said he'd arrange for delivery of the package later,' she said. 'He'd work something out and let you know.'

A voice on the public-address system announced the last call for the KLM to Amsterdam. 'You better hurry,' Ash said.

Ash rode the escalator to the observation platform on the second floor, and waited the half-hour until the plane took off.

Reese found him there. 'You blew the whistle,' he said. 'You warned him off.'

'He wasn't coming.'

'What about the girl? In her condition, she's got to be taken care of.'

'Sullivan made other arrangements.'

'And the money? He never picked up the money. Two hundred and seventy-five thousand dollars. Are you telling me he just walked away from that?'

'He'll pick it up another time.'

'He'll be killed,' Reese said. 'Bet on it. He's going to be put down.'

Ash stripped the cellophane from a cigar, the first he'd had time for that day. 'When they try,' he said, 'I hope they give the job to you.'

CHAPTER TWENTY-ONE

There was nothing more for Ash to do. He had the limousine driver drop him several blocks from his apartment. He was in no hurry to go home; there was nothing to go home for. He missed Eleanor and dreaded the idea of the empty apartment. He was lonely but could think of no one else he wanted to be with. He kept himself from thinking of her in Hong Kong, of whom she might be with.

He was tired. He stopped in a place and had a drink. He knew that his life with Eleanor was over, and he wondered what he would do now. He felt distant from his own life, detached, more weary than unhappy.

He thought about Sullivan, and about the girl. They'd go after them; Sullivan would kill some of them, they'd kill him. Ash wanted Sullivan to live, at least long enough to spend his money and have some good times with his girl. Sullivan was his friend. Ash came suddenly to understand him, his need to live on the edge.

It was nearly eleven when he arrived home. He stopped at his mailbox with only the faintest hope there'd be something from Eleanor; and of course there wasn't, merely a bill from Saks and his American Express statement.

He said good night to the hallman and took the automatic elevator to his apartment. The instant he opened the door, he knew something was wrong. The place was dark, just as it always was; there were no unusual smells, no cologne or aftershave, nothing out of place, not a sound. But Ash knew someone was in the apartment.

He stepped away from the open door and stood for several seconds until his eyes grew used to the dark. He was unarmed; he tried to think of what to do.

He was suddenly convinced it was Eleanor. She had come

back to him. He switched on the lights; Sullivan was sitting in a chair at the far end of the living-room.

'Did you know it was me?' he said.

'I knew you'd have to get in touch with me.'

'You weren't frightened?'

'Why should I be?'

'And you don't have a gun, do you?'

'Are you frightened?' Ash said.

Ash went to the bar and made two drinks; Jack Daniels, three inches, without ice in two tall glasses.

Sullivan said, 'Everybody get off all right?'

'Just fine.'

'And the money?'

Ash took the envelope from his pocket and gave it to Sullivan.

'What will you do now?' he said.

'A little trip,' he said. 'Maybe somewhere by boat. I've earned my rest.'

'Why not send the money to the girl?' Ash said. 'Then go and talk to Justice. Give them just a little. You know the way. Justice will help you, and help its powerful friends. That way, in a couple of years, you go to the girl and you both live to enjoy the money.'

Sullivan seemed not to have heard. 'I've got an envelope for you, too,' he said. 'Man of my word. You give me the money, I give you the life insurance.' He held a stamped envelope in his hands, the address neatly typed: Mr Ash Morgan, 60 Sutton Place.

'You're setting it up for a shoot-out,' Ash said. 'Look around corners and check your car before you start it. That's the way you want it, because you can't live an ordinary life.'

Sullivan looked coolly at Ash and then said, 'Let's see how long I can,' he said.

He put down his glass without touching the bourbon and walked past Ash to the door. Ash followed him to the mail chute in the hall. Sullivan pressed the elevator button.

'The Astra file is in a safe-deposit box. All the original documents. The key is in this envelope, with all the details you'll need.'

The elevator door opened. Sullivan smiled, showing his chipped front tooth. 'I trust you, Ash,' he said. 'But I'll need a couple of days' head start.'

He dropped the envelope into the chute and stepped into the elevator. The door closed and he was gone.

Ash returned to the empty apartment, closed and locked the door, and made himself another drink. One needed help with an ordinary life.

Eric Ambler

A world of espionage and counter-espionage, of sudden violence and treacherous calm; of blackmailers, murderers, gun-runners—and none too virtuous heroes. This is the world of Eric Ambler. 'Unquestionably our best thriller writer.' *Graham Greene*. 'He is incapable of writing a dull paragraph.' *Sunday Times* 'Eric Ambler is a master of his craft.' *Sunday Telegraph*

Fontana Paperbacks

Anthony Powell

'Powell is very like a drug, the more compelling the more you read him.' *Sunday Times*

A Dance to the Music of Time

'The most remarkable feat of sustained fictional creation in our day.' *Guardian*

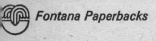 *Fontana Paperbacks*

Fontana Paperbacks

Fontana is a leading paperback publisher of fiction and non-fiction, with authors ranging from Alistair MacLean, Agatha Christie and Desmond Bagley to Solzhenitsyn and Pasternak, from Gerald Durrell and Joy Adamson to the famous Modern Masters series.

In addition to a wide-ranging collection of internationally popular writers of fiction, Fontana also has an outstanding reputation for history, natural history, military history, psychology, psychiatry, politics, economics, religion and the social sciences.

All Fontana books are available at your bookshop or newsagent; or can be ordered direct. Just fill in the form and list the titles you want.

FONTANA BOOKS, Cash Sales Department, G.P.O. Box 29, Douglas, Isle of Man, British Isles. Please send purchase price, plus 8p per book. Customers outside the U.K. send purchase price, plus 10p per book. Cheque, postal or money order. No currency.

NAME (Block letters) _____

ADDRESS _____

_____

_____